★

BILL PRIEST HAD SUFFOCATED, WIDE-AWAKE ALL THE WAY.

The sensations he felt while it went on would not have been pleasant.

With this realization came uneasy speculation. All around me, medical students were studying: anatomy and physiology, biochemistry and pathology. And pharmacology.

As a medical student, Bill Priest would have studied those things, too, which meant he would have known pancuronium was not just a bad drug for suicide. With the possible exception of strychnine, it was the worst. And while I supposed he might have killed himself, I doubted very much that he would have deliberately tortured himself to death in so horrid a manner.

Very unhappily, I began to wonder who had.

★

---

addicts do it all the time. But then, they aren't paralyzed.

MARY KITTREDGE
DEAD AND GONE

W❂RLDWIDE®

TORONTO • NEW YORK • LONDON • PARIS
AMSTERDAM • STOCKHOLM • HAMBURG
ATHENS • MILAN • TOKYO • SYDNEY

DEAD AND GONE

A Worldwide Mystery/July 1991

Published by arrangement with Walker and Company.

ISBN 0-373-26075-X

Printed in U.S.A.

This book is for John Ellerson Squibb

ONE

FOUR HYPODERMIC NEEDLES had been driven with some force through the corners of the sign on the bulletin board in the "Staff Only" lounge of Mercy General's emergency room.

Hand-lettered in black magic marker, the sign read:

THIS IS NOT A REHEARSAL. WE ARE PROFESSIONALS AND THIS IS THE BIG TIME.

Other notices littered the board: minutes of staff meetings, in-service lecture schedules, a placard for the senior surgical residents' Halloween Bash BE THERE OR BE SQUARE, and a reminder that vacation requests would not be honored during the Christmas and New Year's holiday weeks—NO EXCEPTIONS, THIS MEANS YOU!

Rude remarks had been scribbled over this last memo.

It was 5:05 P.M. Somewhere outside, an ambulance screamed, getting nearer. Flipping to a fresh page in my notebook, I trudged back out to the emergency admitting area, where beyond the sliding glass doors of the foyer the siren cut off as the ambulance careened into the driveway, stopping at the floodlit receiving ramp. Then the glass foyer doors jumped aside, letting in a gust of exhaust fumes along with the ambulance technicians, who sprinted through, trundling an aluminum stretcher. One held an IV bottle as he ran; one pumped the chest of the guy on the stretcher. A third pressed a black rubber mask with his left hand while squeezing the resuscitator bag with his right.

It all looked good, like a fund-raising commercial for the Red Cross. The next sequence would show the recovered victim smiling over his get-well cards from his clean white hospital bed.

Not this victim, though, blue not being the skin color most admired by emergency-room salvage experts. It was, as they said, a bad prognostic sign. And this guy was blue, all right: deep, sullen blue, like a statue cast in lead.

I followed him, notebook at the ready, down the corridor toward the major-medical treatment room. Just entering this room horizontally dropped the guy's chances way below even money, but from what I'd heard before he arrived, his odds had been slimmer than that when the ambulance got to him.

A prognostic sign, by the way, is one aimed the same direction as the patient: in this case, down. Aside from his color, he'd been out too long; the West Haven medics had radioed ahead an estimated arrival time of twenty minutes, but the actual transport had taken nearly twice that. To make things worse, they'd called it apparent suicide.

Apparent, not attempted; bad news. The techs had gotten an IV into the victim's arm and started pumping on his heart right there at the rescue site. That made it worse still: no pulse, no breathing.

It's hard to pump a guy's heart while hauling his body into an ambulance. It's even harder to get air into his lungs. And every second both those things aren't happening, he gets more dead.

In a few minutes the techs had called back to say they were finally on their way in, and this time they'd added one more detail: an empty glass vial and fallen syringe on the bathroom floor next to the victim. The vial's label said pancuronium.

At that, the charge nurse broke out a shroud kit and stuck a blank death certificate on a clipboard. A couple of the ER aides checked their watches, to see if they might still make dinner. One of the patient-transport aides caught the action and ambled down the hall, returning with a morgue stretcher—one of the newer, shinier models, with a green canvas cover over a false bottom so the other patients wouldn't know there was a dead person rolling by.

Now it seemed there was going to be. Through the open doors of the treatment room, I watched the nurses and technicians pounce on him, intent on jump-starting him back into this mortal realm.

Looking grim, though; I guess this pancuronium stuff must be pretty bad. Hunting for someone to ask about it, I spotted Harry Lemon and caught up with him as he hurried toward the activity.

Harry was the resident physician in charge of acute medical emergencies on this shift; to Harry, however, this shift was thirty-six hours long. I planned to spend a full day with him, sometime when I felt superhuman.

Superhuman qualities, I thought, were definitely going to be required. Tolerating the shift would be bad enough, but on top of that I would have to tolerate Harry.

"Ah," he said, ignoring my question, peering down at me over his wire-rimmed glasses. "Our visiting scribe. So heartening—our labors to be preserved in your deathless prose."

Harry was in his early thirties, tall and tubby with a good half-dozen strands of blond hair slicked back from his wide, smooth forehead. His plump pink cheeks and rosebud mouth combined with the wire-rimmed spectacles to make him resemble a large and freakishly studious baby, except that no baby ever looked so self-satisfied for so little reason. He was a good doctor, just lousy at everything else. Perhaps that was because to Harry there wasn't anything else.

"You might save your effort on this one," he said, gesturing at my notebook. "I believe our new client has per-

manently punched his exit visa''—he shook his head—
''although I suppose I shall have to attempt to revoke it.''

Harry didn't like suicides. To him, the only good suicide was a dead suicide, because, as I'd heard him remark, they wasted his time.

''After all,'' he went on, ''if this fellow thought his existence not worth continuing, who am I to say him nay?''

His actions, though, contradicted his words once he got
into the thick of things. There was in fact a spark of hu-
manity in Harry, but like some shy ghoul it only came out
when folks were trying to die and Harry was trying to stop
them.

Green-tiled and fluorescent lit, the treatment room ordinarily had even more warmth and charm than your
average mortuary cooler. Now, to complete the atmosphere, it also had the perfect tenant: a guy who wanted to
be a corpse.

As I entered the room, his clothes were being scissored
away and his naked body swung onto a sheeted examining
table. Almost all of his existing orifices were being inspected or invaded, and several new ones were being
created in a manner that struck me as both messy and
hasty.

I sidled into my usual observation post in the corner just
as the on-call anesthesiologist arrived: a tall black man in
a green paper cap and baggy green scrub suit, assessing his
patient as he made his way to the head of the examining
table. His name tag read Burton Dunn, MD.

''Aw, hell,'' Burton Dunn said, ''Somebody gimme a
Yankauer suction and a curved laryngoscope, please. And
grease the tube.''

Then with a silvery medical tool he maneuvered the thick
plastic tube down his patient's windpipe. A technician
pulled the mask off the breathing bag, stuck an adaptor on
the tube, and resumed giving oxygen. The sweet, sharp
reek of benzoin rose up as the anesthesiologist sprayed

some of the sticky stuff around the tube, then secured it with a loop of white adhesive tape.

"What's pancuronium?" I asked him when he had finished.

The blue man stayed blue. His lungs made a sound like a sodden sponge being squeezed and slowly released. Burton Dunn looked unhappy.

"Pancuronium," he said, "is a drug that keeps you lying still. You don't move a muscle, see, not even your breathing muscles. It's related to the stuff South American tribesmen used to stick on the tips of their arrows, to paralyze their prey."

"Curare," I said. "And he gave it to himself? To kill himself?"

"That's what the ambulance folks say. A big thirty cc's of it."

Dark brown hair curled tightly to the blue man's head, above neat, classically-modeled features now half obscured by tubes and swatches of tape. He wore a gold Rolex on his left wrist and a chunky gold link bracelet on his right. Two thinner chains, also gold, lay in the hollow of his throat. His lashes were long and black, curled gently over the purplish circles beneath his eyes.

What I could see of his face looked familiar, but that had to be an illusion. I'd only been in town six weeks, so I hardly knew anyone. Besides, the way he looked right now he wouldn't have known himself in the mirror.

Burton Dunn rubbed his right hand tiredly over his jaw. "Not a good way," he said. "Not at all a good way to kill yourself." Then he picked up the small glass vial that the ambulance fellows had brought along and peered at it, looking a little puzzled, I thought, or perhaps just fatigued.

Meanwhile the nurses finished wrapping the EKG leads and we all looked up at the cardiac monitor screen—even me, who couldn't ordinarily read it.

This time I could, though. Nothing. "Resume compressions, please," Harry Lemon said, and the burly aide doing heart massage straight-armed the blue man's breastbone again.

After that, one of the interns got lucky and hit the left external jugular with a needle the size of a railroad spike, and for the next twenty minutes they pumped that big vein full of enough stimulants to power the Kentucky Derby, along with glass ampules of calcium and epinephrine and sodium bicarbonate and anything else anyone could think of.

Finally there was a tickle on the EKG readout. Only a cockeyed optimist would have called it fibrillation, but it was all they had so they slapped the defibrillator paddles onto the guy's chest and shocked it anyway: 500 watt-seconds.

The smell of burnt hair drifted up. The jolt would have made you or me jump off the table and dance out the door, but this guy didn't twitch. Then the line on the monitor went flat again, and as a last resort, Harry Lemon threaded a split wire down a needle straight into the guy's heart. He hooked the wire to a pacemaker box, secured the connections with alligator clips, switched the box on, and cranked up the power.

All he got was the pulse from the battery: bump, bump, bump on the EKG readout. Nothing from the heart. It was like trying to make a Chicken McNugget stand up and squawk.

At which point the whole scene looked less like working on a live person, and more like mutilating a dead one. I couldn't help wondering what they thought they were doing for the poor stiff. At least he wasn't feeling any of it; by now the feeling equipment would be long gone.

I'd have been wondering what I was doing there, too, except that I knew: it was my job. As a freelance non-fiction writer, I've often thought my work consists mostly of standing around feeling like an idiot, asking a lot of stupid questions so my readers won't have to. The assignment at hand was no exception, just a little gorier than usual.

I was gathering material for a mass-market paperback on how to survive being in the hospital, meanwhile trying to survive, myself, on the publisher's advance—which of course put me at major risk for the two medical conditions most feared by writers: exposure and malnutrition.

I had my reasons for sticking with it, though, and the book itself was decent product: part American Hospital Association promotion, part genuine self-help. My longtime friend and agent, Bernie Holloway, wanted to call it *Tricks for the Sick!*

But then, that was Bernie, safe and cynical in his office in Manhattan. I, on the other hand, was on the spot in Mercy Hospital in New Haven, where I'd learned right off the bat that blueness was bad. As a prognostic sign, in fact, it rated just above coldness, stiffness, and mummification of one or more vital organs.

Now Harry thumbed the guy's eyelids open and frowned as he shone a penlight into the glassy eyes. "Have a look," he invited, so I slid up alongside.

"Note the dilated pupils, the absence of reaction to light."

I nodded, speechless. The pupils I saw were huge and motionless, which meant the brain underneath them was starved for oxygen. As a rational, thinking being, their owner now had all the social and intellectual potential of a rutabaga.

What really stunned me, though, was the color of the irises around his eyes' fixed black pupils.

Colors, rather: brown on the left, green on the right. I scanned the rest of him again, feeling stomach-punched and hoping against hope. But if he hadn't been so blue, I'd have recognized him sooner.

"This is Bill Priest," I said.

Harry's eyebrows went up. "Friend?"

"Friend of a friend." That was putting it mildly.

Harry's lower lip bulged with unhappiness. "Nevertheless," he said, "I believe we have done all we ought, and refrained from that which we ought not." Wincing slightly, he switched off the pacemaker box and pulled the wires off the terminals. He didn't like suicides, but he liked losing even less.

"Thank you, everyone," he said, and went out.

There was a moment, just a little moment, when everyone was silent. Then the heart-massage aide stepped down from his stool and began shaking the stiffness out of his arms. One of the technicians turned off the oxygen and popped the flowmeter from the wall outlet. Nurses started pulling IV bags down off the skyhooks, throwing them in the trash bins.

Bill Priest's left arm flopped off the examining table, swung a couple of times, and stopped. A few blackish dried blood crumbs still clung to the hole just opposite his elbow.

He'd had everything. Also, my friend Helen was in love with him, and on that count alone his death mystified me. Anyone who had Helen had plenty to live for.

Unless maybe Helen had given him more to live for than he could handle. Biologically speaking, recent events put Helen in for the long run, and from what I knew of Bill Priest he was just not a long-run type of guy. Still, an imminent first-born was no reason for suicide, even if you weren't exactly Ward Cleaver.

Thinking these things, I left the nurses readying Priest for the morgue, the more junior doctors still playing Monday-morning quarterback over his corpse. If she knew what had happened, Helen was probably around here in a waiting room somewhere. If she didn't know, I would have to find her and tell her.

It wasn't a task I welcomed. When she got the news, Helen Terrell was going to be worse than mystified. Billy Priest's death was going to damn near destroy her.

X-RAY MACHINES, wire central-supply racks, laundry hampers, and housekeeping carts crowded the corridors around the emergency room. Up and down the halls, lab runners and blood bank technicians hustled, rattling metal baskets of specimen containers; clerks and secretaries hurried, clutching insurance forms and folders of billing information.

Outside the orthopedics clinic, a pretty girl in a denim jacket lowered herself into a wheelchair, morosely regarding the toes at the end of her plaster-encased foot. A few doors down, a towheaded toddler glimpsed a nurse with a needle, but his howled objections to the theory and practice of tetanus immunization were to no avail.

Meanwhile, oblivious and unhurried, housekeepers wearing blue hospital-issue uniforms and closed, silent expressions wiped sinks and emptied waste baskets, filled soap dispensers and swept floors, stripped emptied beds of dirty linen and bore it away. Anonymous, meagerly paid, and unlikely to be recognized or promoted, they were perhaps the most necessary of all hospital personnel, for while a medical center may improvise almost any service or supply, there is no substitute for clean sheets.

Making my way among these unsung heroines of the public health, I found Helen at last in a little waiting room near the canteen. Six feet tall and eight months pregnant, she wore a pair of bleach-white cotton painter's pants and a white smocked tunic brilliantly embroidered with suns, moons, and stars. Beneath them her narrow body bloomed out at the middle like a flower about to bear fruit. Her lips were full, her cheekbones startling, her posture taut and anguished. Her wavy red hair, haphazardly pinned up, fell in loose strands about her stricken face.

Her eyes were like two gray stones. "It's a mistake," she said tonelessly. "It isn't him."

I didn't say anything, just sat down beside her as she sank into a chair and bent over the knot of her clenched fists.

"Uh, excuse me. I'm Walt Krusanke."

His shoulders were nearly as wide as the doorway and I thought he wore a padded vest beneath his gray sweatshirt, until I realized that was his chest.

He frowned with concern at Helen, then looked back at me. "I live right downstairs from Bill. I was doing my workout, and I heard him fall, or something fall, anyway. When he didn't answer his door, I—"

Nervously, he pushed up his sleeves, revealing forearms the size of mutton roasts. His brown hair was clipped very short, his face stolid but not stupid. It was the face of a man determined to absorb a great deal, and I thought he was about to get his chance.

"Oh, god," Helen said very softly.

"Well, I'm the building super," Walt went on, "so I ran for the keys. I let myself in and found him, started CPR, and called the ambulance. Helen was just getting there."

Glancing at her hunched-over form, he shrugged, shifting muscles like boulders. "Maybe it wasn't too smart, though, bringing her in here."

Something like a strangled laugh came out of Helen. "Oh, that's good, Walt. What do you think? If I didn't find out, then he wouldn't be..."

She straightened, gazing at Walt and me.

"Dead," she said brokenly, but behind her grief I glimpsed a secret, vanishing flash of caution that made me realize how little I really knew her any more.

We'd had pillow fights and milk-drinking contests in first grade, when Helen's glorious hair was just a couple of fat, messy braids and her fantastic smile wasn't even in braces yet. We'd stayed close even after high school, when she went off to an expensive, exclusive women's college and I didn't.

But in recent years I'd wound up a California hack writer with a small reputation and a smaller emergency fund, while Helen stayed East, rich and gorgeous, with a degree in architecture and design and more freelance clients than she knew what to do with. Lately she'd beaten out several bigger, more established firms to remodel Mercy's lobby, and with that in her track record she would never need the blue-chip safety net I knew she had.

Not that she cared about any of it; at least, not recently. What she cared about was Bill Priest. Six weeks ago, when I'd come back East and she'd offered me a place to stay, he was the first thing I heard about. In fact, he was all I heard about: Helen was in love.

Although I thought love wasn't really quite the right word, because if Bill Priest had told Helen to jump off a twenty-story building, she'd have put on her lipstick and taken the elevator to the roof.

Somehow that didn't sound like love to me. It didn't sound like Helen, either. Looking as if she descended from heaven every morning on a pearl pink shell had always gotten Helen plenty of mileage in the personal-services department, so that for better or worse she'd come to expect considerable front-and-center snappiness in the attentions other people paid her.

Which meant that jumping when Bill Priest whistled just wasn't her style. And now, as it turned out, old Bill had taken the jump himself.

And I wasn't even sorry, because I'd met him. Only once: he didn't seem to care for Helen's friends. Still, once was plenty on top of all she told me.

He loved her, she said, and he was perfectly willing to marry her, with one proviso: that he would be free to see other women. He simply could not curtail an activity so essential to his personal development.

Billy, I gathered, was a big fan of personal development, as long as it was his own personal development.
Helen wouldn't marry him under his conditions, of course,
but she loved him; she understood.

I'd understood, too. He didn't plan to stop screwing
around, Helen or no Helen, baby or no baby. Bill Priest,
in my book, was an utter slime toad.

Now Helen began to rock violently, her face hidden in
her hands. Little moans escaped from between her fingers, each one rising more toward the shriek that was imminent.

Meanwhile I heard another siren wailing in, which
meant everyone would be involved with that new emergency, not realizing there was one developing here.

"Walt," I said, "have you got a car?"

He nodded, looking frightened.

I grabbed his big arm and shoved him nearer to her. It
was like shoving Mount Rushmore, but he moved. I
guessed he didn't much mind getting closer to Helen; I
didn't have time, though, to follow up on that thought.

"Look," I said. "I'm going to try to find someone to see
her, but there's something else I have to keep track of, too.
You stay with her, and take her home afterward, and keep
staying with her until I get there. Can you do that?"

Walt nodded and knelt beside Helen.

"Hey," he said uncertainly, reaching out to touch her,
then drawing his big hands back. I could see why he hesitated; she was a bundle of hysteria getting ready to erupt.
Anything might set her off.

"Listen, Helen," he said, "it's going to be—"

He stopped, looking up in helplessness at me. What he'd
been about to tell her was ridiculous and he knew it; nothing was going to be all right.

Out at the desk I found Harry Lemon, and told him
what was going on.

"OB or shrink?" he said, stuffing the remains of a cold hamburger into his mouth with one hand while scribbling notes on a chart with the other.

"Huh?"

He swallowed hard, wiping his mouth with his sleeve. "Is she losing the baby, or her marbles?"

"Maybe both, if somebody doesn't get down there. Isn't there even a minister? Or a social worker, someone trained?"

Harry pointed at the acute surgical room; the doors were closed. "Three-car crackup. God squad's doing last rites on the leftovers. You know, Charlotte, I think children ought to be issued six-packs and driver's licenses at age eight. That way, people intrinsically stupid enough to drink and drive wouldn't get a chance to reproduce. Bingo, you see—right there you've cleaned up the gene pool."

He glanced up, and got a look at my face. "Never mind," he said hastily, "I'll find somebody."

He reached for the telephone on the desk, at which point my beeper went off, my heart came up into my throat, and I headed for the elevators at a sprint.

I'd been trying all day to keep my mind off the real reason I was there: why I'd come East, why I'd taken on *Tricks for the Sick!*, why I'd accepted Helen's hospitality in the first place. I'd stayed in the emergency room, working hard on not thinking about another area of the hospital: the operating room on the sixth floor.

Now, though, all my avoiding was over. The signal on my beeper, courtesy of a sympathetic operating-room secretary, meant that Joey Dolan was coming out of surgery, where he'd been for just—I glanced at my watch—a little over seven hours.

If I was fast and lucky, I could be in the corridor when they wheeled him by. I would get a glimpse of him then, before he vanished through glass double doors marked Intensive Care.

A twinge of guilt prodded me as I pounded the elevator buttons in the main corridor. Joey, at the moment, was surrounded by the best neurosurgeons in the world, the best nurses, the best equipment, the best everything.

Which meant there was nothing I could do for him, nothing that was not already being done. Probably I wouldn't be able to get within three feet of his bed, assuming they even let me into the intensive care unit any time at all soon.

Meanwhile, Helen's world was falling apart. I should stay with her.

Right. I hammered the elevator buttons and cursed as all three doors opened at once, all going down. They would stop in the basement and come back up: thirty seconds, tops.

I ran for the stairs.

Helen would live. Joey might not.

HE WAS fourteen years old, my son in all but blood, and his choice had been simple: surgery or paralysis. If he chose the surgery, he might be paralyzed anyway. Or he might not wake up.

"There was a small problem," Claire Bogan said. "It was why we took so long."

Until that moment, I'd thought that on Joey's account I could endure anything. That word, though: *problem*. The green linoleum swam beneath my feet.

Still in her olive-drab OR scrub suit, Claire faced me across the high, side-railed bed where Joey lay naked except for a white towel draped across his midriff. Tubes and wires snaked away in all directions from his motionless body; a boxy blue respirator forced air down into his lungs while numbers flickered, radium green, on the electronic monitor screens over his head.

I found my voice. "What kind of problem?"

Claire was fortyish, blond and brilliant, the chief of Mercy's neurosurgery department, and she had removed the tumor that surrounded Joey Dolan's spine.

Or maybe she hadn't; I didn't know which, yet. The operation had come with a lot of cautions and no guarantees; it was, strictly speaking, experimental, which meant among other things that the department of surgery gave it to him free.

"The mass was more extensive than we expected," Claire said. "We had to do some damage getting it out."

"Damage," I repeated stupidly. "How much?"

She shook her head. "We're not sure. The spinal cord is intact at this point, but there could be some swelling. We're giving him drugs to reduce that. And we won't be waking him up as soon as we thought. We don't want him injuring himself."

"Not wake him up? How can you—"

"We're going to sedate him, and keep him still. We have drugs for that, too. It will be better. We can keep everything under control." As she spoke, her gaze ranged over the boy on the bed: measuring, assessing. In spite of myself I began to shiver, my fingernails digging bright separate crescents of pain into the palms of my hands.

I'd never meant to keep him. I'd taken him in, but the arrangement wasn't permanent—or so I'd thought then. On the other hand, I have noticed that as a mark of maturity, the ability to make long-term decisions is almost indistinguishable from the ability to notice that one has made long-term decisions.

Which is to say that I loved him.

"What drugs? And for how long?"

I got the words out, then bit my lip hard. I trusted Claire. I admired her. I even liked her. But I didn't like her enough to cry in front of her, and if I wasn't careful I was going to do that in a minute.

She looked at me cautiously, as if gauging my ability to digest any information whatsoever. I was merely a relative, after all. But apparently she decided I wasn't going to come apart right there on the spot, because after a moment she grudgingly gave me a few spare particles of fact.

"Valium, mostly," she said. "Morphine. And pancuronium. A paralytic, so he won't move. His spinal cord is vulnerable—I don't want to take chances with it."

"Pancuronium," I heard myself repeating dully. A sudden picture of Bill Priest, blue and motionless, flashed into my head. *"Nice and still. Even your breathing muscles..."*

The scant growth of beard on Joey's cheeks made him look like a half-fledged nestling, which he was; soon, I thought, watching his chest rise and fall and imagining his leaving. In his backpack now were blueprints for the cabin he meant to build, at home in California, when he was well.

A place away, he'd told me simply, a place where he could be on his own. Not far; just a few hundred yards into the redwoods, behind the cottage where he'd lived with me since he was twelve.

Listening to him then, I'd felt the apron strings tug for the first time. They'd seemed attached more vitally, though, than to my waistline: higher, and deeper.

Now I touched the guitar calluses on his fingertips, the dimple in his left earlobe, which he had insisted on piercing with a darning needle. The blood had ruined one of his best Iron Maiden concert T-shirts, or so I had thought until he informed me that blood only improved Iron Maiden concert T-shirts.

Claire seemed to read my mind. "Nothing is going to happen. The respirator won't fail, the tubes won't come unhooked, and even if they did, he's watched every minute in here, you know that."

I did know that. But knowing it for someone else was different from knowing it for Joey.

In the cubicle's dim light, a thin scar showed faintly across his forehead, reminder of the terrible winter day when a chainsaw had kicked up at him. Joey's response, once the bandages were off, was to save up his money, buy a new saw with a chain guard and a safety handle, and spend the next winter supplying not just my stove but the stoves of everyone else along our country road. With part of his earnings he'd bought me a year's membership in a private research library in San Fanscisco.

Now the scar seemed just one more badge of Joey's quietly remarkable courage, and I wanted him to get more of them. Ordinary life, with its ordinary hurts, its ordinary, nonfatal scars: I stood by his bedside demanding them for him.

A couple of nurses came into the cubicle then, armed with tubes and bottles and syringes, and carrying several thick plastic IV bags full of dark red blood. B-negative: I'd donated it the day before.

"Give him five of valium every four hours," Claire said to the nurses, neither of whom looked much older than Joey and both of whom I wanted to shake. How dare they be walking when he can't, I thought unreasonably; how dare they be well. Then I stopped myself.

"First valium whenever his pressure starts rising," Claire said, "Five of morphine if he needs it, and pancuronium four milligrams every four hours. If he needs an extra dose, give it and call me." Then she turned to me again.

"I'm not going to insult you by telling you everything will be all right," she said. "But it will be as right as I can make it." I nodded, biting hard on the insides of my cheeks, and she went out.

"You can visit every hour for ten minutes," one of the nurses told me kindly. "But honestly, he isn't going to look any different for quite a while. You could get a cup of coffee, or go home and get some rest. Really, there isn't an awful lot you can do here now. We'll take good care of him.''

She meant well. I nodded again, because I did not trust myself to speak to her without screaming at her, and finally I went out to the waiting area where a half-dozen anxious visitors sat stiffly on the brown industrial-strength upholstery of the low chairs, smoking cigarettes and drinking coffee from styrofoam cups.

Bypassing them, I called the emergency room from the pay phone on the wall. Helen was only now being seen by a doctor, the charge nurse told me; they were sorry she'd had to wait, but other patients needed more immediate care. Yes, they expected she would be there for some time; yes, she was still quite upset.

Poor Walt, I thought, imagining him summoning the strength to comfort her from somewhere in his mooselike frame. I started to ask how long it might be before Helen went home, but the nurse had hung up.

So there I was, alone in the middle of a hospital in a strange city with Helen grief-stunned down in the emergency room and Joey drug-stunned in the intensive care unit, talking into a dead telephone with tears streaming down my cheeks.

After a moment, though, I hung up the phone and scrubbed the tears from my eyes because the other visitors in the waiting room were looking at me. I suppose they thought whoever I'd come for was dying; their faces, while sympathetic, said *better her than us*.

I didn't blame them. I felt the same way. Better them than me; better anyone than Joey. Sooner or later someone's number would inevitably come up; we all knew that. It was why they built places like this.

I had another hour to wait before I saw Joey again; surely I could not stay here where misery hung in the air like nerve gas. I felt certain its effects would seep from my system into Joey's, poisoning the tender young tissues struggling to heal themselves even as I thought.

So, after stopping in the ladies' room to splash my face and blow my nose into a paper towel, I did what I always do when I am in a strange place, in dreadful circumstances, without an idea in the world of what to do next.

I went to the library.

TWO

DESPITE WHAT YOU may have heard, it is perfectly possible for a normal person to read a medical book. The difficulty is simply that doctors do not like normal persons to do it, because the reading of medical books by normal persons leads to fright. Symptoms of rare and exotic subtropical diseases tend to leap directly from pages of medical books into the imaginations of normal persons, after which they may never be entirely normal, ever again.

The trick for preventing this, I have learned, is to ignore the color plates, no matter how divertingly grotesque, and to remember that the parasites swarming so hideously on page 321 do not flourish there by nature. They infest the river Ganges, and only the steamiest, most glutinous part of it at that.

Approached in this way, a medical book may do little more than narrow one's choice of swimming holes. The other trick, however, is a bit less easy to manage: getting into a medical library at all.

This latter feat I accomplished by means of my special ID card, a strip of plastic stamped with my name and my signature, vouchsafed to me by a solemn hospital administrator. Apparently I did not look to him like someone who would, on purpose, acquire an imaginary subtropical disease. Besides, if all went well, *Tricks for the Sick!* was going to give his hospital some good press.

Of course, I did not call the book that when I talked to him about it; *Johnny Goes to the Hospital* was more his style. Hospital administrators, it seemed to me, were steadily getting younger and younger; at least that was my theory, the alternative being just too dismal to think about.

At any rate, I got into the library, and there I discovered that the drug pancuronium binds, in just a very few seconds, to the junction between nerve and muscle, blocking the signals that tell muscles when to contract. Breathing muscles, for instance.

Around me hung a studious hush, broken only when someone got up from one of the long oaken tables or turned a page. The room smelled of floor polish, steam heat, and ozone from the continuously running Xerox machine back in the card catalog room.

Despite the smells, though, the atmosphere was of books: thousands of volumes above me in stacks and galleries and attics, below me in basements and subbasements. Loaded onto carts for reshelving, heaped in carrels with pink slips stuck between their pages, piled on tables and ranked on racks, open on desks: books. On their shelves they stood shoulder to shoulder, forming walls so sturdy I thought that if the library building should collapse, the books themselves would go on standing, a solid bulwark against the dark of ignorance.

I found it all immensely comforting. But then, that is my private method of reassurance: what can be learned can be controlled. And if I cannot learn it myself, well, someone else already has, and I can go to the library and look it up.

Before me on the desk lay the new edition of *Pharmacological Basis for Therapeutics*. From it I learned that the drugs Claire Bogan was giving Joey had side effects; none, however, were as bad as the side effects of not giving them to him. That made me feel better.

The other thing I learned, though, made me feel worse. I didn't want to think about Bill Priest any more, but the book gave me no choice.

In my ignorance, I'd assumed that as drug-induced paralysis came on, awareness slid away. What I'd imagined must happen when a dose of pancuronium took hold was a sort of general fading-out, the fog descending and thickening peacefully to darkness.

I couldn't have been more wrong, as the pharmacy text made clear. Pancuronium was not a sedative or anesthetic. Patients given pancuronium, the book warned, should be as thoroughly sedated as their condition allowed, since their awareness was otherwise in no way diminished.

Which, I realized, was why Claire had ordered valium and morphine for Joey. It was also why pancuronium wasn't the drug of choice for would-be suicides.

Without much wanting to, I thought back to the emergency room; *not a good way,* the helpful anesthesiologist had said. I hadn't understood; the stuff seemed pretty damned effective.

Now that I'd done my homework, though, I got a clearer picture; so clear, I wished I hadn't. It was, in fact, a lot like the color plate of the swarming nasties on page 321: ugly and true to life.

Bill Priest had suffocated, wide awake all the way. The sensations he felt while it went on would not have been pleasant. The three to five minutes between paralysis and unconsciousness would have seemed to him like a very long time indeed.

With this realization came uneasy speculation. All around me, medical students were studying: anatomy and physiology, biochemistry and pathology. And pharmacology.

As a medical student, Bill Priest would have studied those things, too, which meant he would have known pancuronium was not just a bad drug for suicide. With the possible exception of strychnine, it was the worst. And while I supposed he might have killed himself, I doubted very much that he would have deliberately tortured himself to death in so horrid a manner.

Very unhappily, I began wondering who had.

OVER THE next few hours Joey's condition remained unchanged, and from the emergency room I learned Helen had been discharged, so I drove to her house. By now some clever pathologist might be getting the same idea I had: that Bill Priest had been murdered.

Which meant there would be questions. And knowing just how unpleasant those questions could get, I thought Helen had better hear them first from me.

The idea hurried me down Chapel Street, past the mall and the Schubert Theatre and the Green. Since I'd been in New Haven last, the downtown area had been turned into a sort of yuppie theme park where one could now buy a chocolate-chip bagel, a pair of pink Reeboks, and a pound of Jamaican Blue Mountain without ever encountering a person less privileged than oneself. Even the old-age pensioners' hotels had been transformed, their bricks sharply repointed and their rents raised, their rooms combined and track-lit for graphic-arts studios.

Helen lived a few blocks farther east, in a three-story brownstone on Lodge Street, a gentrified upscale ghetto of wrought-iron fences, fake gas lamps, and brass door knockers shaped like the heads of endangered beasts. Each front stoop bore a tub of geraniums; each first-floor window flashed a security sticker. Saabs, Volvos, and BMW's stood at the cobblestone curbs.

On the other hand, when you go to park a Datsun you learn the value of the little things in life. I pulled Helen's tiny sedan neatly in between two of the larger machines and, gripped by sudden apprehension, shut off the key without stopping to enjoy my triumph.

Helen's windows were all dark.

"Helen?" I dropped my bag on the table in the marble-tiled entrance hall, tossed my coat at the antique bentwood coatrack, and went on through the cream-and-rose-chintz living room to the kitchen, where rows of polished copper pans mooned me like so many pink babies' bottoms from the exposed brick walls.

No Helen.

Her drink was white wine and seltzer; it was an acquired taste, and to make sure I wouldn't acquire it I'd stashed a fifth of Cutty under the sink. The gizmo on the refrigerator hummingly disgorged three ice cubes into one of Helen's chunky cut-crystal highball glasses. When the ice cubes floated, I stopped pouring Cutty.

Where the hell was she?

I flipped through her address book, on the butcher-block counter just under the telephone and had just found Walt Krusanke's number when, as if by mental telepathy, the phone rang and it was Walt.

Which was how I learned Helen had indeed been discharged from the emergency room. She had not, however, been discharged home. Instead, according to Walt, she had been admitted to the hospital, supposedly suffering from a number of serious diseases I knew she didn't have.

Also according to Walt, who sounded quite upset and as if he didn't understand any of this any more than I did, Bill Priest was missing. Or rather, his body was.

Somewhere between the emergency room and the morgue it had simply vanished.

IT WAS nearly midnight when I found Harry Lemon on the medical ward where Helen had been sent.

"Harry," I said as politely as I could, "there's been some mistake. Helen doesn't have blood clots, diabetes, high blood pressure, or heart disease. She's perfectly healthy, always has been, so what in the world ever made you think—"

Harry smiled, which was in itself unusual and should have alerted me.

"Pardon?" he murmured, signing his name to Helen's chart with a jerky flourish and slotting the chart into a rack behind the nursing desk. "I seem to be having trouble hearing you. Would you mind not repeating that?"

"I *said,*" I began, and then stopped. Harry's smile fairly dripped with dangerous sweetness as he glanced toward Helen's room, just a few yards away down the quiet corridor.

Outside her room sat a man in a familiar blue uniform. The uniform included handcuffs, a badge, and a large, imposing-looking leather holster containing a large, imposing-looking .38 caliber police special revolver.

"Oh," I said faintly, and Harry nodded.

"I should shut up, right?"

He nodded again. "Charlotte, I am going home now. I am going to hand over my beeper to the next poor miserable sucker—ah, I mean, dedicated professional, and get some sleep."

He eyed me. "You and your friend don't object to my sleeping, do you, Charlotte?"

I assured him that we did not.

"Good," he said, rubbing his plump hands together. "Because in addition to my emergency room duties I am chief resident on this ward, and if anything goes seriously wrong here tonight, the nurses will call me. And then, Charlotte, I will call you. And I will be very irritated."

He fixed me with a look that communicated perfectly just how irritated he would be.

I nodded. "Can I see her?"

"That is between you and your opthalmologist. But certainly you may see her. My orders state specifically that you must be allowed to. Besides, she's not under arrest—yet."

The man in the uniform turned a page of the *New York Post.* Beside his chair stood a stack of other reading matter, several cans of diet soda, and a sack from a local fast-food place. He looked relaxed, secure, and as if he had settled in for the duration, which to me meant that Helen Terrell was in deep and serious trouble.

Uniformed men sitting outside hospital rooms can afford to look secure, because they do not have to worry about catching people. They have already caught their people, and they know it.

"There have been a few questions," Harry said.

There'd been a few Mongol hordes, too, I seemed to remember. I edged Harry a few steps down the hall, out of earshot from the uniformed man.

"Harry, how are you going to get away with this?"

Harry was not in the habit of drumming fake diseases up out of thin air in order to keep their supposed owners out of jail cells. Harry's habit was to beat even real diseases back into thin air, where he thought they belonged and where they would certainly cause a good deal less trouble for everyone, especially himself.

"We're all entitled to a mistake now and again, Charlotte," he said, widening his eyes in feigned innocence. It made him look incredibly foolish and I could have kissed him for it, because when all Helen's tests came back normal he was going to look more foolish still, and he clearly didn't care.

He'd fallen for her, of course; everyone did. Better men than Harry had done much more foolish things for Helen Terrell.

But from this thought a host of others bristled unpleasantly like the legs on a centipede; someone, after all, had recently done something very foolish indeed, not to mention wicked. And unless I missed my guess, Helen was about to be blamed for it.

Down the corridor, the uniformed man finished the *Post*'s Jumble puzzle and unhurriedly began to fill in the crossword.

"At any rate," Harry said, "not only is there the question of where William Priest's body has gotten to, intriguing as that may be, but it seems there's a question of how it got to be a body in the first place. As opposed to a live person, I mean."

Harry's smile became positively beatific. He hadn't, I realized, been warning me about future possible irritation. He was irritated already.

Very irritated.

"Remember our friend from the anesthesia department," he continued, "who came down and gave us a hand earlier in the emergency room?"

The one who'd gotten the tube down Bill Priest's throat, and told me about pancuronium. "Burton Dunn?"

Harry nodded. "Right. Well, Burt called me later. Some of these foreign-schooled fellows really are quite conscientious, I must say. And it seems he'd gotten to thinking about the drug. It wasn't the standard pancuronium. This was new-generation stuff. Kicks in almost instantly—good for traumatic airway emergencies, crushed throat and the like, when you need your customer limp without a moment's delay.

"Anesthesia boys." He shook his head patronizingly. "They don't know much, but they are tops in pharmacology, I'll give them that."

I thought about how grateful the anesthesia department was going to be, to have Harry's endorsement.

"And what Burton wanted to know," Harry went on, "was how anyone could self-administer that much of that particular drug. A piquant query, I had to admit."

Right. Piquant. Now I understood Burton's puzzled look.

It's perfectly easy to give yourself a shot, once you get over the initial fear and squeamishness. Diabetics and dope addicts do it all the time. But then, they aren't paralyzed.

Bill Priest had been, seconds after the drug began entering his bloodstream. He wouldn't have had time to push it all in, whether he'd wanted to or not.

"It's not just unlikely," Harry continued, "it's impossible. Which meant I had to notify the authorities. Suspected felony—regulations are clear. And that meant that in addition to all of my other obnoxious chores, I spent half an hour this evening with a police detective, one Lieutenant Malley."

He shuddered faintly. "Horrid fellow. When the body came up missing, he looked at me as though he thought I'd done it."

"Who does he think done it?"

Harry winced.

"I mean, did it? Assuming it was done?" In my stunned state of surprise and fatigue I clung to hope, but the answer was obvious.

"Oh, it was done, all right," Harry said. "Pancuronium in the vial, pancuronium in the syringe. If we had the body, pathology would no doubt find pancuronium in it, too. Consider the absence of myoclonic response to defibrillation—definitively diagnostic of neuromuscular blockade, wouldn't you say?"

He looked at me, remembered where he was and who I was, and came down from the podium of his dreams with a visible jolt.

"Ahem. At any rate, Charlotte, statistics do indicate that most of us are done in by our nearest and dearest. After all, who has better reason?"

He glanced toward her room. "However. I can keep her here for forty-eight hours, perhaps seventy-two. Four days at the outside, Charlotte. After which..."

I took his meaning. After which, even Harry wouldn't be able to disguise the fact that Helen was healthy as a horse, no matter how utterly smitten he might be with her.

"Besides," he added, astonishingly for Harry, "any man who would give that woman a moment's pain deserves murdering."

And with that he turned away; woe betide the person who gets between a medical resident and his bed, once he is finally able to go there.

RULE FOR murderers: if you must kill by injection, don't get busted for narcotics first.

"I need a lawyer, don't I?" Helen said.

Her hands lay limp, palms upturned, on the white thermal hospital blanket. She looked spent, her shoulders slumped and her face oddly slackened, as if she'd aged twenty years in the past few hours.

She also looked guilty as hell, at least when viewed through eyes other than my own. Motive, method, and opportunity: I could imagine a jury believing she'd had all three. The missing corpse was the only hitch. How could she have gotten rid of it?

The trouble was, any jury that got a look at Helen would also believe she'd easily managed to attract an accomplice, and this idea also seemed already to have occurred to her.

"In fact, I need more than a lawyer," she said.

Then she waited, not wanting to ask. Wanting me to offer. You don't solve murders in California without your old East Coast friends finding out about it.

You don't turn your back on those friends, either, no matter how long ago you made them. Not if you want to walk anywhere near the path of the righteous, anyway. And not if you want to sleep at night.

On top of which, there was the question of where to sleep at night. If fish and visitors smell in three days, I'd been reeking of low tide for six weeks now. Meanwhile Helen had gone on providing drinks, dinners, and lavender-scented sheets, along with constant assurances that if

I went to a hotel, she would be devastated—not that I could afford a hotel, a fact Helen had perceived with perfect clarity.

Now I saw her imagining, with some justice, that I might want to do something in return. Find out who killed Bill, for example. Prove, by the deep and mysterious methods known only to me, that Helen hadn't. Deliver the true culprit into official custody, and live happily ever after.

Never mind the little matter of an ongoing police investigation. Never mind that I'd have sooner—and safer—stuck my hand into Joey's chainsaw than get involved in one of those.

Still, without Helen I'd have been napping in bus stations and washing up in public lavatories. The least I could do was lend her a sympathetic ear.

"So listen," I said, pulling a chair up beside her. "How come the cops think you killed Billy?"

She shot me a look of trepidation and right away I knew I was in the soup, because I'd seen that same look twenty-five years earlier, the day she broke the transistor radio I'd earned by selling garden seeds. She'd been sorry then, too, but it hadn't fixed the radio.

"Well . . . I guess because I said I would."

Terrific. "And did anybody hear you? Say you'd kill him?"

Her laugh was bitter. "Everyone in his building, probably. I didn't say it, I screamed it. Twice, maybe three times last night, after—"

I waved a hand to silence her. First things first.

There was an intercom panel in the wall behind her bed. Its lights were off; no one was eavesdropping. Still, I didn't even whisper the words, only mouthed them:

"Did you? Kill him?" Then I stopped her again before she could reply.

I will do a lot of deeds, but they don't include perjuring myself at a murder trial. Perjury wouldn't help, anyway;

when those guys know enough to ask, they know the answer.

Still, I didn't want to be able to confirm it for them.

After a puzzled moment Helen understood. She looked down at her hands, then back at me. "No," she said, "No, I didn't."

I let my breath out, and began speaking aloud. "Okay. What did the police say?"

Her lips tightened. "They haven't charged me yet, if that's what you mean. That policeman outside is to keep me from running away, though, I think, so they can when they get ready."

Right, and to bust her stones a little, too, playing hardball right from the start so she'd know they meant business.

Her eyes filled with tears. "I wish I hadn't screamed at him, Charlotte. I didn't know I'd never see him again."

I wished she hadn't screamed at him, too. I wished she'd never met him. In fact, I was beginning to wish I'd never even met her, but I'd wished that before and probably would again. It was just one of those things about Helen: sometimes she seems like a nut, sometimes she don't.

"What did you tell them when they questioned you?"

She shrugged. "Not much. I almost did, I was so out of it. But I'd only told them my name and where I lived when that doctor came in, and he said—"

She drew herself up, frowned, and deepened her voice in a credible imitation of Harry Lemon.

"'Young woman,' he said, 'have you been charged?' And I said no. And *he* said..."

Her eyebrows knit again. "*He* said, 'As your physician, I order you not to speak one more word until you are represented by competent legal counsel.'"

She smiled; almost a real smile. "And he told the policemen that if they upset me, and I lost the baby, and it turned out I wasn't guilty of anything—or maybe even if I was—I could probably sue the city for millions of dollars. After that, they didn't want to talk to me any more. I guess they'll be back, though."

They would. They'd be visiting me, too, probably.

"How about today? Did anyone see you at Bill's? Getting out of the cab, or going through the lobby? Or in the elevator?"

Helen's fingers plucked nervously at the blanket. "No. I didn't take a cab—I walked, for the exercise. There was no one in the lobby. And I didn't take the elevator, I always take the stairs. Somehow I've got to try to hold onto my figure—"

The ghost of a smile came onto her face, vanished when she took in my expression. "Why? What difference does it make?"

"For one thing," I said, "it makes it hard to prove you were going in when Walt met you. Instead of leaving."

Comprehension dawned. "You mean, leaving after—"

I nodded. "And they know you could have injected him. If they don't know, they will."

She sagged into the pillows. "I wasn't addicted, Charlotte. I got involved with the wrong people...."

"You got arrested and convicted for possession of narcotics and narcotics paraphernalia. Needles and dope. They know you've shot up, they know you know how. The *why* doesn't matter, Helen."

"But that was fifteen years ago. In college, for heaven's sake."

"Have you forgotten how to find a vein?"

She stared at her hands for a moment, then shook her head. "No," she said quietly. "No, I haven't forgotten."

She took a deep breath and became again all at once the practical, hardheaded overachiever that was the other side of her character. The switch was boggling unless you were used to it or remembered it as well as I did.

"Jim Crichton's number is in my book at home," she said. "He's in corporate law, but he'll refer me. I guess I need a criminal lawyer."

I guessed so, too. Once the police got their ducks in a lawsuit-proof row, they would be back. Mad, too, probably.

I stood. "Let me have your keys, will you? The copy you made is sticking in the Datsun's ignition."

Obediently, she fished her own set of keys from her bag; I took them and left, jingling my next move in my pocket.

What the hell; we were old friends, but I'd never promised I wouldn't lie to her.

On the other hand, she hadn't promised she wouldn't lie to me, either. Thinking this, I stopped jingling the keys, because I'd just realized another thing about Helen that hadn't changed. She was still the type of person who would answer your question before you finished asking it.

At least, she was until I asked her if she'd done murder. Then she'd paused: just a split second, but long enough to jab me with a ragged needle of doubt.

Her answer satisfied me. Her hesitation didn't. I didn't want to think that Helen Terrell had killed Bill Priest.

Suddenly, though, I wasn't sure.

THE BUTCHER-BLOCK table in Helen's kitchen was big enough to handle the entire Chicago stockyards, but there wasn't a knife mark on it so I carved salami on the little cutting board beside the brushed aluminum sink. When I went back to the table, I had a deck of salami slices, a chunk of toasted French bread heavily smeared with Brie, a quartered tomato, and a handful of Oreo cookies.

Amidst her chic decorating scheme the simple food looked all wrong, so I decorated my own interior with it. Then my empty glass looked wrong so I filled it a final time with Cutty and carried it into the living room, where I sank into one of the chintz armchairs.

I already knew what I was going to do; I just wasn't looking forward to it. Besides, it wasn't time to do it yet. Darkest before dawn, they say, which is why the hour before dawn is the best one for snooping.

I used the time remaining to take a nap and a shower, and change into fresh clothes. By a little after four I had dumped two scoops full of fresh-ground French roast and black Kona into a paper filter and put the kettle on. When the water boiled I poured it through the coffee and dosed the resultant brew with plenty of sugar and a dollop of whipping cream.

While I drank this potent ambrosia, I examined Helen's keys. There were a fistful of hospital keys to places she had to get at for the lobby-remodeling job; it wouldn't be politic, for example, to cut through the ventilation system while installing the recessed track lighting, and Helen wasn't the type to believe what was inked on blueprints. She'd been checking things herself.

On a smaller loop, however, were six other keys. Three were to Helen's own house: the front door key, the key to her inside door, and the one to the deadbolt. A fourth stamped UNIVERSITY PROPERTY—DO NOT DUPLICATE, belonged to her office at the hospital. Two more were standard Nissan issue.

The fifth and sixth hung together on a yellow metal chain. I didn't know for sure what they unlocked, but if I was right, they were the keys to Bill Priest's apartment.

And that meant at least four people with access to Bill Priest's place: Helen, Walt Krusanke, Bill himself, and now me.

Sometime soon, I thought, people were going to start asking questions again. They might even lock her up while they asked them; never mind that she was innocent. Or that I hoped she was.

Innocent didn't count. What counted was an ambitious district attorney's ability to build a case, close the case, and get a lot of favorable newspaper ink in connection with the case.

Which was why, despite my earlier intentions, I planned to be asking a lot of questions myself in the next few days. And prosecuting attorneys aren't the only ones who like a head start on the answers.

For my head start, all I had to do now was screw my courage to the sticking post and hope it didn't screw me back.

PRIEST'S APARTMENT building was tan, square, and modern, with all the homey appeal of a cinder block. Inside: banks of mailboxes in the foyer, big glass doors that one of the keys on Helen's ring unlocked. Silence boomeranged off the mirrored walls of a lobby so empty it felt as if it could suck itself inside out.

The green indoor-outdoor carpeting bore a mud-colored stain that led from the glass doors to the elevator, which turned out to be a metal box lined with walnut contact paper. I didn't have claustrophobia when I got in, but I did by the time it reached the third floor.

The hall there was more of the matted green carpet, long tan walls set too near to each other, and silent door after silent identical door all down the corridor like the stage set for the opening act of a bad dream.

The yellow sticker on Priest's door said that inside was a crime scene, and I should KEEP OUT.

I looked up and down the hall. It smelled of bleach and laundry detergent, and I guessed that the unnumbered door at the end of it hid a couple of washers and dryers. From one of the other apartments came the faint voice of John Wayne, telling somebody to listen up and listen up good. Nothing else moved or made a sound, and the lighted numeral 3 over the elevator stayed lit.

I loosened the yellow adhesive paper from Priest's doorjamb with a small battery-powered traveler's steam iron that I keep for taking the wrinkles out of official stickers. Then I unlocked the door, covered the knob with a tissue, turned it, and went in.

The room was dark, which suited me fine. A deep gray oblong in the blackness told me I was in the living room, and that the curtains were open. I crossed to the window, taking care not to stumble over anything, mindful of Walt Krusanke asleep in the apartment below. At least, I hoped he was asleep.

On the way out of the hospital, I'd filched a pair of thin plastic gloves from a cart outside one of the isolation rooms. Now I put them on. It seemed a dramatic sort of precaution to be taking, but then, getting arrested as an accessory to murder would be dramatic, too.

The curtains were cheap but useful for my purposes: fabric facing the room, a rubberized lining on the window side. I drew them shut, then felt my way along the wall until I found a light switch. It was a rheostat and I turned it just past the click.

A plastic Tiffany-style hanging lamp lit dimly above the wood-grain formica dinette set by the window. A few circulars and bits of junk mail lay scattered on the table; beyond it was a small kitchen with the standard appliances.

A few cups and glasses stood in the sink. On the stove a jar of instant coffee was flanked by a battered saucepan. The refrigerator held a six-pack of Miller Light, a quart of orange juice, a tub of margarine, and a loaf of white bread.

The freezer's contents looked like a supermarket display case: TV dinners, pizzas, boil-in-bag vegetables, a plastic sack of french-fried potato puffs, and a carton of fish sticks.

It was the food supply of a man who ate because he had to. The rest of the apartment gave the same impression: he lived here because he had to live somewhere. The remaining furniture consisted of a sofa with a green chenille cover thrown across it, a red beanbag hassock, a thrift shop coffee table, and an old Zenith black-and-white TV. On the TV stood a pair of rabbit ears with foil wrapped around the tips. The bedroom was a mattress, a lamp, and a dresser; the bathroom held the usual men's grooming equipment and nothing more.

Whatever Bill Priest's interests were, and I knew he had plenty, he kept them elsewhere. Presumably, a man who took such care to keep his interests out of his living space would also keep his elsewhere securely locked, which meant there had to be a key to it.

In one of the kitchen drawers lay a key case and a checkbook. Not hidden; he hadn't expected a search and clearly there hadn't been one yet. The door sticker was to keep things pretty for when there was. The balance in the checkbook was twenty-two thousand and change; stuck in the back of it was a sheet of lined looseleaf covered on both sides with names and addresses, each name tagged with a letter and a number.

I dropped the keys, checkbook, and notepaper into my bag, turned off the lamp, and opened the curtains. Outside, it was threatening to get light. A few cars moved slowly in the street, their taillights cherry smears in the drizzle that had begun.

In the corridor, I locked Priest's apartment and pressed the yellow sticker back onto the door. Now, inside was the scene of several crimes, all of which I was indeed guilty of. Unlawful entry, tampering, withholding—the list went on and on.

Which should have turned me and sent me scuttling for home. Instead, it made me feel better than I'd felt all day.

I didn't know who had killed Bill Priest. I didn't know for sure that Helen hadn't, and that alone disturbed me badly. But she was the oldest friend I had, and when I came East with Joey after not seeing her for years, she hadn't stopped to wonder if my presence was going to be convenient. She'd offered her home, car, money if I wanted it. Any way at all, she'd been ready and willing to take care of me.

Now she was in real trouble, and with Joey lying comatose and beyond any help I could give, my own caretaking machinery was revved to a high, steady whine. If she was innocent, she needed me. If she was guilty, she needed me more.

Besides, Claire Bogan's assurances to the contrary, Joey was in real trouble, too. Claire's voice had said he might make it, but her eyes had said, regretfully, that he might not.

If he lived, I felt nothing could hurt me. If he didn't, I didn't have anything to lose. And what I needed now, desperately, was something to keep me from thinking that, every waking minute.

Maybe, in fact, I needed Helen's trouble even more than she needed my help getting out of it.

I rattled Priest's doorknob to make sure his door was securely locked. Then, turning, I walked into a wall draped in a damp gray sweatshirt.

Which turned out to be Walt Krusanke's muscular chest.

THREE

"THOUGHT I HEARD SOMEONE," Walt said, a look of alarm fading from his blue eyes.

I rubbed my nose, which felt as if I'd bench pressed a bowling ball with it. A wet bowling ball: Walt Krusanke was soaked from the bristles of his clipped brown hair to the cuffs of his gray cotton running suit. Clearly the rain hadn't stopped him from putting in his early-morning mileage.

"I was just checking to make sure the ambulance guys left Bill's door locked," I said. Gesturing with the key in my hand, I noticed too late that I still wore the plastic gloves.

Walt nodded, dripping. The water trapped in his running suit could have irrigated Oklahoma.

"Heard you inside," he said. "Thin ceilings. I was just about to make some breakfast," he went on. "Want some?"

I blinked, and looked again at Walt Krusanke. Under all the beef, I thought I detected a flicker of humor. Behind the beef and the humor I though I detected a man who wanted to talk.

As I followed the squish-squish of his sodden sneakers down the hall toward the stairwell, I thought also that I had misread the look I'd seen fading from his eyes.

He hadn't been alarmed. He'd been relieved.

His apartment was the identical twin of Priest's: bedroom and bath just off the brief entryway, then a long room that was both living and dining areas with the same kitchenette just to the left of the big front window. Except for the bare bones of the layout, though, it couldn't have been more different.

"Coffee?" Walt asked from the kitchen.

Ranged neatly on the counter were a toaster-oven, a set of canisters for flour, sugar, and so on, and a cookie jar in the shape of a smiling cat. A clean dishtowel hung from the handle of the refrigerator door.

"Yes, thanks," I called back. In the bookcase at the living end of the long room stood several trophies, the largest a bronze figure of Atlas on a walnut pedestal. The engraved plaque read WALTER FRANCIS KRUSANKE—NEW ENGLAND CHAMPION 1985.

He saw me looking at it and gave a faint, embarrassed laugh. "I used to fool around in competition."

"Used to? Why'd you give it up?"

He shrugged; only about 4.5 on the Richter scale. The floor hardly trembled at all. "It got in the way of other stuff. Listen, I'm going to take a shower. Pour yourself coffee when it's ready. Make yourself at home—I'll have breakfast fixed in a jiff."

He disappeared into the bathroom; as the shower hissed on, I used his absence to discover what the "other stuff" was.

Only one shelf in the bookcase held trophies; the rest held books. A row of orange paperback spines turned out to be the complete Penguin set of Jane Austen. Beside them stood all of Stephen King's novels, and all of John Le Carré's. A few Parker mysteries and Colin Wilson's *The Mind Parasites* filled out the fiction collection.

All the others were textbooks: human anatomy, physiology, biostatistics, and a shelf of sports medicine manuals. I thought about Walt's big, blunt head, embarrassed at having assumed there was nothing in it, and resolved for perhaps the millionth time to learn from my mistakes.

And from Walt, if I could.

Something brushed my ankle; I looked down to find a pair of blue eyes regarding me. Crossed eyes, with a Siamese cat behind them.

"Meerowryowow," the cat said. I sat down on the sofa, which was mostly covered by a large rose-and-black crocheted afghan. The cat leapt up beside me, whiskers twitching and crossed eyes glaring.

"Mrmmph," it remarked skeptically.

The shower went off; Walt appeared in jeans, a sweater, and athletic socks.

"Nice afghan," I said. The cat kept glaring at me. "Was it a gift?"

The embarrassed smile again. "Nah. I made it, actually."

He crossed to the kitchen, poured coffee, and brought a cup to me. "It's real good hand therapy. I figured I ought to know how to do it. I'm looking to be a professional trainer. Do you want cream or anything?"

I did, until I tasted the coffee.

He gestured at the Siamese. "Watch out for her, by the way. Her name's Cat Dancing. She's nice but she's nippy."

I put my cup down on the end table and looked at her.

"Cat," I said in a normal, conversational tone. "Hey, Cat."

Cat Dancing walked calmly onto my lap, eyeing me as if to make sure I knew just how great a privilege I was receiving, and settled down.

Walt grinned. "A cat person, I presume. Ordinarily, she'd be getting ready to rip your lungs out."

She was a chocolate point, no kitten; ten or eleven years old to judge by the darkness of her fur and her floppy belly. She was not purring, and I did not make the mistake of trying to scratch her ears.

Instead, as Walt headed for the kitchen, I reached for the coffee again; Cat muttered and resettled herself. "I thought you health guys didn't go for this caffeine stuff."

"Yeah, and the Pope's Jewish." All of a sudden I thought I was going to like Walt Krusanke, and when I tasted his eggs Benedict, I knew I was going to.

"So," he said as I scraped up the last bit of Canadian bacon and washed it down with a final swallow of coffee, "I put the trophy on the shelf, took the scholarship that came with it, and here I am. Beats playing football—those guys might as well just hop knees-first into a meat grinder."

"And you met Bill . . . ?"

A regretful look came into his broad face. "Anatomy lab." He rubbed his forehead with a big hand. "You know, I still can't believe he's gone. He was that kind of guy. When I was with him, I always wound up doing crazy things, going places I never would have gone. Last year, we did a two week backpack through the Texas desert."

He shook his head again. "He wasn't always an easy guy to be around. You kind of had to know how to handle him. He could be...I don't know. Pushy. Manipulative. I think I was probably one of his few real friends, he was that overwhelming. But once you knew him—if you didn't let him shove you around—you couldn't imagine life without him."

"Yeah," I said. "Helen's having a hard time doing that right now."

His expression changed, something sad closing off behind his eyes, back there where I wasn't invited.

"Right. I guess she must be. Helen is . . . a nice person."

"And Bill wasn't."

Walt looked up, ready to be angry; then his eyes met mine.

"No. Like I said, he was interesting, energetic. Exciting, even. I envied him in a lot of ways. But you couldn't call him nice. Especially . . ."

"Helen told me," I said.

The big hand massaged the broad forehead again.

"When I met her with Bill, I wanted to warn her. I'd seen it before, the way he was with people, women especially, like he had magic powers. Lots of women saw through him, but Helen was different. She was really in love with him."

"And you," I said quietly, "were in love with her. Are, I mean. That's why you're talking to me now."

Cat Dancing hopped off my lap and into his. "It's that obvious, huh? I guess I might as well be, now that—I mean, wait a minute. I don't want you to get me wrong. I would never have horned in between Bill and Helen. No matter what."

I swallowed the last of my orange juice. "I suppose you heard them fighting, though."

He nodded reluctantly. "A lot, towards the end. They'd be right upstairs, and I guess by then he was just driving her a little crazy. With the baby coming and all."

Yeah. And driving Walt a little crazy, maybe, too.

"How about last night?" I asked. "Helen says they had a big disagreement."

He shrugged. "Nope. Missed that one. I was on the re-hab ward. Guy I used to know dove into the wrong end of a pool—I'm teaching him to type."

My eyebrows must have gone up. "He pokes the keys with a stick in his mouth," Walt amplified, "because his mouth is what he can move."

"Oh," I said. Outside the big front window it was full light now, at least as full as it was going to get on an autumn day of pouring rain. And seeing as I could still move more than my mouth, it was time I did.

"Are you going to help Helen?" he asked as I got up.

"If I can. Are you going to help me?"

"Sure. She couldn't have killed him, you know. She just . . ." He lifted his hands in a gesture of frustration, let them fall.

"Right," I said. "She just couldn't. Any idea who could have, then? Was Bill having trouble with anyone?"

Walt shook his head. "He never mentioned anything. But that was another thing about him—he might complain about little things, but he didn't give himself away much on the big stuff. Actually, when classes were in session he spent most of his time working. Put in more library hours than anyone I ever saw."

I pulled Priest's keys out of my bag. "How about these? Familiar?"

"Sure, those are Bill's. The little one is to a locked study carrel in the medical library, up on the third floor. If you make honors, you can get one."

I looked at him. "Honors, huh?"

A final flash of the embarrassed smile, like sunshine coming out from behind a big, burly cloud. "Us muscle-bound guys gotta break the stereotypes somehow."

At the door, I looked back at the cozy room with the cat and the afghan, the trophies and books and the lingering smell of good breakfast. Where breaking stereotypes was concerned, he was doing a pretty good job.

Hurrying through the rain to Helen's car, I thought also that in spite of everything he'd had a pretty good reason to kill Bill Priest. I'd seen Walt by Helen's side in the hospital waiting room. Just now I'd watched his face when I said her name. I'd heard him insist she couldn't have done violence.

He was in love with her, all right, and in his thin-walled, thin-floored apartment, he'd been a captive audience to all that had gone on between her and Bill.

Also, he was big—big enough for the hardest part of injecting a grown man with poison. Bill Priest, after all, would hardly have stuck his arm calmly out for the killing shot.

Assuming he'd known what it was, someone had to have held him down, to give it to him.

THE UPPER FLOORS of the medical library smelled of floor polish and old wood. It was just eight-fifteen; early enough, I hoped, to get in ahead of the gossip. Maybe people here didn't know yet that Priest was dead.

But they would soon. In the medical center, gossip spread faster than subtropical diseases. I hurried to the third floor and went into the first office I came to.

The young woman behind the typewriter looked up with pallid irritation, her hands poised impatiently over the keyboard.

"I'm supposed to pick up some notes from a friend's study carrel," I said, rushing the words and looking as harried as possible.

She swallowed the toffee she was chewing and plucked another from the foil-covered box on her desk.

"He gave me the key," I went on, flashing it, "but he forgot to tell me which carrel he's in. His name's Bill Priest."

At the name, a hint of color came into her complexion; she dropped the toffee wrapper into the wastebasket and brushed back one of the mouse-colored curls that looped tiredly over her plump cheeks.

"Oh, sure. He's here all the time. Isn't he a nice guy, though? His carrel's this way."

She went ahead of me out of the office and down the dim hall, wearing a matching wool sweater-and-skirt set whose style was as faded as her hopes. Her sensible heels and heavy support hose made her short legs look like beige fireplugs.

"I help him all the time," she confided. Behind her thick glasses, her sparse, colorless lashes batted coquettishly over watery gray eyes. "References and things. It's so fulfilling being helpful, don't you think?" she finished a little anxiously.

Clearly she wanted me to put in a good word for her; perhaps my reference would turn the trick where helpfulness had failed.

"Yes," I said. "It certainly is fulfilling." I knew I was patronizing her, but I couldn't help it; she looked as if she would gladly fling herself down onto the linoleum to be walked on.

"Well, this is it." She gestured at a door, which had an opaque glass window with *304* stencilled on it. "Listen, say hi to him for me, will you? Tell him Felicity Dunwoodie says hi."

"Um, if I see him," I began, wondering what Felicity would do if I told her Bill Priest was supposed to be in a drawer in the morgue's cold room, only no one could find his corpse. Then her phone began ringing and she hurried off to answer it.

The carrel was about twelve feet square, its walls lined entirely with books. On the desk stood a computer: keyboard, screen, and disk drives. Above were several shelves full of boxes of disks. A bulletin board displayed lists of assignments, with due dates still several months away.

A heavy-duty printer sat on the floor, on a sound-muffling foam pad. The printer featured a ratchet for running form-feed paper, several cartons of which were piled in the corner of the room along with boxes of printer ribbons.

I sat down in the chair in front of the computer. To judge by the number of reference books and style manuals on the shelves, being a medical student involved a lot of research, not to mention writing. And it was writing, not calculating; a number-crunching specialist wouldn't need as much paper as I saw in the cartons on the floor.

Two filing cabinets held up the desk. The drawers were full of manila envelopes, stick-on address labels, rolls of stamps. There was even a postage scale, at which I paused.

This place didn't look like a student workroom, no matter how industrious the student. It looked, more credibly, like the office of a fair-sized medical journal.

Mistrustfully I regarded the computer screen, which stared back with a blank, unwavering eye. Then I took down the first of the floppy-disk boxes. Since, when I am not out chasing other people's wild geese, I am supposed to be a writer, I do have some knowledge of word processors. And a word processor, I suspected, was what Bill Priest's computer primarily was.

With some trepidation, I turned on the machine and loaded it, and brought the information from the first disk up onto the display. Then I began loading and unloading disks one after another, pausing at each just long enough to see what was on it.

I stopped scanning halfway through the third box. All the disks were the same: A double-blind study of this, retrospective review of that, outcome of twenty-five chronic nonfatal cases of the other. Except for the first disk, they were full of medical research papers.

The first one was a ledger. Whatever Bill Priest was doing with all this research, it was costing him twenty bucks a week in postage alone. He had, it seemed to me, been compulsive about his record-keeping, even noting the price of a bottle of White-Out.

The disk also held a list, which looked almost the same as the one from the back of his checkbook. This list, however, also noted dates, dollar amounts, and a single asterisk in place of an omitted name. Some of the dates went back almost two years.

Swiftly I compared the looseleaf sheet with the list on the screen. Except for the asterisk, they matched name for name. The asterisk was extra; whoever it stood for, he or she was not identified on the paper list.

Names and addresses; dates and prices. And research. What was he doing with it? After a minute, it hit me: He was selling it, of course.

Bill Priest was an academic ghostwriter.

I looked at my watch; I'd been in the carrel almost half an hour. Any minute Felicity the Helpful would be outside the door, wondering what the hell I was still doing in here.

Meanwhile I sat wondering what the hell else Bill Priest had been doing in here, because ghostwriting didn't explain all of it. His little term-paper factory was the literary equivalent of a hot-sheet motel: unsavory, but profitable.

Only not this profitable. I ran my eye again through the ledger displayed on the screen. Plenty of students, I supposed, earned spending money doing other students' work, but not many made thirty thousand a year at it. Fewer still billed a single customer—the asterisk—for half of that. And he'd been collecting it, too, to judge by the balance in the checkbook.

In the hall, footsteps approached: brisk, sensible footsteps.

Hastily, I unslotted the disks, shut down the machine, and opened the final unexplored file drawer. It was full of more disk boxes; beneath them lay a single thin sheaf of typing paper. As the door to the carrel opened, I lifted the papers out.

"*Here* it is," I exclaimed to Felicity, whose eyes had narrowed to suspicious little raisins that squinted meaningfully at her wristwatch.

"I thought..." she began, a doubtful crease wrinkling her forehead. Then, like a blessing from heaven, the phone in her office rang again.

"I'll be right back," she said in a warning tone. Clearly, she did not like doubts or betrayals, unpleasant foreign lumps in the smooth thin whey that was her life.

Clearly, also, she meant me to stay where I was.

Fat chance. I slammed the file drawer and the door to the study carrel. Hurrying down the corridor with the sheaf of paper tucked under my arm, I heard her voice rising.

"Who? He *what?* Oh, my *god*...Listen, I'll call you right back. No, listen, I—*no*. Will you shut *up?*"

The phone gave out a sharp, concussed *brinng!* Felicity's sensible heels pattered into the hall.

Two flights away, I heard her little moan of distress.

"Oh, you *stinker,*" she called down the stairwell. "You said you'd say *hi* to him for me!"

THE OFFICE for Graduate Student Affairs was at the other end of the library building, in a wing that housed medical-school research areas. Wheeled metal racks loaded with huge glass flasks and beakers stood at intervals along a hall reeking of bunsen burners and formaldehyde.

The doors here were unnumbered, and the corridors angled into one another like a psychology student's maze; this was what life was for laboratory rats. Stopping a young blond woman who happened to be pushing a cart full of these animals, I asked her for directions.

"Onward," she said, pointing, flashing a smile that made her look like Ingrid Bergman. "That way."

"Thanks." Inside their cages, the rats scrabbled madly at wire mesh. "What are you going to do with them?"

"Well," she said cheerfully, "first I'm going to give them all a nice snack of crackers and cheese, and then I'm going to cut their little heads off and dissect their brains."

"Mmm," I said, swallowing hard and plodding firmly on. A few doors down I found the one I wanted and went in, trying not to listen for tiny rodent shrieks.

The grad-student office was strictly utilitarian, all battered gray file cabinets, yellowed venetian blinds, and metal chairs upholstered in early electrician's tape.

Utilitarian, that is, except for the personnel.

"Good heavens," said the willowy young man behind the metal desk. "You found this where?" He blinked at the papers I laid before him.

The top right-hand corner of the first sheet bore a ragged patch where a sticker had been torn off; name and address, probably. The work itself was a thesis: introduction, materials and methods, data, discussion, and conclusion. The title was "Predicting Sudden Death: A Retrospective Application of the Manners-Moreheim Scoring System."

"On a chair in the hospital cafeteria," I said. Much more of this and my nose was going to start growing.

His violet eyes regarded me, then returned to the papers. Gracefully he pushed his long fingers through the yellow-white curls above his forehead.

"No name," he said musingly. "That is odd."

"And so I was wondering," I went on, "if there's some sort of register where prospective theses are recorded, preferably by title and name of author, so I can return it."

"Of course," he said, and I could see him wondering, in his gentle way, what the hell my angle was, because it was clear he didn't believe me for a minute.

"Well," he said after another moment. "There is a register for the medical school, and one for the graduate school of nursing. Another one still for public health. I could check and see if this paper's title is listed anywhere."

He looked up. "The thing is, it's rather a lot of trouble and even if it is there, I can't give out the names or addresses of students."

"I see. A sensible precaution." He was going to be sticky about it. "But I'd really prefer to return it myself." I picked up the papers again.

He wore navy wool slacks, a white silk shirt, and a cashmere sweater of purest robin's-egg blue. His manicured right hand caressed the chunky gold ring that adorned the pinky of his left.

"I'm afraid that's a problem," he said. "Because much as I sympathize with whoever lost this paper, and much as I do appreciate that you would like to return it, it just wouldn't be worth my while, would it, to go through all that work and then get into trouble with my boss?"

The operative phrase there, unless I was mistaken, was "worth my while." Considering the size of the diamond in that pinky ring, I couldn't quite believe it, but I opened my bag and slid out a twenty-dollar bill, to test my theory.

The slender white hand moved casually over the gun-metal-gray desk and closed around the bill. "Of course, for an intelligent, trustworthy person such as yourself—"

"Right," I said. "The name?"

A hint of pique flashed in his eyes, an adder among the violets. Then, shrugging ruefully, he got up and left the office.

I'd scanned the thesis on my way over, forcing through its academic style: the prose equivalent of barbed-wire fence. But once I'd sorted the passives from amongst the subjunctives and optatives, I'd learned what the Manners-Moreheim scoring system was.

Simply, some patients who didn't look too awfully sick were in fact close to dying; not many, but some. To identify them, you could take a lot of lab values and the result of physical exams, and assign scores to them. Then add up the scores, and just like that you knew which ones were secretly fitting themselves for long wooden boxes.

"Retrospective" meant Priest had gotten his raw data out of medical records, and applied the scoring system to fifty hospital patients who'd checked out unexpectedly.

It was this sort of thing for which someone had been paying Priest one hell of a word rate. Either that, or he'd had something else to sell.

Meanwhile, a name was missing from Priest's ledger, missing also from the sheets on the desk before me. Maybe its owner would be able to tell me who thought Priest was worth more than fifteen thousand bucks.

Or didn't. Maybe someone hadn't liked watching all that money vanish down a rat hole, and decided to poison the rat.

In a few moments, the secretary returned with an unfamiliar name inked in angular, backhanded script on a scrap of lined paper. I took the paper, folded it, and slipped it into my bag.

"No address?"

He tilted his head in mild exasperation. Apparently twenty was the bare-bones price, rating bare-bones service.

"Okay. Thanks." I was halfway out the door when he spoke again.

"Don't expect a reward when you find him—the guy whose paper you're, um, returning."

I turned. "Why not?"

He plucked a bit of imaginary lint off the blue cashmere. "Well, I suppose I shouldn't say, but . . . well, I've gone this far, haven't I? What a little weasel I've turned out to be in my old age." Tiny crinkles appeared at the corners of his eyes as he smiled self-mockingly.

I revised my estimate. He wasn't in his twenties, as I'd first thought. The high, smooth forehead below the yellow curls wasn't only high; it was receding.

Thirty, at least; maybe pushing thirty-five. Still clerking in an obscure office. And for him, thirty-five wouldn't be just pushing it; it would be more like a painful, unrelenting shove.

"Anyway," he said, "he was in here Friday. I remembered him right off, actually, but—"

But remembering right off doesn't lure out twenty bucks.

"And this is his name, the one you've given me? Steve Marino?"

"Mmm. Changed his mind about the thesis, so he said."

"So the upshot is, he's doing a different thesis now?"

"Mm-hmm. And terribly urgent about it. Insisted I get the copy he'd already submitted right off Brockway's desk. I'd say it was that one, except the one I gave him back still had the sticker with his name on it."

"Who's Brockway?"

He looked surprised. "Wes Brockway. Doctor. Professor in the anesthesia department, and Marino's thesis advisor. Marino's a medical student, you see, and before they graduate they have to write—"

He stopped, flashing that wry, self-mocking smile again.

"Anyway, I don't think he'll thank you for returning it," he said. "And now if you'll excuse me?"

I wondered just how urgent Steve Marino's reasons had been; more than twenty dollars' worth, surely, if angle-face here had to sneak right into his boss's office. I was about to pursue this question along with the missing address when his telephone rang.

"Grad schools," he answered unenthusiastically; then his voice perked up. "No, I didn't. What news?" He paused. "Who? He what? You're kidding."

The violet eyes lit with malicious pleasure. "Dearie," he said into the phone, "I don't care how warm you were for the brat's form, I think he got just what he deserved. Yes, I do, and you know I'm right. He'd have eaten you up and spat you out, just a little pile of bones and hair like all the others."

I made a getting-out-of-here face; waving a slender hand in farewell, he settled into a down-and-dirty gab session with, I'd bet any money, Felicity Dunwoodie.

Which put paid to the idea of calling the cops on me, at least for the time being. Apparently, a truly meaty chunk of gossip did not often come Felicity's way, judging at least by the swiftness with which she had begun chewing it.

On the other hand, if she happened to realize later what a prize twit she was being, she might still end up describing the woman who rifled Priest's carrel to a composite-sketch artist. The thought urged me very efficiently out of the library and away from the scene of the crime; once it had performed this function, however, I pushed it into my mental "to deal with when absolutely necessary" pile, where it joined the fact of my dwindling bank balance, the necessity of doing some laundry sometime very soon, and the question of what really happened to Judge Crater.

Thus, as I stepped briskly along the sidewalk towards the hospital wing of the medical complex, I was able to contemplate the diversity of the architecture looming all around me, in styles ranging from Early Greek Revival to Inadvisable Glass Monolithic.

The oldest of the medical buildings was marble fronted, copper domed, and handsomely supported by sturdy Doric pillars; this structure was, however, unfortunately connected by a glass-walled bridge to the newest building in the complex: a twenty-story monstrosity featuring hundreds of shiny black glass windows, which together resembled the compound eye of a large, malevolent insect. Just looking at those windows made one wonder uncomfortably what could possibly be going on behind them, all the while suspecting unhappily that one knew.

It was this tendency of modern medical architecture to frighten and appall, I knew, that Helen had been working against, another fact about her that put me squarely, if so far rather uselessly, on Helen's side.

Meanwhile, thoughts of malevolence and incongruity led me smoothly to more thoughts of Bill Priest, who had written a research paper for someone named Steve Marino, after which Marino had handed the paper in to his advisor. But then Marino had wanted the paper back, wanted it badly enough to lie and even pay to get it. After that he had, apparently, returned it to Priest, or someone else had. And then someone had killed Priest.

Musing over these things, I crossed the hospital lobby, rode up in the elevator, passed through the glass doors marked Neurosurgical ICU, and stopped as the nurse behind the desk shot me a guarded look.

Something had happened, something that wasn't in the program. I could almost smell it: guilt and anxiety spiced with tentative relief. Joey still lay in his high, railed bed, his face still nearly as white as the sheet drawn up to his chin. The respirator still whush-puffed through its regular cycles, and under the sheet his chest still rose slowly and fell with breaths and exhalations.

But his arms were tied down with loops of white gauze, the tape on his face was pristinely fresh, and the tube in his throat wasn't the one that had been there before. The old tube lay where it had been flung, in the metal wastebasket, while a tool kit of medical instruments stood open on his bedside table, its contents in disarray as if hastily rummaged.

Something had happened, all right, and it hadn't been expected, and it hadn't been good.

"Joey?" His eyes fluttered open. His cracked lips moved, making no sound.

A paper cup of ice chips stood on the table. I spooned a few of them into his mouth, wanting instead to gather him into my arms. Joey sucked on the ice chips, his eyes sending a message of woozy gratitude. Then they closed again, as he relaxed once more into drugged sleep.

When I could get my fingers unclenched from the side rails, I left the cubicle.

"DAMN," CLAIRE BROGAN said. Slapping an orange cardboard folder onto the long table in the conference room behind the nursing desk, she began sticking a series of X-ray films onto the light panels on the wall.

Unnoticed, I stood in the doorway. Lit from behind on the films, Joey's spine showed: a stacked column of bony white disks.

"I can't believe it," Clair said, glaring at the films. "I can't believe they left his restraints that loose. Any kid wakes up with a tube in his gullet, he's going to yank it out if you let him."

"Well, listen," said the scrub-suited man studying the films with her, "a kid with that much sedative on board, no one expects him to get so purposeful. He's a vigorous kid, that's all. And this still looks okay. In fact, it looks better than it did."

He gestured at the light panel. "Still a lot of swelling around the cord, but . . ."

"Yeah, and we had to retube him on top of that swelling." She yanked the film down and snapped the light off, shaking her head. "I agree, the films do look better, god knows why. Maybe something did get shifted into better position, but this sure as hell is not the way I'd have picked to shift it."

"Why did he?" I asked quietly. They turned. "Wake up, I mean?"

"Gotta roll," the scrub-suited man said to Claire, "I'm late for rounds. Give me a yell if you run into any trouble." With a nod to me, he left.

Claire waved me into a chair and poured two styrofoam cups full of coffee from the urn at the end of the table.

"Charlotte," she said, "I'm sorry about this. I know it can't be boosting your confidence any. The thing is, you've got to wake them up once in a while, to check their neuro status."

She handed me one of the cups. "And the other thing is that we're unbelievably short-staffed. Florence Nightingale is dead, and I must say I applaud her demise. But until hospital administrators wake up to that fact, they're not going to reward people appropriately for skilled nursing, which makes it hard to get people to do it. Which means the nurses we've got work harder. Lots harder.''

I nodded. ''Want to translate that into right now?''

She gulped coffee. ''Right. The nurse covering Joey had another patient, too, and the other patient lost his blood pressure. She was out of Joey's room five minutes, tops. But during that time, he got out of his arm restraint and pulled his tube out, and we had to put it in again. And that's the story.'' She shrugged in elaborate disgust.

''He's okay, though.'' I made it a statement, but one with challenge in it.

Claire nodded grimly. ''No damage on the films. They're better, in fact, and don't ask me how that happened either, but believe me, he won't be doing it again. Besides,'' she added, ''he promised me he wouldn't wiggle any more. God, he's a nice kid. Where the hell did you find him?''

The coffee was strong enough to float ball bearings, which was exactly what I needed. I hadn't slept much in forty-eight hours, and relief at Joey's being all right made me suddenly want to put my head down on the table.

''He was the boy next door,'' I told her. ''His folks were into pot parties and airhead politics, but they weren't into kids.''

''And you were.'' She looked at me consideringly.

''Much to my surprise, yeah.'' I shrugged and changed the subject; in the process of getting Joey into my life, I'd nearly lost my own, and the memories were still painful.

Meanwhile, just at the moment, I didn't care if Helen had shot Bill Priest with a curare-tipped blowgun dart. ''Listen, I'm staying here with him.''

Claire shook her head. ''No,'' she said flatly. ''That's out. You don't know the first thing about assessing this kind of patient. You'll freak him out, you'll antagonize the staff, and you won't even be doing him any good.

''Besides''—she got up—''you'll drive yourself nuts. I know a good private-duty nurse who's looking for hours.

Private duties aren't usually allowed in ICUs, but they're so short here right now I think nursing administration might bend the rule a little. And don't worry about the money, either—neurosurgery can spring for a couple days of private duty. Hell, we owe the kid one.''

How she was going to wangle all that, I didn't even want to ask; instead I sat silent as she made the call and gratitude flooded me, because in fact she was right. I didn't have the faintest idea how to care for Joey now. And I could no more pay for private nurses than I could finance a moon shot.

"Okay, she's coming over,'' Claire said as she hung up, then glanced at the papers I'd dropped onto the conference table. "What's this?'' She frowned at the pages.

"Oh, just something a friend of mine is...'' I stopped as the doubt in her expression deepened into outright skepticism.

"Your friend's got a problem. We use Manners-Moreheim scores pretty intensively here. If they only worked this well, we wouldn't bother.''

"You mean there's something really wrong with the numbers?''

She nodded. "Math errors, or sloppy data. It shows up right here, see?'' She pointed to a column headed "Outcome.''

"Patients with scores like these''—she ran her finger across the page—"well, they just don't die. Not this many, anyhow. One or two I could believe, but not...eight? Uh-uh.''

She straightened. "Tell your friend to check it. There's a glitch here—Manners-Moreheim is very reliable.''

I gathered up the papers. "Thanks. And...thanks for being straight with me about Joey.''

Her grin was genuine, and I thought again that we were fortunate to have found her.

"Habit of mine," she said, briskly pushing her cup into the trash can. "Cuts down on lawsuits. If the sky starts falling, you'll hear it from me first. And now I think the OR's got a crunched backbone with my name on it." She left.

I stayed, smelling burnt coffee and thinking of crunched backbones, waiting for the private-duty nurse to arrive and looking at the thesis Bill Priest had written for Steve Marino.

If he had. Suddenly I wasn't so sure. The scoring system worked, but this paper held an error big enough for Claire Bogan to see at first glance. Which meant Priest had built a sizable ghostwriting business while still being able to turn out a paper with a large, obvious mistake in it.

And that didn't make sense, for two reasons. First, Priest had been running a tight ship; I couldn't see the owner of that neat, well-organized little office making careless errors of any sort. Beyond that, though, the only way to publicize an illegal business is by word of mouth, and that depends primarily on reliable product. Sloppiness wouldn't fuel what Priest had had going in that study carrel. Not for two years, anyway.

Stuffing the thesis into my bag, I went back to Joey's cubicle, where I found him asleep. Behind his bed, one of the IV pumps began beeping; looking for someone to deal with it, I nearly walked into a small, slender woman in a crisp white cap, white stockings and shoes, and a short white nurse's uniform.

She was perhaps twenty-five years old, with the bright eyes and lively expression of a chipmunk, only no chipmunk was ever so pretty or intelligent looking. Her glance darted about the room, taking in the equipment, the monitors, the IVs, and the boy in the bed. I could almost hear the brain-cogs whirring as she made sense of it all. Then she turned back to me and stuck out her hand, her smile businesslike.

"Hi, I'm Twyla McKay. I'm here to take care of Joey."

A small red-and-blue butterfly spread its tattooed wings on the inside of her right forearm, just above the wrist. Her hand was warm and dry, full of small determined bones.

Withdrawing it, she flushed Joey's IV line until the beeper on the pump stopped beeping, checked his wrist restraints and secured one of them, jiggled an EKG lead until the monitor's tracing satisfied her, inspected the respirator's dials and dumped water from its tubings, snapped the wrinkles from his bedsheets, and cleared a clutter of instruments from his bedside table.

"There," she said, not even breathing hard. "Oh, and I brought a few things."

From her bag she pulled a big calendar, hanging it on the wall where, when he woke up again, Joey could see it. Popping a tape into a small cassette deck, she set acoustic guitar music playing sweetly where Joey could hear it. Finally, and this won the last stony outposts of my heart, she slid her small white hand into Joey's larger brown one, where he could feel it.

"Joey," she said into his ear. "Everything's okay, guy. Your operation's over, Charlotte's right here, and we're going to get you well and get you out of here, starting now. Okay? Okay."

Maybe he couldn't hear her, and maybe he could, but I could hear her and I felt better. Lots better. The phrase "therapeutic personality" didn't even begin to describe Twyla McKay; I didn't know where she had come from but I didn't bother asking, either, because as far as I was concerned she had come from heaven.

"And," she said, turning, "what about you? Do you think you could get some rest? Because you look like you could use it, if you don't mind my saying so."

I didn't. Right about then, she could have told me to walk on hot coals and I'd have tried it. No problem, Twyla.

Besides, I'd just caught a glimpse of my own reflection in the window between the cubicles. I'd seen better looking faces on smashed clocks. My hair stuck up in untidy spikes, the circles beneath my eyes were deepening to trenches, and the fresh clothes I'd put on a few hours earlier now resembled something dug out of the rag bag.

"Try not to worry," Twyla said.

Right. It would be easy, like not breathing in and out. Still, I had the strong sensation that something good had just happened, and I decided to go with it.

Not that I had a lot of choice. I was wiped.

"Bye, guy," I said. Joey slept on.

In the visitors' lounge I stopped by the telephone again, resisting the impulse to collapse full-length onto one of the industrial-strength sofas.

The information operator informed me that the number for Marino, S., was unpublished, which meant there was one; score a point for me.

Then I checked Priest's looseleaf sheet again. Marino's name was on it, near the bottom of the second side. Whoever the asterisk was, it wasn't Marino. Minus a point for me.

No address for him, either; only a local zip code. Two of the other names were missing addresses too, which made sense when I realized that all the ones that were present were out of town, many out of state.

Priest wouldn't have wanted a high local profile, so he did most of his business with students who lived some distance away. And he hadn't bothered handwriting the addresses of his few nearby customers, since most likely he already knew them. Maybe they all even lived in one place—say, the medical school dorm. A further glance at the sheet confirmed this; the missing addresses shared a single zip.

And there I stopped, fatigue and spent nerves ringing in my head, a high, humming jangle. Driving back to Helen's,

I took care to stop at red lights and go at green ones instead of the other way around. In Helen's apartment, I set the alarm for four P.M., dialled the bedside phone's ringer to its loudest setting, set my beeper by my pillow, and turned the electric blanket to "toast."

Drifting into sleep, I thought again about names and numbers, theories and theses, and especially about Bill Priest's beefed-up bankbook. Someone, it seemed certain, had been paying him for more than ghostwriting. The question was, for what?

Meanwhile there were some other big questions, too, ones I hadn't even touched yet in my first headlong rush of peeping and snooping. Such as, who took his body? And why? And where the heck was it now?

FOUR

"BERNIE HOLLOWAY CALLED," Rob Solli said.

This change in subject, transmitted perfectly by the miracle of long-distance telephone, indicated what Solli thought of my interest in murder. The last time I'd gotten involved in one, Solli had used up four hours, forty stitches, and most of his surgical skills repairing the result. On me. Which was how I'd met him.

It was just after four P.M. in New Haven, three hours earlier where Solli was: in my armchair, in my cottage, deep among the redwoods of the Northern California coast. I could almost hear the foghorns, the big waves booming in on the rocky Pacific shore.

I'd been standing at Helen's kitchen counter, but at the mention of Bernie's name I sat down. In the good old days when I'd been a thrilled and aspiring young writer, a call from my agent had made me feel like a professional.

Now it made me feel like a professional, too, only now I knew what one was: a professional writer is a writer who shuts up and does the fifth revision while awaiting the first paycheck.

"What's he want?" I managed faintly. Chances were good I hadn't been nominated for a Pulitzer. That left only bad news.

"*Home Health* wants you to make a few cuts in the opening chapters of *Tricks for the Sick!*" Solli said. "And the new editor is sending along a few queries on what's left."

"Uh-huh," I said with what was left of my breath.

A few cuts. The difference between surgeons and editors is that editors use blunter knives. Also, they don't stop the bleeding until the writer is weak enough to stop arguing with them.

As for the queries, I should have expected those. New editors are always confused, and the only thing *Home Health* used up faster than writers was editors. That was because there were only two kinds of people who wrote for *Home Health* at all: a few cutthroat hacks like me who needed the money, and a vast sea of terminally befuddled folks who always thought they could be writers if only they got the chance.

As a result, *Home Health* editors often went from promising careers to institutions for the intensely amused, sometimes in a matter of weeks. They usually held off the giggles just long enough to screw up my manuscripts, however, and this time looked to be no exception.

"Okay," I sighed. "Bernie's sending me the changes they want?"

Bernie Holloway is a good, honest agent, and he pegged my literary niche the moment he met me. No rich husband, no trust fund, no teaching job. This, to Bernie, is the definition of a natural hack writer, and on top of his other irritating habits, Bernie is also frequently correct.

"Uh-huh," Solli said. "You'll be completely occupied in a couple of days, tops." He made me sound like a fiendish brat who might set the house on fire if not kept amused.

"Couple of days," I thought aloud. "I could check out a lot for Helen, in that time. Of course, whatever I turned out to be checking out..."

I sighed and let this part sink in.

"...I'd be checking it out all alone."

The silence now was of this idea giving Solli pause.

"But," I brightened, "if you helped, I'd be calling you every few hours. Instead of off somewhere without anyone knowing where I am or what I'm up to, in case I run into..."

I paused for effect, and for Solli's imagination to work. "...difficulties," I finished innocently.

Now the silence was of Solli knowing he was beaten. Nobly, I did not laugh out loud.

"I suppose you realize," he said, "that what you want me to do is illegal. Tapping hospital data banks and ripping off wads of confidential information is out of my line, Charlotte."

"But if I got you the phone numbers, you could just call them and check this stuff for me?" How I would get them I would worry about later.

"Right," he said reluctantly. "It's not quite as simple as that, but I could do it."

I'd figured as much, because when he wasn't busy being the north coast's star general surgeon, stitching up everything from split lips to aortic aneurysms, Solli was also a major-league computer hacker and underground phone phreak. Very discreet, very effective. Top-of-the-line felonious, too, but for a good cause.

"Charlotte, with the right phone access and those patients' hospital ID numbers, I can get Social Security numbers. With those, I can get bank balances, credit ratings, criminal records, employment histories, selective service stuatus—"

"Fine," I said. "I want all of it. And the raw data from Priest's thesis checked, too."

Another silence; I was asking for a lot. Despite his expertise, Solli didn't snoop much, except very quietly into the records of rich political groups whose manifestos leaned somewhere to the right of Adolf Hitler's. These records he found and trashed with the happy zeal of some long-haired commie hippie weirdo, which was what he was, only in yuppie disguise.

What I wanted was different. This was snooping on the good. Good and dead, though. Dead and gone.

"Solli, dead people don't care who knows their business. It can't hurt them just to have a look. Besides, what if Priest's thesis results aren't some kind of mistake?"

More silence, as Solli caught the drift. If the thesis results were right, a bunch of people were dead who shouldn't be, which brought us right back to murder.

"Anybody else know you're involved in this?"

"A few," I admitted.

"Because I don't want you to be. Dead and gone, I mean. Or involved, either, for that matter."

"I won't be. And I can't help it, I am involved."

"Yeah." He didn't sound convinced, but he promised to help. That's bottom line on Solli. Also, he flosses regularly.

At any rate, he sent his best to Helen and told me to kiss Joey for him and I said that I would, and I told him he should remember to close the cat door or we would have a house populated by raccoons, foxes, and skunks, not to mention dead cats, and he said that he would, and he said I should be very, extremely, unreasonably, ridiculously careful, and I said that I would be, and then we hung up.

And then I went out to interview a mugger.

"COPS AXED me this before," Myron Rosewater said.

Myron was the patient-transport aide who'd been assigned to take Priest's body from the ER to the morgue. Found and persuaded by Harry Lemon, he had agreed to meet us at the scene of the crime.

Or one of the crimes, anyway, since snatching dead ones, I gathered, was just as illegal as making dead ones out of live ones, not to mention breaking into their apartments afterward.

Myron, Harry had told me, knew plenty about what was and was not illegal, and when I met Myron I understood.

"Axed me all about it," he repeated, lounging against an unoccupied stretcher near the hospital's employee entrance. Distantly, time clocks *chunk-clunk*ed as the seven-to-seven shift punched in and out. Myron was ready to go home, or wherever he went.

Just sixteen, he already had the sullen look of a man who thinks he is way too good for his work. He didn't like school, either, according to Harry, so he didn't go much, and when he did go he scared the teachers.

He scared me a little, too. I tried not to let it show, but Myron knew. That was his real job: scaring people, and letting them give him money so that he would stop. Myron the mugger had racked up a dozen juvenile offenses already, and only showed up for his hospital job because his supervisor was also, in effect, his parole officer.

Still, he was surprisingly cooperative. I suppose it was because he wanted something in return, and that before too long I would find out what it was.

"I know they asked, Myron," I said. Looking bored, he fingered the gold stud in his left earlobe. His denim jacket bore embroidered colors of a notorious street-prowling gang; *Constrictors,* it proclaimed in scarlet silk, above the grinning visage of a serpent whose fangs looked ready—even eager—to strike.

"But," I went on, "Doctor Lemon here feels that if you could go over it again, he might manage to find something better for you to do here in the hospital. You'd like that, wouldn't you?"

"Anything's gotta be better'n wheelin' stiffs downstairs to the icebox." Myron shrugged, shifting a radio the size of the sound system at Madison Square Garden. It hung from his shoulder by a thick strap that resembled, but of course could not be, braided human hair.

Or perhaps it could. Myron's dark eyes met mine.

"What kind of better?" he asked challengingly.

"Ah, maintenance," Harry Lemon put in. "Or cafeteria? Something can be found, I feel sure, that will challenge your, um, considerable talents."

Myron squared his thin shoulders, leaned back, and folded his long, wiry arms. "Computers," he said, and I thought for a moment that he had been reading my mind.

"That's where the money is," he went on. "That's where I want to be."

Harry made a choking sound that turned into a cough. "Now, Myron, you must know that computers are highly technical—"

"Bullshit." Myron made it four syllables. "They got a program here. High-school kids, work four hours, go to class four. Hospital sponsors 'em, sets 'em up, you know? White kids, from the sub-burbs."

He looked at me. "Just 'cause I'm mean," he said, "that don't mean I'm stupid. You dig?"

I dug. I looked at Harry, who nodded with slow resignation.

"I am aware of the arrangement," he said. "In fact, I helped design—"

"Yeah," Myron said. "But see, alls I want, man, I just want in. I make it, fine—I flunk out, ain't no skin off your ass. Ain't that right?"

Harry blinked several times. Then he looked at me.

"Can you do that, Harry?" I asked.

He nodded. "Actually, I can. But I hope you realize, Charlotte—"

"Never mind that," Myron said, shifting the enormous radio to his other shoulder. The strap had to be hair; nothing else short of braided steel had that kind of tensile strength. "Let's go. I got to get across town, tell some dudes to get themselves a new lieutenant. I'm gonna be busy, now on."

Harry's eyebrows went up. "Lieutenant? May I infer, my upwardly-aspiring friend, that you hold a post in some local civic responsibility?"

Myron turned, a grin spreading over his face. I'd seen a shark grin that way once, and been glad it was in a tank on the far side of some grin-proof glass.

"Yeah," he said, "you can infer it. You just don't wanta know 'bout it, that's all."

Harry nodded, no doubt wondering how he would lever Myron Rosewater in among a lot of privileged white kids from the suburbs. Myron could not only buy and sell them, without much trouble he could chew and swallow them, too.

Harry would do it, though. He would do almost anything to help me, and it hadn't taken much conversation to discover why: he'd seen Helen again.

"A truly delightful specimen of young womanhood," was his comment, and he'd blushed when he said it. It looked to me as if Walt Krusanke was in for some serious competition, assuming the prize didn't wind up in the slammer.

So far, I couldn't promise she wouldn't. I'd come up with the motives all murders boil down to—love and money—but only one motive had a known associate of the victim conveniently attached.

From the cops' point of view, it was all so neat it could have come in a kit labelled "Contents: Prime Suspect."

"Come on, come on," Myron Rosewater said, jitter-bugging on down the corridor towards the room where Bill Priest had died and from which he had vanished.

THE ROOM was small and clean, green tiled and furnished with a sheeted examining table, mirrored overhead lights, and various gleaming instruments for poking, prodding, palpating, and peering into human bodies.

"This is where I was s'posed to come and collect him," Myron said, "only he wasn't—"

"Wait a minute," I interrupted. "If he had been here, what would he have looked like?"

Myron eyed me as if I were brain damaged. "I didn't have no prior personal acquaintance with the dude," he said.

Harry's sigh had the sound of patience drawn to its snapping point. "She doesn't mean him *particularly*, you wretched little—"

"Harry," I said mildly. Then I turned back to Myron, who was scratching a spot just below his right ear and staring at a spot just below Harry's. On Myron, the patch of skin was dark brown, shadowed and protected by the corner of his taut, angular jaw.

On Harry, the spot looked pink, plump and vulnerable. Myron kept smiling. The silence lengthened. Catching the drift, Harry fingered his neck uneasily, then caught himself at it and jerked his hand down.

"Yes," he said, pressing his palms together and forcing a smile, "well, at any rate, what Miss Kent means is—"

"I know, I know," Myron said. "Any old stiff, right? Like I would pick up. Well, they look like a mummy. Always the same, lyin' here on this table all wrapped in a white sheet. Tape around 'em, tag on the toe end to show who they was."

He moved to the head of the examining table and pantomimed pulling a stretcher in alongside it. "What I do, I roll 'em off this table into the holder in the bottom of the stiffmobile"—he motioned swinging up a side panel—"close 'em up"—he swung the imaginary panel down—"and roll 'em away."

"But this time," I prompted, and Myron nodded significantly.

"This time there ain't no passenger to collect. I mean, to me, that shows nerve. You feature it? Sneak in and grab some guy, he's cold stone dead, weasel him out?"

He shivered in mock fear and real apprehension. "Man, I like to meet that dude."

I shook my head. "Uh-uh. Probably you wouldn't."

Myron's dark eyes flashed comprehension. "Oh. I get it. You mean like whoever snatched him prob'ly stiffed him, too?"

"Seems like," I said.

"Well, I like to meet him anyway," Myron asserted. "So, what you want to know next?"

"I want you to show me the route you usually take to the morgue," I said. "On the way, I want to see anywhere you think might be a good hiding place for a body."

"Hey," Myron said admiringly. "You really gettin' into this, ain't you?"

"Right," I said, wishing I weren't. Then Myron turned to Harry, who by now was jabbing impatiently at the elevator button.

"You know, Doc," he said, "I hear in a few years the dudes that run computers be ruling the world. You think that's true?"

Massaging the bridge of his nose, Harry peered at Myron. "Good lord," he said. "I'm creating a monster."

IN THE hospital basement, Myron ushered us through a pair of sulfur yellow doors, their paint chipped to bare metal at about the level where a rolling stretcher would crash into them, if no one bothered to walk ahead and open them first.

Inside, the smell clapped itself to my face like a wet rag: formaldehyde. The tiled floor was damp, and from the slick green tiles to the high, fluoroescent-lit ceilings the walls were lined with lockers, each about two feet square.

Beside the counter in the entry area stood a young Chinese man wearing a plastic apron, rubber gloves, and black rubber galoshes. His glossy black hair was pulled back in a low ponytail, and his face had a clear, lemony translucence made striking by thick black eyebrows and a black goatee.

He looked as if he had just stepped off a four-thousand-year-old vase, and he was about as old-world ethnic as a slice of Mom's apple pie.

"Hey, Myron," he said, "how's it goin'?" In the room behind him, Steely Dan was singing about station WJAZ.

"These here are my friends," Myron said. "They want you to show 'em the deal down here. This here's Louie. He's the boss man of the pathology techs. Louie's not his real name, but nobody can pronounce his real name, so I changed it. Right?"

"Right," Louie said. His face expressed the serene good humor of a man with forty centuries of heritage and an unending supply of completely satisfied customers.

"Myron is my favorite of all the transport runners," Louie confided. "No one else will come down and eat supper with me."

"Yeah," Myron laughed, "just as long as you ain't havin' liver. Show the folks around, will you? They want to see where they gonna end up one of these days."

"Not, I trust, any time very soon," Louie said politely. "You I recognize," he said to Harry Lemon.

"Indeed." Harry offered his hand, then pulled it back. Louie glanced down at his rubber gloves, still slickly wet.

"Sorry," he said, pulling them off. "Busy afternoon."

I introduced myself, since Harry was apparently not going to do it for me; shortly thereafter, he and Myron departed, Myron apparently feeling that if he was going to rule the world, he had better get started.

"What I need to know," I told Louie when they had gone, "is what happens to a corpse. The routine, that is."

"Ah," Louie said. "You are interested, I think, in one that it didn't happen to?"

"Exactly. I guess the police have been here already."

Louie nodded. "Old Chinese proverb. Always hide with a lot of the same things." He winked.

It wasn't old, and it wasn't Chinese, but it was precisely the theory I had in mind. There aren't many spots you can put a dead body where it won't look out of place.

"Well, it's all pretty cut-and-dried," Louie said. "The remains come in through the double doors and we check them in here."

He indicated a metal gurney and a row of battered filing cabinets.

"One section of the ID tag stays with the chart, which goes here," Louie said, waving a chart rack like the ones on the wards. "One section goes on a locker door"—I noted the sulfur yellow slips on some of the lockers—"and one stays on the patient. Do you want to see?"

He gave me a look that on anyone else I would have called inscrutable. I nodded; I didn't want to, but I was going to.

Louie strode to one of the doors, and opened it. "Cadaver number and locker number goes on all three copies of the tag, and also in the admissions book. That way, nobody gets lost."

He slid a metal tray out of the locker. "When the body is released," he went on, "one tag goes with it, along with the death certificate and a few other papers—the rest, and the chart, go back to medical records."

In the refrigerator locker's tray lay a man who was dark grayish blue. His upper lip had begun to wrinkle peevishly, as if of all his body parts it alone knew that it was dead and didn't much like it. Also, there was no room in the drawer for an extra occupant, which was what I'd been wondering.

Louie slid the drawer shut. "The hearse comes to a loading dock down the hall, but those doors are very secure since two years ago. Some guys were caught taking stolen typewriters out that way."

"And they go directly from a locker to the hearse?"

"Unless there's an autopsy. This way." He gestured for me to follow him into the room where all the activities of his busy afternoon were occurring.

A long soapstone table stood in the center of the room. The object on the table resembled a hastily repaired mattress.

Twitching a sheet from a rack, Louie covered it. "Very sad, sometimes," he commented. "I try to keep a scientific point of view."

I tried to keep one too, but with only fair success.

"Anyway, this is where I prepare the bodies, make necessary incisions, ready everything for the pathologist, and clean up afterwards."

Counters, shelves, and sinks lined the room. On some of the counters stood plastic squeeze bottles of solutions in purple, green, amber, and red.

"Fixatives, stains, preservatives," Louie said. "Slides, equipment for preparing frozen tissue sections. Specimen jars; canisters for larger specimens. The pathology department is very good about supplies and equipment. Everything the best, and well maintained—a pleasure to work with."

Somehow I couldn't imagine the pleasure of scissoring snippets off dead folks. But then, amateur sleuthing wasn't turning out to be any real treat, either.

"What's in there?" I pointed to a large metal door like the entrance to a meat locker.

"Meat locker," Louie said. He shot me a worried glance in case I was shocked, but my capacity for shock was wearing thin. "Also the preserving tank. I am afraid we call it the aquarium."

"Working down here, I guess you'd have to develop a fairly efficient sense of humor."

He nodded. "Takes some getting used to, though. You sure you want to go in there?"

"Not at all," I said. "Let's get it over with, before I decide."

As it turned out, it wasn't so bad. Cold as hell, but you could pretend you were in some big restaurant's freezer if you ignored the dozens of hanging shapes swathed in sheets of nearly translucent plastic.

In an adjoining room, a big aluminum tank was set into the floor. The reek of formaldehyde here was stunning. Chains hung from a rack set into the ceiling; at the end of each chain, through the tank's slowly rippling fluid, a pair of metal tongs could be dimly glimpsed.

Gripped in each pair of tongs was an object I did not want to glimpse, not even dimly.

"Medical school's cadavers," Louie said. "They are here until the students finish dissecting."

"They've all been checked?"

"Every one," he replied. "Also the lockers and the cold room. The police were very thorough. They had many questions."

He led me back out to the main room, with its banks of lockers. "I showed them the entries for the afternoon," he went on, "and that our records and procedures are extremely careful."

He gestured at the doors with their yellow tags. "You may think that the morgue is the best place to hide a body, but the fact is, it is the worst. These are my patients, you see, I feel as responsible for them as if they were alive. I know all their names, birth dates, causes of death. Except for segments, that is; I couldn't possibly keep track of all those. Some are older than me."

At my questioning look, he explained. "Some cadavers are retained, if they are of interest. And if the next of kin permit, of course. Mostly skeletal remains, but we have some brains, spinal cords, other organs. The bones we preserve with special varnish. Soft tissue is pickled.''

His voice grew enthusiastic; clearly he felt privileged to be the curator of such an exotic museum. "It's an extensive collection. We even have Siamese quintuplets. Do you want to see them?''

It took me about a second to decide that I didn't. I asked a few more questions, he answered them, and I thanked him.

"No problem," Louie said and bowed, fingertips pressed together. "Well, back to work. Chop-chop." When he looked up the grin above his dark goatee was mischievous.

From the phone in the upstairs lobby, I called Harry Lemon and got him to call security for me. Ten minutes later, he called back. No body had been dispatched from the loading docks since before Priest's death until ten this morning, when Mrs. Wilma Riddington, age ninety-one, was picked up by drivers from the Cedar Grove Mortuary.

I called Cedar Grove. Wilma's funeral was tomorrow, open casket. So much for the old switcheroo: even if Louie had been fooled somehow, the dearly departed's relatives wouldn't be, at the wake.

Meanwhile, security cops worked all the hospital's doors except for emergency exits, which were wired with alarms and couldn't be opened without attracting a lot of attention. Carrying a package shaped like a dead body past a security cop would attract attention, too.

There were plenty of plumbing-and-steam-pipe-lined tunnels leading from the main hospital building to everywhere else in the medical center. I happened to know, though, that those tunnels were kept locked, to keep kids from sneaking in to play Dungeons and Dragons there. One hungry, thirsty, and badly frightened thirteen-year-old son of one very eminent cardiac surgeon had taken care of that; it had been in all the papers.

Besides, even if someone did get Priest's body out through a tunnel, there was still the problem of getting rid of it somewhere else. A body, I was learning, is a pain-in-the-neck thing to have to hide.

All of which made me think it was still in the hospital. Any other theory was just too complicated, and I was sure now that whatever had happened, it was simple. That was why, so far, it had worked so well.

Next I called the ICU. No change on Joey: still comatose from all the sedation he was getting, still on the respirator, his condition listed as critical but stable.

How a person could be stable while also comatose and on a respirator, I wasn't sure. Maybe I would cover that in a sequel to *Tricks for the Sick!*; *Son of Sick*, Bernie would surely want to call it. Still, the nurse at the desk sounded confident and polite, and it wasn't her fault that just the sound of her young, healthy voice made me want to kill her.

Which only made me all the more anxious to find fault somewhere else. And for doing that there is no better place than a hospital cafeteria, so I went there.

In steam-table vats, something gluey and brownish looking lurked. They called it veal scallopine and I got some of it on rice. Brussels sprouts, too, because there is nothing even a hospital kitchen can do to ruin a brussels sprout. Squares of pink-and-white frosted cake looked sweet enough to pop out my fillings, and I took one along with a cup of coffee.

At one of the long cafeteria tables, I spread a napkin on my lap and cautiously sampled the main dish. It still looked like the dog's dinner, but it was also thick and hot, studded with chunks of veal so tender that threads of it fell away into the gravy, which was fiery with garlic.

I guessed they must have had to disguise it so that no hospital-food inspector would come along and say it was too good, and while I ate it, I tried to think like a murderer.

Never mind, for now, how somebody got rid of Bill Priest's body. Just as important was *why* get rid of it? Why go to all that risk and trouble?

After all, I could testify that he was Priest, and half a dozen people could testify that he was dead. So stealing his corpse wouldn't stop a murder indictment. On the contrary, quite a few murderers have been indicted, and some convicted, with the victim's body absent from evidence. I started on the cake, which was just right: pink frosting a quarter-inch thick, the perfect foil for the carbolic harshness of the brew in the styrofoam cup.

I took a big bite, letting sweetness ring in my ears. Then suddenly all that sugar must have battered open a pathway in my brain; in the next moment I didn't want the rest of the cake, because I had something sweeter.

"...autopsy," Louie had said. If you didn't have a body, you couldn't do an autopsy. And if you couldn't do an autopsy, you couldn't find...what?

Something besides the needle mark. Something, maybe, that didn't show at all. On the outside, anyway. Something on the inside, though, in Priest's bloodstream or even in his stomach. Doping him would have made him easier to inject, after all, and dope would certainly show up on postmortem exam.

The trouble was, dope on the inside wouldn't identify the killer any more than the needle mark on the outside had, which made stealing the body to hide that fairly pointless, too.

And so much for brilliant ideas. Sighing, I consoled myself with the last bite of cake, then looked up into the Ingrid Bergman smile of the girl I'd seen wheeling mice to their deaths a few hours earlier.

She sat one table away, reading a magazine and eating yogurt with wheat germ, and I thought if I were her I wouldn't eat meat either. Still, she'd been helpful once.

"Excuse me," I said.

The smile radiated again, a hundred and fifty watts. I thought she must really like killing mice. Then I saw she was reading *Cosmopolitan* and figured she probably just didn't remember killing them.

"You may think this is a strange question," I said, "but I guess you probably know your way around here."

She nodded and smiled some more.

"So I wondered," I went on, "if you wanted to get rid of a body in the medical center somewhere. A fairly big one. Body, I mean."

Her smile got cautious.

"Just hypothetically, of course."

She nodded again. "You mean, like, let's pretend?"

I looked at her. Dissecting a mouse's brain had to take a certain minimum level of skill and intelligence.

"Like, in your fantasy?"

On the other hand, maybe she just lopped the top of the mouse's skull off and used a little tiny ice-cream scoop.

"Uh, right." Her face stopped looking like Ingrid Bergman's and started looking like the one on the magazine cover.

"Well, if I were pretending to get rid of a body," she said thoughtfully, "I'd pretend to put it where I put all the dead mice, in the lab crematorium. That's where we dispose of animal remains. It's respectful, and also it's hygienic."

Bingo. "Would it be big enough?"

She considered this, and ate more yogurt while she did.

"I think," she said after a moment, "that I would pretend to cut the body up in pieces. That would work, I think, except for one thing."

"What's that?"

She shrugged. "It's broken. The crematorium, I mean. I've been freezing the mice in baggies for two weeks. So if you're pretending, you'll have to pretend to wait until it's fixed. Ten days or so, they say, and I hope they're right. I'm running out of freezer space."

Oh, well. It had been a nice thought for a minute there. "Uh, one more question?"

That smile again. "Sure."

"If you were looking for a medical student and you didn't know what he looked like or where he lived, or even his telephone number, where would you look?"

"That's easy," she replied. "Today's Friday, and Friday night's the medical school happy hour. Across the street, in the dorm lounge. Pay your dollar and take your choice—they'll all be there."

"You're wonderful," I told her. "Has anyone ever mentioned that you look just like Ingrid Bergman?"

The smile wavered. "Who's Ingrid Bergman?" she said.

FIVE

"IT ALL STARTED," Steve Marino said, "when I found out I wasn't going to be a brain surgeon."

The medical school's Friday night happy hour was held in a long, wide room with a wall of plate glass on one side and a big empty fieldstone fireplace on the other. Along the third wall, sheet-draped tables held liters of wine, mixers, soft drinks, and bottles of the hard stuff from which student bartenders were pouring busily and liberally.

Jammed into the room, brilliant ambitious folks whose names graced the mastheads of medical journals stood elbow-to-elbow with students, interns, nurses, and white-jacketed technicians, all gulping from plastic cups of free booze, tanking up and letting their hair down after a rough week taking care of sick people.

"I'm too damn clumsy to be a brain surgeon," Marino said.

He was twenty-five or so, short and pudgy with thinning black hair, horn-rimmed glasses, and pasty skin. His white shirt looked to have been nested in by gerbils, his tie hung askew, and crumbs of tobacco dribbled from the crumpled cigarette he was trying to light, tipping his drink down his rumpled front as he did so.

If the American College of Physicians and Surgeons ever held fertility rites, I thought, this happy hour was what they would look like. Already the prettiest female nurses and medical students had been edged from the gentle herd, tender as lamb chops and as unaware of their peril as the frilly cuts of meat they resembled.

The scene did not bring out my best mood, perhaps because I could no longer by any means be mistaken for a lamb chop. Steve Marino, no tender cut himself, seemed to share my opinion, a fact I found intensely charming under the circumstances.

I signaled a refill to the bartender, who had, I calculated sourly, entered kindergarten on or about the date of my first marriage.

"Does Wes Brockway come to these shindigs?"

Marino glanced sideways at me, his eyes appreciative as if I had answered a question he had been pondering. Then he gestured across the room. "That's him over there."

Brockway sat on a low couch, one arm thrown expansively back, telling a story and sipping, apparently, a white wine spritzer. He wore a light blue warm-up jacket, white Izod shirt, tennis shorts, and white cotton socks that contrasted prettily with his muscular, sun-darkened legs.

He looked like the kind of guy whose picture gets run on the cover of *Money* magazine: fiftyish, zesty, eager for the contest, as likely to swing at a racquetball as at his competitor's head. The students around him weren't quite kneeling at his feet, but they were laughing at all the appropriate places with what seemed like genuine pleasure.

Even from across the room, he resembled the single spot of color in a black-and-white photograph. He had the kind of enthusiasm that can't be faked, all eyes turned effortlessly toward him, his own eyes alive and interested in everything.

Something in the tilt of his head and not-quite-guileless grin told me he knew it, too, though. Knew it, and made the most of it. I was wondering exactly how he made the most of it when Marino's elbow found my ribs.

"Let's get out of here," he said. "We've got to talk."

"What do you think we've got to talk about?" I said, but he was already scuttling ahead of me toward the door.

I'd showed up expecting to have to find him; instead, he'd found me, then spent the next hour lubricating his voice box. I got the feeling he was working himself up to something.

Alcoholic coma, maybe. I hurried to catch up. "How did you know me, anyway? How did you even know *about* me?"

"Later," he said, dropping his cigarette, grinding it under his heel on the polished parquet. Then he opened the glass outer doors and waved me through, suddenly gracious as some old-world gentleman squiring his lady friend to the opera.

We reached the sidewalk just as the last shuttle bus pulled off toward downtown in a rumble of exhaust fumes. Few taxis patrolled the rundown tenement streets around the medical center, and Helen's car was blocks away. Meanwhile, Marino did not look capable of formulating a destination, much less getting to one.

I expressed these concerns, but he paid no attention. Instead, he peered down the darkened street, put his index finger and pinkie to his lips, and let out a whistle that could have been used for riot control.

My jaw dropped as a long, black car glided up to the curb, pantherlike. A uniformed gentleman got from behind the wheel, stepped around, and opened the right rear door with a dignified flourish.

"Good evening, sir," the uniformed gentleman said. He was tall and tailored and very correct; his hair shone silver under the streetlight and his buttons had been buffed with emery paper. Behind him the car idled sweetly with a sound like low thunder.

"Hey, Rawlins," Steve said. "How they hangin'?"

"Very well, sir," Rawlins replied, with a barely perceptible twitch of his stiff upper lip. Then he turned to me.

"Miss?" He indicated the car's interior, which smelled of old wood, old velvet, and old money, all cared for by experts.

Good servants aren't hard to find; it's just that nobody wants to spend what they cost. Steve Marino, it seemed, was an exception. Or somebody was.

Meanwhile, Rawlins's look and gesture as I got into the car were politely communicative. I understood: I was Mister Steve's companion this evening, and I would be cared for just as he was.

Unless, of course, I committed some faux pas: toyed with the young master's feelings, perhaps, or spoke graspingly of his trust fund. Physical injury was the worst but not the only breach of manners implicitly forbidden me; it was, however, the one Rawlins's look most explicitly warned against.

That brief glance told me not only that I was about to be waited on, catered to, cosseted like some member of royalty. It told me also that if I harmed a hair on young Mister Steve's receding forehead, the valued old family retainer with the silvery pate and burnished buttons would be pleased to serve my kneecaps to me.

Then the panthermobile purred away from the curb, bearing us into the night. The passenger compartment was a compact den, fitted with brass and mahogany and deep blue plush carpet. The windows had the chunky, thick look glass will have when it is bulletproof. I wondered again what bunch of billionaires Steve Marino was the scion of, then it hit me:

Marino. Not Steve here, but Steve, Senior. According to newspaper reports, the old man hadn't actually seen a highjacked tractor-trailer in thirty years.

His employees had, though, and unless his lawyers did some fancy stepping, my new young friend's daddy was about to see the inside of the slammer. In fact, he was about to memorize it; stealing trucks is not such a heinous crime, but killing the drivers is, especially when they are afterwards minced, mixed with filler and other anonymous meats, and sold as all-beef weiners.

Even in New Jersey, mislabeling meat lay beyond the pale of civilized behavior; it didn't help any that the A-number-one customer for most of Marino's weiners happened to be the New Jersey public school cafeterias.

Which meant my evening's companion was the son of the East Coast's most major crime boss since Don Corleone.

"So listen," I said, turning to where he sat flicking ashes onto the floor mat. "You want to stop somewhere for a hot dog?"

THE RESTAURANT we wound up in was so classy, it didn't have a sign out front. Knowledge of it was apparently passed from generation to generation.

"I can't eat when I'm nervous," I explained amidst the discreet clunk and tickle of expensive crockery. "So I thought I'd better find out how nervous I should be."

Around me, stiff silent guys in tuxedos kept serving from the right and removing from the left. I took a mouthful of fresh grilled swordfish and just let it sit there, allowing my tongue to get used to the delightful sensations it was experiencing.

"Yeah, well, you can't eat when you're dead, either," Steve replied, gulping at his *premier cru*. "I know guys, they'd have put you in a sack for that remark. I mean, I'm *related* to guys who would've. Anyway, this thing about the thesis."

I swallowed the swordfish; wild applause from my stomach lining. "Did one of your relatives put Bill Priest in a sack, by any chance?"

Marino chuckled and took another forkful of steak tartare. "Oh, come on. You know I wouldn't tell you that." He chewed, swallowed, and gulped more champagne.

"In point of fact, though," he went on, "they didn't. And believe me, I'd have known. My father and I, we have this agreement."

"Which is?"

Steve Marino eyed me levelly over the Waterford and the Limoges. "I don't freak with his business," he said, "and he doesn't freak with mine. You want to hear what happened or not?"

"Can I ask one more question first?"

"What do you think this is, a game show?" He shrugged. "Sure, go ahead. Shoot. Oops, poor choice of words. Ask, I mean."

"Okay. Why me?"

He swallowed again, dabbed his lips with a linen napkin. "Well, it's got to be someone. I can't ask the old man. The last thing he needs is to call out the troops for his punk son while he's on trial. I'm not even sure he could get them now; for all I know, someone's hired them to get him. Or me, although that's less likely. Coffee?"

"What? Oh. Yes."

"Leave the pot," Steve said to the waiter when our cups had been filled, the cream proferred, the sugar lumps deposited with small bright tongs.

"Christ," he said, "you wouldn't think there could be such a thing as too much service, would you? Anyway, where was I?"

"Telling me what I'm doing here." I sipped my coffee. It was coffee, all right. The way sterling is silver. Like the Hope Diamond is a rock.

"Oh, yeah," Steve said offhandedly. "I'm hiring you. Is five hundred enough?"

I didn't exactly drop the cup.

"Seven-fifty? I'll tell you right now, I won't go a penny over a grand. My future isn't worth that much, frankly, even to me. Especially now."

I took another sip of coffee and hunted for my voice.

"All right, all right," Steve said, "eleven hundred, but that's it. That's absolutely—"

"Shut up."

"—positively—"

"Shut *up*."

"—may as well just go home and put a bullet through my—"

"Earth to Steve," I intoned through cupped hands.

Steve stopped, blinking.

I let my face into my fingers and peered through them. "Look, I don't know who you think I am, but you have a mistaken idea about me."

He tipped his head skeptically. I got the feeling Steve was good at skeptical, maybe not by choice.

"I am a writer," I said. "I do sometimes help people solve problems, but I'm not very good at it and right now I'm having a hell of a time trying to figure out my own problems, which is *my* idea of what I'm doing here."

A stony look came onto Marino's face.

"I'm sorry," I said. "But I'm not the one you want for your job. Whatever it is."

Marino took a black leather wallet from his jacket. Moments later, ten hundred-dollar bills lay on the linen tablecloth.

"Your turn to listen," he said. "Don't be stupid. Take the money, for Christ's sake, before the waiter decides it's his tip. Call it a consultation fee."

"But I don't—"

"It all started," he began again, "when I found out I wasn't going to be a brain surgeon. You want a brandy?"

"No."

"Good," he said. "Me, too." He waved; drinks appeared.

He had a way about him, all right. He got what he wanted, and what he wanted now was for me to listen to him.

Quietly I folded the money into my handbag. I could always slide it between the seat cushions of the panther-mobile, on the way home.

I could also pay off some old bills, or reimburse Helen for some of the food she bought every week, or tell *Home Health* to take a flying wing-ding at the nearest celestial object.

"What I *was* going to be," Steve went on, "was a medical student for the rest of my life, or at least another year, which I swear in this Ivy League outback would kill me. Unless I could get a goddamned thesis written in three weeks, I was, you should excuse the expression, rat-fucked."

"So you called Bill Priest." That much made sense.

He nodded. "Discreet guy, quick and reliable. Just what I needed, or so I thought."

"Why couldn't you write the thesis yourself?"

A look of disgust passed over his face. "I could have, if I'd picked a subject that only needed library research. Well, maybe I could have, I'm not much of a writer, either. But no, I had to do a lab project. Which is how I discovered that I am the original Doctor Fumblefingers."

He swallowed some brandy. "It's not Biology 101 in a real research lab, you know. Nobody helps you—you're just a mangy medical student, getting in everyone's way."

He grimaced. "By the time I found out how bad off I really was, it was too late. So I asked around, and two weeks later Priest gave me a thesis and I paid him."

"And then?"

"And then he wanted it back. A couple of days after he gave it to me. I'd already turned it in, it was sitting on Brockway's desk, and this chump calls me to say he gave me the wrong thing, and if Brockway reads it, it's going to screw me royally."

Steve shook his head. "Cost me another fifty bucks to get hold of it again, from that sweet young gadget in

Brockway's office. And I'm still not sure Brockway didn't see it first."

I picked up the brandy snifter, then put it down. On top of the champagne, the fumes made me feel lightheaded. Meanwhile Steve was ahead of me by a half-dozen drinks and had bounced back thoroughly; he looked, if anything, more alert than when I'd met him.

"What did Priest say when you returned it?"

"Never saw him." Marino lit a Camel and took a deep hit. "He said slide it under the door of his carrel, he'd get back to me."

"You did that," I said.

Marino nodded. "Right. Then he got himself knocked off, so I'm stiffed five hundred bucks *and* I'm short one thesis. Sometimes there's no justice, you know? I mean, what am I going to do now, petition his estate?"

He knocked back the last of his brandy. "So. That's the story. You want to go see a movie or something?"

It wasn't and I didn't. "No," I said. "I want to know, assuming I'm going to keep your money, which by the way I'm not—"

Yet another waiter appeared, stopped just short of genuflection as he offered Steve a silver tray with the bill on it. Catching a glimpse of the total as Steve signed, I reached for the brandy; at prices like that, it was sinful to waste.

"—I want to know," I went on when I got my breath again, "what you'd want me to do for it."

"Oh, you'll keep the money," Steve said. "That's simple. You need it. I know you've already decided that. See, I know about that kid you're trying to get fixed up."

I stared.

"I," he said, "know all about you." He pushed his chair back, got up, and allowed me to precede him across the silky carpets, among the gilt chairs, through the dim marble foyer and out of the restaurant.

"What *I* need is simple, too," he went on as the big black car materialized before us in the chilly night.

Then I realized: if he knew all about me—and how he knew, I didn't want to guess; it occurred to me that his family's business probably employed some heavy-duty research talent of its own—he'd known I was a writer.

"Look," I told him, "if you think I can knock out a thesis in time for you to graduate this year, I've got to tell you that's way out of my—"

Steve chuckled richly and strode with jaunty confidence toward the car. All at once I realized how much I'd been enjoying this improbably wealthy young man with his mixture of boorishness and gallantry, his generosity and his stubbornness.

He turned; the look on his odd, young-old face was amused. "Oh, no, that's not it at all."

The venerable Rawlins opened the passenger door; when we were inside, Steve spoke again.

"Look, you're trying to find out who killed Priest, right?"

"Right."

"And the reason you're doing that, as far as I can see, is to prove your friend didn't kill him, right?"

"Right again," I said; he did know all about me.

"Good." Steve sank tiredly back into the plush upholstery. "Then all you have to do, while you're at it, is prove I didn't, either. Because the thing is this, Charlotte, when I found out I was going to have to do another thesis, I got right on it."

I didn't want a client. Besides, I wasn't a real detective, private or otherwise, so I didn't see how I could have a client, and especially not two clients.

On the other hand, Marino did have all that fresh, green money to spend...

"I worked up another goddam experiment," he went on, "and I booked some time in the dog labs, and I got together the animals and drugs and the instruments I needed. Christ, I never learn, but I really hate library research.''

My ears pricked up. "Drugs?"

"Yeah," he said sourly. "Halothane, for anesthesia. Tagged methylene blue—it's a dye I was going to track through the dogs' guts. And pancuronium, a half-dozen vials of the stuff."

He looked at me. "Only now there are only four. Somebody stole two out of my lab the day Priest got murdered."

He sighed. "Priest crossed me up but good, and it's well known my family's heavily into revenge. Also I've got no story—I'd worked all night and slept all afternoon, alone. *And* I'd mentioned to one or two people just how mad I was at the slimy son of a bitch, although I didn't say why."

We rode on in silence as I thought about his problem. Mostly, I have to admit, I thought about stringing him along. It would have been funny if he weren't so genuinely worried, which was what made it sort of sad.

Meanwhile it was now a little after two in the morning; beyond the car's bulletproof windows the city rolled by looking dark and lonely and as if it had a killer in it. Out there, though. Not in here.

"There's nothing else?" I asked. "You're telling me the whole thing?"

"Yeah, I'm telling you the whole thing," he said irritably. "Isn't that enough?"

"Will a simple no answer your question?"

"No, a simple no won't—wait a minute, what are you . . ."

"Look, Steve, I hate to tell you this, but your old man's trial has got you seeing cops under the bed. Or something has." I guessed a long history of watching family members get hauled to the hoosegow might tend to do that to you.

Steve frowned. "What's that supposed to mean?"

"Well, first off, do you even know where Priest lived?"

He shook his head. "We didn't exactly run in the same social circles. But how the hell can I prove..."

"Shut up. You won't have to. Next question— How are you going to get a thesis written now that he's dead?"

"I'm not going to. That's the whole—oh."

"Right. In fact, you've got a hell of a good reason to want him alive, don't you?"

He began looking hopeful. "Yeah, I guess. But what about the drug?"

"Right. I'm getting to that. So tell me, what was it for? That is, what were you planning to do with it, in the lab?"

He grimaced. "Paralyze the dogs, of course, so I could operate on them. Right there is where that idea went to hell. No dog could survive having me for surgeon, and there they all were, licking my hands and begging me to let them out of their cages... that's when I went home and went to bed."

"Uh-huh. But if you had gone ahead with it, how long would it have taken? Before the dog was paralyzed, I mean?"

He tipped his head, thinking. "Eight to ten minutes. I watched another guy work on a dog, once, and that was about how long..."

And that did it. As I'd suspected, the medical school did not dispense pricey, state-of-the-art pharmaceuticals to students getting ready to operate on stray mongrels. I explained to Steve how Priest's murder had come to light.

"They've got the murder vial, Steve, and it's not the one you lost. You're not only off the hook, you were never on it. Knowing you, your vials probably rolled under a radiator or something."

His shoulders sagged in relief and embarrassment. "Christ. I don't need a detective, I need a keeper. Why the hell didn't I think of all that?"

"Probably because you were all freaked out. I can see why things looked dicey to you, especially considering your family situation."

That, of course, was the root of his anxiety. I thought of asking him why he hadn't talked the whole thing over with a friend—almost anyone who heard the story could have set him straight—but realized just in time: if I knew who his dad was, probably everyone else in the school did, too.

It wasn't the sort of fame that encouraged confidences, I thought, which was probably the real reason he'd tried to pay me a thousand bucks to listen to his. Now all I had to do was return the cash.

I was contemplating methods of performing this painful action when, after a long period of silence, his voice came again from the plush gloom.

"You know," he said, "someday I'm going to find a girl who likes me more than she likes my money. I mean, really likes me."

Blinking at the change of subject, I managed to say that this ambition seemed a reasonable one.

"Reasonable, yes," he answered. "But possible? I'm beginning to wonder."

He turned to me. "Let's face it, Charlotte, I'm no calendar pinup. But if I do find her, you know what I'm going to do?"

I wished I had a dime for everyone who knew what he would do if only—fill in the blank. Steve had what most of them wanted, but he still reminded me of a kid with his nose pressed up against a bakery window.

"No, Steve," I said. "What are you going to do, if you find her?"

He sighed again, a wistful sound in the darkness. "I'm going to make her the happiest woman in the world. I swear, I'll wash that woman's feet for the rest of my life."

Moments later we pulled up in front of Helen's place, and Steve walked me to the doorstep.

Upon which Rob Solli stood, wearing faded jeans, Frye boots, and a leather bomber jacket over a blue chambray shirt. He looked like a cross between a stunt pilot and a rocket scientist: sheer animal magnetism, more brains than a Stanford think tank, and mine, all mine.

"Hi," he said, grinning lazily. "Flight out of Sacramento, taxi from JFK. Am I welcome?"

"Yeah," I said. Have I mentioned that he flosses regularly?

"Hi," Steve chimed in, sticking out a hand as he looked from Solli to me and back again. "You must be the main squeeze."

His gaze dropped to a gray case, slightly bigger than a briefcase, that dangled from Solli's other hand. Solli set the case down, draped his free arm around me, and squeezed, whereupon ready-lights winked on in several long-dormant areas of my nervous system.

Steve kept staring at the briefcase. Then he pointed at it.

"Listen, before you two get too deeply involved in the long-time-no-see stuff, how's about hauling that bag up to my place, plugging it into about a zillion kilobytes, and calling up every phone number in the Western world?"

At that, a conspirator's look passed between them. From it, I knew Steve Marino had more cards up his sleeve than he'd been showing.

Also, I could forget the long-time-no-see stuff. For now, anyway.

MARINO'S TINY dorm room looked like a corner of Radio Shack, only with all the merchandise out of its boxes and turned on. Cables and wires, consoles of blinking lights, long banks of switches. The walls were papered with printouts of programs written in computer languages arcane as Hindustani.

"Man's got to have a hobby," Steve said shyly as Solli took it all in, openmouthed. "Some I bought, some I built.

I've been coveting that gadget, though." He pointed at Solli's case. "You want to fire that sucker up?"

Solli did. Within minutes he had his hardware out of its carrying-bag and mated with Marino's, and their two systems were chuckling and muttering to one another like long-lost electronic cousins.

I sat on Steve's bed and watched; no matter how many zillion kilo-whatses they've got, they're just fancy typewriters to me. If they don't print out letter-quality, and in English, I've got no use for 'em.

"So," Steve was saying to Solli, "once I got into NAS-DAQ, I kind of lost interest."

"You broke into the stock quotes? And...manipulated them?"

"Nah." Steve punched a few buttons on Solli's keyboard; the flipped-up screen flickered and numbers began scrolling down it. "Just wanted to have a look around. I got into NASA, too—I was on-line when Challenger went down. Christ, that signal-interrupt scared the shit out of me—for a minute I thought I'd blown up the goddam boosters myself. Anyway, here's what you want."

On the way over, Solli had given Steve an edited version of what I'd asked for, and Steve had said no problem. It made me think Solli ought to be sleuthing instead of me, except how would I know Steve Marino had the phone number of every electronic data base in North America?

He did, though, along with an enormous lot of other stuff.

On a small table lay the inner workings of a gadget that looked to have come out of Bell Labs: a circuit board as big as a thumbnail, wires thin as hairs, pinprick-sized dots of solidified red goo to hold it all together. A soldering iron with a needle tip, a tiny pair of tweezers, and some other delicate tools lay there, too; Steve, apparently, was only clumsy in company.

"It's just a little spy toy I'm building," he said, noting my interest.

"This, on the other hand" —he pointed at a small oblong box by the telephone— "is a Hayes twenty-four hundred baud external modem. It connects that" —he waved at the computer stuff— "with that." He waved at the window, indicating the rest of the world.

As my eyes grew accustomed to the clutter in the room, I saw that he also had a record collection, a coin collection, a gem collection, two maps of the stars (one sky, one Hollywood), dictionaries for Spanish, Hebrew, Greek, and Italian, a book of *London Times* crossword puzzles, and a clock radio that proved on closer inspection to contain a four-inch TV screen. And that was just the top layer. Steve wasn't simply good at entertaining himself; he'd raised loneliness to an art form.

"Uh, by the way," Solli said, seating himself in front of the computer console.

"How'd I guess you were a hacker?" Steve made a wry face. "The little baby you just pulled out of your bag was privately designed and hand-assembled, and it cost a little over twenty grand, cash. Also, it runs some special bells and whistles, or so I've heard."

I once knew a man who kept a Bugatti sports car in his bedroom; his smile looked like Solli's now. Not many people knew much about Solli's toy. Fewer still realized just how special it really was.

For one thing, it could call phone numbers faster than AT&T could send out long-distance bills. For another, it incurred no long-distance bills of its own, because wherever it went it erased its electronic footprints as it stepped out of them. An instant later, it hadn't been there at all.

And that, for Solli's purposes, was very useful, since the kind of people who would like to follow Solli's footsteps were also the kind who liked to stuff bomb shelters full of automatic weaponry.

"If I were you," Marino said, "I'd carry that thing in a shopping bag or something. I don't know about out West, but even the case is getting famous on the East Coast."

Solli nodded, filing the information for future reference as his hands began moving on the keyboard. Eight small red lights on the modem began twinkling as numbers marched across its digital display. The faint electronic click of a telephone number being automatically dialed gave way to a series of hollow clucks, a brief high tweeting sound, and—

"Gotcha," Solli said. Glowing lines of print scrolled up the screen. Consulting a spiral notebook Steve handed him, he entered a swift series of keystrokes.

The screen blanked. A directory appeared on it.

"Ladies and gentlemen," Solli said, "what's your pleasure?"

Not much later, we had everything but the actual hospital charts on Priest's thesis patients spewing out of Steve's printer. Charts weren't stored in Mercy's electronic data base, but consult records—visits from the surgery, dermatology, and cardiology services, and so on— were, and according to Solli they were almost as good as the charts themselves, since if you know who's been called to fix something, you know what's gone wrong with it.

Not until the next morning, though, did I learn that Solli had retrieved even more information than I had asked for.

"WHO'S WES BROCKWAY?" he asked.

Him again.

Propped up with pillows, Solli spoke from the guest bed in Helen's apartment, where he sipped coffee and studied the printout of his data base raid.

From the bathroom where I stood towelling my hair, I told him who Wes Brockway was. "Why?"

"Because of the fifty deaths in Priest's study, eight didn't conform to the Manners-Moreheim scoring system, right? That is, the patient's scores say they shouldn't have died, but they did anyway, is that the deal?"

"That's it. So what's it got to do with Wes Brockway?"

"Well, for one thing, all eight were Brockway's patients."

It was seven-thirty in the morning. Solli's recuperative powers were astonishing and I was feeling reasonably spiffy, too, because Solli's were the paws that refreshed.

This last bit of information, though, snapped me fully awake.

"Are you sure?" I sat down on the bed beside him, peering over his shoulder at the page he was examining.

"Yep," Solli said. "Different diagnoses, different services, different treatments, different consults. But sooner or later they all got anesthesia for something, and Brockway gave it to them."

On the printout page were eight lists of names, each headed by the name of the patient from the thesis. The lists were of the students, interns, residents, consulting doctors, and private physicians who had cared for each of those patients during their doomed stays at Mercy General.

Brockway's was the only name common to all the lists.

"He's also who Marino handed his thesis in to," I said, "before Priest told him he'd better get it back. Hell, what do you suppose that means?"

Solli shrugged. "Who knows? Thing is, he's the common factor here, but he wasn't around when any of them died."

"Not around? Not for any of them? How can you tell that?"

He turned a page. "Once I realized he was what they all had in common, I tried to link him with the death dates. For that, I pulled his charges from the hospital's accounting file and sorted them by date. See?"

I shook my head. "Not really. What do charges have to do with it?"

"Everything, Charlotte," Solli said patiently, "because if you want to see what a doctor does, you look at the bills he sends out. Follow the money, you know? Look here and you'll see there are breaks in Brockway's billing, sometimes a few days or as much as a week when he didn't charge anyone for anything. And during each of those breaks, someone died who wasn't expected to."

"Could he have been billing out of his private office, or doing charity cases? Not charging at all?"

"Uh-uh. If any of his hospital work gets billed through the hospital, then all of it does. Too confusing otherwise. And here's a couple of 'no charge' items, which means Mercy General keeps track of those, too."

He flipped another page. "If he's got a private office, he might have some private billing. But a guy this active— if he's in town at all, he'll have something going on in-house. No, I think he was off somewhere during these breaks. Conventions, maybe, or vacations."

He frowned and set the printout aside. "That's odd enough by itself—being away when they died, almost like it was arranged that way. But it's starting to look as if something else odd was going on, too, because I also checked Priest's calculations and they're right. And so's his raw data."

"So the patients on this list really weren't that sick."

He shook his head. "Nope."

"And they died anyway."

"Uh-huh."

"And Priest's thesis says so without coming right out and saying so, and a couple days after it hits Brockway's desk, Bill Priest is dead."

"Looks that way."

"So if the Manners-Moreheim scoring system is so good, how come no one noticed this before?"

"Because," Solli said, "it's not just good, it's also new. There've been earlier attempts at predicting who's going to give his doctor a nasty surprise. But none of them were reliable, and besides, they were for predicting outcomes in the critically ill, not for heading off complications in patients who looked good."

"Nobody applied it to these patients when they were alive," I said slowly. "It wasn't being used yet."

Solli nodded. "Right. Priest actually did something very interesting. Instead of using Manners-Moreheim to see into the future, he took a look back. And his study should have validated the system, by showing that if it had been in use it could have prevented these patients' deaths."

"And instead," I said, "he found something else. Deaths that didn't make sense, sitting there in the statistics. Only no one had ever looked for them before."

"Maybe," Solli said doubtfully. "There's one thing more, though. Think about it, Charlotte; fifty patients in the study, and eight show up screwy. That's a little under twenty percent."

I looked at him. "I don't suppose," I said slowly, "that nearly twenty percent of Mercy's deaths are suspicious."

"One would sincerely hope not," Solli said.

"Which means Priest didn't pick study-subjects at random. If he had, he might have found one or even two of them just by chance. Eight, though..."

"...is darned unlikely," Solli finished.

"*Which* means...uh-oh." I looked at Solli. "Does it mean what I really hope it doesn't mean?"

"You got it," he said. "Whatever went on here, and I hate to say what I'm starting to think it might have been, Bill Priest didn't just happen to find out about this study. I think he already knew."

SIX

DRIVING OVER to the hospital, I reviewed my options. It took about ten seconds.

Option One: I could walk up to Brockway and ask him if by any chance he'd knocked off eight of his patients by some as-yet-unknown long-distance method, for some as-yet-unknown reason, and oh, by the way, had he killed Priest, too, to cut off Priest's blackmail demands?

Assessment of option one: possibly dangerous, definitely stupid, and in either case premature. Tipping one's hand to a multiple murderer easily leads to loss of said appendage, and while I certainly didn't know Brockway was a murderer, I didn't know he wasn't, either, or who else might be.

Which led to option two: I could go to the cops, like this—

Hi, guys, I'm an out-of-town hackwriter snoop, and have I got a story for you. How did I get it? Let's see, burglary, theft of evidence, theft of confidential data—right, my boyfriend the phone phreak helped me with that, you can lock him up, too, and this here's my buddy, the mobster's kid; he'll make a great character witness.

Assessment of option two: cut your throat. It's quicker.

I couldn't take the Manners-Moreheim numbers to the cops, because I wasn't supposed to have them or the data that went with them. Ditto for Priest's checkbook and thesis-writing stuff; I wasn't supposed to have them, either. And telling how I got them could get me dropped swiftly and seriously into the clink.

What I could do was trade things for immunity on how I found them out. That left me with option three: getting the whole story myself, preferably with proof. *Then* I could go to the cops.

And that led to the first business of the day: Helen. I needed more information on Priest than I had, and probably by now Helen would have calmed down enough to give it to me, or so I thought until I saw her.

The guard outside her door looked terminally bored, and when I got inside I understood why. Helen did not appear likely to motivate herself from one side of her bed to the other, much less to think about escaping it.

She had on a faded blue hospital gown in which she would not ordinarily have been caught dead. Her hair was a ratty tangle slung up on the back of her head with two bobby pins. She wore no make-up, and to judge by the redness of her eyes she had been crying since last I'd seen her.

In fact, she was crying now, which made me feel awfully sorry for her. It also made me want to swat her with a rolled-up newspaper until she came to her senses. Tragic grief was all well and good, but Harry Lemon's diagnostic inventiveness wasn't going to last forever.

"Helen," I said, "I am sorry for your loss."

There, that was over with. She was my friend, she was bereaved, and certain phrases had in decency to be pronounced. Besides, whatever he'd been or done, Bill Priest had not deserved murdering. Clobbering, maybe, but not murdering.

Decent phrases, however, were not uppermost in my mind. Also they had no effect on Helen, who continued weeping steadily and hopelessly. So I cut to the chase:

"Listen, Helen, did you know Bill was blackmailing someone?"

"That's ridiculous. His father owns half the real estate in New Haven."

She broke into sobs again, reaching blindly for a tissue. "Excuse me, but I just can't seem to stop this."

Ordinarily, I would have begun comforting her. Under the circumstances, though, that seemed about as sensible as putting painkiller on a septic wound. Making her feel better was not my number-one purpose, here, much as I wanted to.

"Okay, let's try something else. Like, what was it with you and Bill? I know, he was a gorgeous hunk, but there are lots of those around. So what else? Was he rich, sexy, a good dancer, what?"

I was just fishing, hoping to hook her. She winced at "rich," though; bad sign.

"Give, kiddo. What's the rotten news?"

She blew her nose, controlling tears for the moment. "You're not going to like it. On top of everything else, I've got one of those wonderful financial motives you read about in the tabloids."

She was right. I wasn't going to like it. "Which means?"

Helen shrugged, gesturing impatiently with the tissue.

"He insured himself. Two hundred and fifty thousand. Once the baby's born I turn into a trustee, I'm not sure just how."

"A controlling trustee, though? You can get at the money?"

She nodded. "He did it for the baby, in case anything happened to him. The one responsible move he ever made, and it's going to hang me. But it proves he wasn't as bad as you think, doesn't it?"

"No," I said, "it doesn't." Her situation was as bad as I thought, though, and it just got worse and worse:

I'd been thinking maybe someone had tried to make Priest's death look like suicide, possibly someone who didn't understand the drug. The body-snatch, then, would have been to cover some other part of the method, one that would show on autopsy and incriminate the killer.

But suicide would nix the insurance payoff. A prosecutor's version would go more like this: Helen kills him, meaning all along to make it look like murder. That lines up the bucks. Then the body vanishes out of the ER, with Helen in plain sight. That knocks the prime suspect, or would have if Walt Krusanke hadn't seen her at Priest's place.

And that was the heart of the matter. None of the other evidence against her was more than circumstantial. Her threats against him might actually be turned to her advantage, since no reasonable jury expects a murderer-plotter to shout her intentions in advance. And her presence in the ER was neither here nor there, since it was as good an alibi as any other for the time when Priest's body was being stolen.

No, the thing that nailed her, simply, was getting spotted at the scene. That pulled the circumstantial stuff together; that, the cops would say, was where she had slipped. They would also say that for a piece of a quarter million, plenty of people would sign up to steal a corpse.

Plenty of people knew how, too: people who'd worked in the hospital for years, who knew the physical plant and all the routines, and how to move around in them. It might not be easy, but it wasn't impossible, obviously, since somebody had done it.

"Everybody else always tried to impress me," she said dreamily. "They took me to fancy restaurants and nightclubs and told me all about their investments."

She smiled through fresh tears, remembering. "The first time I went out with Bill, he took me to a crummy gay bar and we played pinball with all his friends. Then I took him to a Sarah Vaughn concert, and he took me to a punk club. And then—"

Her voice dissolved; she pressed the joint of her thumb very hard against her front teeth.

"Oh, I want him back," she said wretchedly. "Oh, hell."

I put my arms around her. Her hair smelled like chamomile and I thought Bill Priest had been stupid.

But that was also unfair; I'd known guys like Priest, too. Lovely to look at, delightful to hold. And securely wrapped in a shield as invisible and impenetrable as Plexiglas.

You could want all you wanted, but you couldn't get there from here. I'd seen it the minute I saw him, and sooner or later Helen would have seen it, too. But the bottom line now was still that Helen would no more have killed Bill Priest than a junkie would rub out his dealer.

No one else was going to think that way, though, because the ante had just been upped by a cool quarter million. To anyone who didn't know Helen, the money was going to look like a damned attractive consolation prize.

Meanwhile the background material had just gotten a lot more interesting, too, since by every recent report Bill Priest had barely had time for all his female conquests.

So, I wondered, how did New Haven's prime example of relentless and omnivorous heterosexuality also happen to have a lot of friends in a local gay bar?

THE NEW Age Cafe sat on a side street in a not-quite-seedy residential district, plunked down between a barber shop and a gas station. It had a working-class look about it: small neon sign in the front window; pool table and pinball machines inside.

The jukebox was a burnished old beauty, though, candy-apple red and enough curving chrome to fit out an antique Chrysler. When I walked in, it was playing "Where the Boys Are" by Connie Francis, and couples were dancing.

I was the only woman in the place.

The bartender shot me a measuring look as I slid onto one of the red leatherette stools, but he gave me a white wine politely enough and he didn't throw my change at me. He was fortyish, balding, with a thick dark mustache and sad basset eyes, and he rang my drink up on an old hand-cranked National cash register that was worth more than any amount that could be in it.

I rotated the barstool a quarter-turn, noticing that it moved soundlessly and that it was not leatherette after all, but real leather. The felt on the pool table was green as a summer lawn, no burns or stains. On the wall behind one end of the bar, water sparkled endlessly in an electric display sign for Hamm's, The Beer Refreshing.

The bar itself was solid oak with blond inlay, a big rounded rim, and the dull glimmer that came from twenty years of well-rubbed beeswax. I took another swallow of my wine. On the jukebox, Connie Francis gave way to the Everly Brothers and "Let It Be Me."

The guy behind the bar eyed me with an amused expression. After a moment he wiped his hands on the clean white towel tied around his waist and strolled back to me.

"You feel like telling me why you came in here, or are you going to need another white wine for that?"

I sipped and set the glass down. "Meeting somebody."

His eyebrows rose and fell minutely. "Nice fern-bar a few blocks down. Why don't you try it?"

I met his frank gaze with one of my own. "I dispense that type of information on a need-to-know basis."

He chuckled. "Uh-huh. So what do you need to know? You'll excuse my persistence, bu you've got annoying questions written all over you, and I don't like my customers annoyed. It plays hell with my tips."

He was pleasant, but he wasn't kidding. I didn't see any hulking bouncer-types lurking, but a couple of the fellows at the bar beside me looked like they might be hiding plenty of tensile strength.

Besides, if I got unwelcome here I could be made to feel it without anybody's lifting a hand, and from the look on the bartender's face, I was on probation now and coming fast to the end of it.

What the heck, I thought.

"I'm trying to help out a friend of mine," I said. "Her boyfriend was Billy Priest. She said they used to come in here."

The bartender didn't flinch, but his not-flinching was more expressive than a grimace. He went away thoughtfully, and after a while he came back with the Almaden jug, holding it like a question mark.

I nodded. He refilled my glass, wiped the sweating jug, and put it away in the cooler again. Then he took two singles from the small pile of bills on the bar and rang them into the register.

I sipped the wine and waited. Frank Sinatra started singing about how he'd done it his way. More men wandered in, gathering at the bar, at the wooden tables, and in front of the pinball machines and pool table.

The bartender moved efficiently back and forth, pouring and mixing, serving and making change. Today was Veteran's Day, and the crowd was a holiday-afternoon crowd, quiet and well behaved. The rest of the barstools were full now, and a couple of their occupants nodded at me, friendly but noncommittal.

I wondered where the hell Walt was. He'd said noon; it was twenty past.

At the end of the bar, near the leather-clad door to the kitchen, which bore an ancient "Closed" sign, the bartender set a bottle of Rolling Rock in front of a skinny redhead with the face of an angel and the eyes of a skip-trace artist. Those eyes flickered briefly over me as the bartender spoke and I felt as if my X ray were being taken.

I sipped more wine, thinking I'd better start on Coca-Cola pretty soon, or get out of here. The redhead finished his beer and asked for another. The jukebox started thudding out "Thriller" and almost everyone who wasn't playing pool or pinball moved onto the dance floor. No one was any good at disco, but everyone seemed to be having a pretty good time.

I looked at my watch again. Walt hadn't sounded delighted about the idea of meeting me here. I got the impression he knew what I wanted to talk about. He hadn't sounded delighted about that, either.

Ten minutes later I looked at my watch again, decided I'd wait until the big hand was on the nine. As if he'd read my mind, the redhead picked up his beer and brought it over.

"Walt's not coming," he said. "He changed his mind."

I must have looked surprised.

"Just call it fag ESP."

He slid onto the stool beside me. He wasn't as young as he'd looked from a distance; not as angelic, either. The eyes, though, were the same: unsurprised. He angled them toward the bartender then back at me.

"I don't call anything fag anything," I said quietly. "Why isn't Walt coming?"

Redhead shrugged. "Doesn't want to be seen here, I guess. People get confused, you know? Don't know what they want. Some decide, you see them. Some decide, and you don't."

"Does that mean he doesn't want people to know he comes in, or that he really doesn't?"

"I mean he never really did. Only once or twice, with his buddy Priest. But this isn't the place to be seen at all for a guy like Walt. Maybe in New York or San Francisco, but not in this town, not the way things are lately, and especially not now that his friend is dead. You know?"

I didn't, but I could imagine. What with AIDS-fueled homophobia, gay wasn't okay any more in a lot of minds. Maybe even in minds that decided on scholarship renewals.

Whatever questions Walt might have been asking himself about his sexual identity, though, he'd apparently answered them—or he'd decided he had. I didn't think he was faking his feelings for Helen, at any rate.

Meanwhile a gay murder scandal could ruin his whole career. He didn't want anything to do with it, and I could understand why; maybe if I'd given him a chance on the phone, he'd have said so.

"Anyway, Walt called here a little while ago. Said to tell you not to wait for him. I'm Paul Whiteside, by the way."

I shook the hand he stuck out and introduced myself.

"I always liked Walt," Whiteside went on. "He seemed like a decent sort. You know Bill at all?" His tone implied that Bill was not a decent sort.

"Met him, that's it."

He considered this. "You like him?"

I didn't hesitate. "No."

The corners of his mouth quirked. "His many charms didn't persuade you? Not even once?"

"I guess I'm just not the persuadable type."

His smile spread, nearly reaching his eyes. "Fancy that. Billy Priest struck out. Maybe that's what killed him."

"How come he's so well known in here?"

"You mean, was he gay too?" Whiteside shook his head. "Not that anybody in this place ever found out."

He finished his Rolling Rock, signalled for another. "See, Bill had his own game. What he liked to do was break up happy marriages. You could say it was his hobby. Sort of the way some boys pull the wings off flies."

He dug his wallet out, thumbed through it until he came to a photograph. The man in the snapshot was dark haired with deep thick-fringed eyes, a smiling mouth, and a twinkle in his merry expression.

"His name was Martin," Paul Whiteside said flatly. "He's dead now. He ate pills. Bill Priest's last conquest."

"I'm sorry," I said, and I was; Martin looked like a decent fellow. "How long ago was that?"

"You mean, was it recent enough so I might have killed Priest myself?" His smile flicked on and then off again, eerily.

I didn't say anything. Around me the music and laughter, the clink of ice and the jangle of the pinball machines was rising to a dull roar. The atmosphere was getting crazy, but it was a happy kind of crazy.

Whiteside was crazy, too, but not the happy kind. From his disconnected, on-off smile, the soft voice I had to lean forward to hear, and the way his pupils kept dilating and contracting in his flat blue eyes, I thought I'd found the one real loony-tune in the outfit.

I didn't think Whiteside had murdered Priest, though. The method was wrong. If Paul Whiteside had wanted to kill Bill Priest, he wouldn't have bothered with drugs and syringes.

He'd have just knocked the neck off his bottle of Rolling Rock and carved Priest's heart out with the jagged end of it.

"It was six months ago," Whiteside said. "And it wasn't Priest's fault, any more than a locomotive is at fault when it rams a bus full of schoolkids. He was just a rolling disaster, that's all. A goddam rolling disaster."

"But—"

"He'd get tight with a couple of guys, see," Whiteside went on, "hang out with them, maybe eat dinner at their apartment. Just buddies, you know? All on the up-and-up. I think he even got jobs for a couple of the guys. His old man's got a lot of things going, real estate and construction and so on."

He grinned bitterly. "Anyway, next thing you know, the two original guys have broken up. And pretty soon old good-buddy Bill isn't hanging out with either one of his two pals any more, either."

He swigged the last of the beer and his voice hardened. "And that's the way it happened. Accidental, you know? Except once is accidental. Twice is coincidence. Three times is wake up, stupid, and Martin made three times. And Martin died of it."

It was an ugly story, and something about the way he told it made me believe him absolutely.

"You mind my asking why you decided to tell me all this?"

He shrugged, met my eyes in the mirror behind the bar. "I saw the girl, the redheaded one. Bill brought her in, sort of flaunted her. But she seemed like a nice enough person. And now this morning's newspapers are making it sound like she might get nailed for killing him."

"That's it? She's a nice person, so you spill your guts?"

I said it as mildly as I could, but he still looked sideways at me. I couldn't blame him; I mean, what did I want? He'd given me the gist of it, and telling the story couldn't have been pleasant for him.

Which was why I wanted to know why he'd told it at all.

"It's like this," Whiteside said slowly, as if explaining to someone not-quite-bright. "If she didn't kill him, but she gets blamed for it, then he's taken another one down, hasn't he?"

He paused to take another swallow of beer.

"Which," he went on after a discreet belch, "is exactly Bill Priest's style of going-away present. A blast from the past for his nearest and dearest, a smear on everything he touched. On the other hand, if she *did* do it—"

He turned to face me, his voice cold. "More power to her. I'd have done it myself, only I didn't have the nerve. We're all such sissies, don't you know."

Mincing faintly, he lisped the last few words, and that chilled me worse than anything so far. If Walt Krusanke was a smashed stereotype, I thought, then Whiteside was a poisoned one. The snapshot in his wallet was his own little blast from the past, courtesy of Bill Priest, and I knew he would keep it with him always.

His dead gaze went past me to the door.

I took the hint. All of a sudden the New Age Cafe didn't feel even remotely friendly any more. Instead, I felt as if I'd stuck my hand somewhere dark and landed it on something unexpected.

Something cold—like maybe Bill Priest's heart.

He hadn't, I saw now, been just a selfish, irresponsible fellow. Instead his behavior made a pattern: search and destroy. Find a vulnerable heart and break it, not just once but over and over. I didn't know how he'd managed to hide that side of himself from Helen, but I did know something else.

To find who killed him, I would have to find someone a lot worse than Paul Whiteside.

To find who killed Bill Priest, I would have to find someone worse than Bill himself.

"...THREE CHAPTERS," Bernie Holloway said from his office in Manhattan. "And work up the outlines, too, Charlotte, will you? With that, I think I can get you some money."

I pressed the phone to one ear and stuck my finger into the other, to block the clackety-clack of Steve Marino's printer.

I'd come to the dorm room to fulfill my promise to Solli: I would check in with him every few hours, minimum. He could not, he said, do anything at all effectively while also worrying that I might be dead in an alley somewhere.

My first reaction to this had been fury. Then I'd realized: turnabout is fair play. I would feel the same way if he were out snooping.

Meanwhile Bernie had been leaving messages on Helen's phone machine all morning and the messages had been getting shifted over here through some magical finagling of Solli's, so that it had all turned out very well.

For Bernie, anyway.

" . . . sign you up for six or eight in the series," he said, "get you out of hock for a change . . ."

Marino's room now resembled the cockpit of some very casual and poorly supervised lunar module. Littered with clothes, cups, and papers, it was also crammed full of screens, keyboards, and gadgets all cabled, plugged, or extension-corded together.

"You can write these books with one hand behind your back," Bernie went on, "they're that easy."

In one corner of the room, Solli punched keyboard control keys and stared at a glowing screen. In the other, Marino poked a calculator, made a noise of disgust, and poked it again. In the third, the printer spewed form-feed paper like some maddened electronic Vesuvius.

The result of all this activity, I had just learned, was the following nugget: big cash withdrawals from Brockway's checking account coincided closely with big deposits into Priest's. The asterisk from Priest's ledger, then, was Wes Brockway; this to me spelled blackmail in even larger letters than before.

In the fourth corner, Steve's man Friday, Rawlins, sat with a cup of Grey Oolong tea, looking dignified and oblivious to the clutter and racket all around him. The book he was reading was *Getting Rich in Distressed Real Estate!* and the pistol inside his neat suit jacket was only just visible.

In my mind's eye, the translation of Bernie's patter was visible, too: "easy" meant boring, "get you out of hock" meant I wouldn't quite be writing the damned things for free, and "six or eight" worked out neatly to "until you drop dead or go blind."

"All the same format," Bernie said, "just like filling in crosswords...."

Writing the bunch of home-health books Bernie now wanted me to sign for would indeed be like filling in crosswords, but before I could express any of the cross words six or eight of them brought inevitably to mind, he was talking again.

"...steady paychecks," he said, transforming my irritation into a premonition of inescapable doom.

When Bernie dragged out the steady paycheck line, it meant just one thing: he had already sworn to some publisher that I simply adored being chained to a typing chair, and wouldn't the publisher please make his X right here on this dotted line, so Bernie could put the check in the bank and earn eight percent on it over the three or four weeks that would elapse before he passed the money on to me, minus his tithe, of course.

Meanwhile *Tricks for the Sick!* wasn't even half finished, and Bernie knew it. But as he had long ago taught me, writers do not make money by writing their current books. They make money by writing outlines and chapters for future books, and by signing contracts promising to deliver these future books, which more to Bernie's point also pays their agents 10 percent of any advances tendered against these miragelike commodities.

Also meanwhile, my own checkbook had been stripmined for living expenses, which made it the most distressed piece of real estate I had seen recently, since although Steve refused to take back his thousand dollars I also refused to spend it.

I did not tell Bernie this, however, because if I did he would want me to start writing bodice-rippers for quick bucks, on the side. And before I did that I would go out and get my own bodice ripped, down to the ankle and in through my ribcage, if necessary.

Bernie knew, though. He let me sputter and swear a while longer, then mentioned a figure lower than the one I might have earned picking lettuce but higher than the one I'd been expecting to hear.

"*Taming the Wild Endocrine System,*" he said happily. "Charlotte, you're going to love it."

I wasn't going to love it, but I was going to do it, which was another thing Bernie Holloway had known all along.

"Okay," I promised ungraciously, "I'll send outlines and chapter-one rough drafts."

This last bit was a flat-out lie; I would as soon introduce Little Bo Peep to Mack the Knife as I would send rough drafts to Bernie Holloway, because while Bernie is a wonderful fellow and a supremely competent agent, his editorial suggestions have all the grace and subtlety of an iced switchblade.

Still, there were those steady paychecks. Besides, I had an obligation to Bernie's revolving accounts-payable fund; if it ever collapsed, Bernie would be hawking home-health manuscripts out of the trunk of an old Buick somewhere north of 125th Street, and I would be hunting another agent.

"Thanks, Bernie," I said, not meaning it.

"Not at all, Charlotte," Bernie said, not meaning it either, and after a few more pleasantries we both recognized as code for "Okay, the deal's done," we hung up.

As soon as the telephone was free, Marino and Solli began sucking what looked like all the information in the world out of electronic memory somewhere. As it flashed past I imagined data banks shrinking and collapsing, dry hollow husks crumbling suddenly to powder under the weight of their emptied shells.

Marino thought there might be another thesis in it; solving a murder by searching medical records, he said, was just novel enough to get him past graduation and out of New Haven for good.

Solli kept at it because I was, as he said, his only true love, a fact I had found eminently touching until I found out the reason: I was too busy to have a social life. Heaven, he had told me on one of the few occasions when he was in his cups, had finally sent him a woman whose free time he didn't have to keep filling, because she had even less of it than he did.

As a result, when he did have free time, he spent it with me or went fishing, which meant that on Solli's days off I either got pursued as a hobby or fed a fresh fish dinner, and sometimes both, a situation which, after some reflection, I found perfectly satisfactory.

Now, though, Priest's murder had not only coincided with Solli's annual vacation from Mendocino Coast General Hospital, it had also brought out the guard dog in him. This to me was not only satisfactory but also somewhat amusing, since when Solli did go fishing, he brought the fish home alive in a bucket and I had to kill them.

All of which was why he and Steve kept searching for common traits among Priest's thesis-patients. There had to be, they both insisted, something that linked them.

Other, that is, than the strong possibility that they'd all been murdered.

"Maybe it's not here," Solli said, as screenfuls of fresh data flashed before his eyes. "Maybe it's in their medical histories. Let's see, two depressions, one mania, a goiter, two fevers of unknown origin, and a case of exophthalmos."

"Weird glandular disease," I muttered to myself, thinking unhappily of months spent up to my neck in these unglamorous disorders. But Marino looked jubilant.

"Thyroid! It's thyroid!" He pulled off his horn-rims and smacked his wide, shiny forehead with the heel of his hand.

"Exophthalmos," Solli explained to me, "is bulging eyes. It's a sign of thyroid disease, and so are those other things. And that could be it, I guess, but . . ."

He turned to the screen again, punching up a new bunch of numbers.

"Terrific," I said, trying to put some enthusiasm into my voice. Now that I had agreed to write on them, gland cases had dropped to the bottom of my interest list—sudden disinterest being another common occupational hazard among hack writers.

"But who," Solli asked frowningly, "cares about thyroid?"

"Maybe someone did," Marino enthused. "Cared enough to make 'em dead, even. Hello, thesis, and goodbye, New Haven."

"Hear, hear," Rawlins agreed, not looking up from his book.

"I don't know." Solli's tone expressed more doubt. "It's not the kind of connection I was hoping for."

Still, they agreed they had better check into it, and shortly thereafter I left them conspiring to raid Mercy's endocrine clinic files, a plan I thought might yield up useful results in a hundred years or so.

While they busied themselves at it, I meant to give seeing Walt Krusanke another try, since now I had even more questions to ask him about Bill Priest. Also, I wanted to check Paul Whiteside's story with someone who had not been directly involved.

Another question had occurred to me, too, though, and as Felicity Dunwoodie's office was not far off my intended route I decided to get it answered immediately.

I had, after all, talked my way into Bill Priest's carrel just hours after his murder, and even Felicity would have figured eventually that there was something fishy about that. And the more I thought about it, the less likely it seemed that she would gab only to her friends and co-workers in the medical center.

Secretaries, after all, do not often have occasion to pass on such thrilling and possibly important bits of information to the police, who could easily have found me if she had and they'd wanted to.

Which made me wonder: Why *hadn't* Felicity called the cops on me?

"BECAUSE," she said, "I was afraid to."

Popping another chocolate nervously into her mouth, Felicity Dunwoodie chewed and swallowed. Her office was a reflection of herself: cleanliness, in her case, was next to featurelessness. The lighting was standard overhead fluorescent; the calendar came from a medical publisher. The surfaces in the room were dustless and devoid of knick-knacks, and there were no prints or posters, or flowers, photographs or other personal objects anywhere in evidence.

Felicity wore a pink nylon blouse, a white vest crocheted out of bargain-basement acrylic, and a navy skirt. Her shoes were low-heeled brown oxfords and her stockings resembled some hosiery I had seen once in a documentary film about East Berlin.

Felicity herself was very nearly in tears.

"How did I know who you might be?" she demanded. "I just didn't want to go making a spectacle of myself. And then you'd turn out to be someone who had a perfect right to go in there, and I'd come out looking like a fool. As usual."

Her fingers unwrapped another candy. "Everybody already thinks I'm some kind of weirdo," she said resentfully. "I can't help it, but they laugh at me anyway, and feel sorry for me. Even Jerry in the grad school office feels sorry, but at least he doesn't show it to my face."

She bit angrily into the chocolate. "I just try to help, that's all. But do you think anyone here ever asks me to go out for lunch, or for a drink after work, or anywhere?"

She crumpled the wrapper and flung it at the wastebasket. "No," she answered herself, "because I embarrass them. Because I don't know how to carry on one of their stupid, meaningless conversations. The only reason anyone told me he was dead was so they could all have a good laugh over what I said about it."

Resentfully, she chewed the candy, swallowed again. "And after I didn't tell anyone about you right away, well, after that I couldn't tell at all, could I? Because then they'd want to know why I waited, and then I'd look like a fool about *that*."

She stuffed another chocolate into her mouth. "I have feelings, too, you know," she mumbled around it.

I could see that she did, and also how she might embarrass people. She embarrassed me when I remembered how cruelly I had thought about her, earlier. Felicity was not pretty, or witty, or graceful, and so I had dismissed her.

But she wasn't stupid, either; she knew when she was being dismissed, which was almost all the time, by almost everyone. And now despite her resentful manner I thought she would answer almost any question I put, so relieved was she to be thought worth asking anything at all.

Except perhaps another favor: Felicity's desk was piled high with typing, most of it unloaded there, I suspected, by people who should have been typing it themselves.

But of course everyone knew Felicity didn't have anything else to do; she wouldn't mind staying late. Or wouldn't object, anyway.

Suddenly I felt intensely, helplessly sorry for Felicity; then I looked up and saw her watching me.

"Now you're doing it," she said. "Pitying me."

"I'm sorry. I don't know anything about you really, and I have no business forming any opinions, do I? But I do think I understand about this. You'd decided not to be noticed at all any more, is that it?''

I asked it gently; she relaxed, mollified.

"To fade into the background," I went on, "as much as you could. So no one would laugh at you or...whatever."

"That's right," she said. "I just want to be let alone."

"And then," I probed carefully, "you caught me at something you thought was wrong, but calling the police would only have meant calling attention to yourself again."

She bit her lip, nodding. "Yes. That's exactly it. It's what they would have said, you know. Poor Felicity's freaking out again, she's so weird. To them I'm just some kind of nerd."

Her look turned defiant. "So why should I have told?" she finished. "Why should I care what anyone thinks of me, or what they think I should do? They don't care about me."

Her voice softened. "Are you finding out who killed him, though? That's why you came, wasn't it? To find out?"

"If I can. You might help," I offered cautiously. I was handling her with kid gloves, now, and she knew it, but she took it peaceably enough.

"Did Bill Priest ever say anything to you," I asked, "about who disliked him, or might want to hurt him? Anything like that?"

Her answering laugh was bitter. "Bill Priest never spoke a word to me in his whole, entire life."

I just stared.

"That was a lie I told you," she went on. "About me helping him, I mean. The only reason I've got keys to the carrels is to let the janitors in. And snoops like you," she added sharply as her mood turned resentful once more.

"So, he didn't ask you to look things up for him? Or check references for him?"

Felicity shook her head. "No, he never asked for anything. He never needed anything, did he? I just watched him, you know, when he went by. He didn't even do that very often. Mostly he came up the back staircase, I think."

Her fingers worried a chocolate-foil. "I only wanted you to think I was friends with him. He looked as if his friends would be... well... like I used to want to be."

Her eyes were wistful for a moment; suddenly she turned back to her typing.

"Anyway, is that all? I don't really know anything about him and I can't sit here wasting time. This paper is going to the *New England Journal of Medicine* and they're in a hurry for it."

Not waiting for an answer, she began rolling a blank sheet into the typewriter.

It was all; I moved toward the door. "Felicity, listen, if you ever..."

If she ever what? Wanted to talk, go out? Beer and pizza, see a movie?

Her shoulders moved impatiently. "Sure. If I ever. Why don't you go away, all right? I told you, I'd really just like to be let alone."

"Right." It had been a dumb idea. "Thanks for your help."

No reply. When I looked back a final time, she was reaching for the candy box again. The hollow sound of her typing echoed down the corridor, past the other offices closed for the evening, and out into the chilly night.

LAST STOP: Walt Krusanke's. I shouldn't have pushed him, I told myself as I crossed the street to his building. I should have just asked him why he didn't want to meet me at the New Age, then met him wherever he said.

Now he might not want to talk to me at all. But he would have a harder time saying no to my face than to an intercom, so I let myself into the building with Helen's key and took the elevator up.

The second-floor hall smelled of dinners cooking and echoed distantly with three networks' version of the evening news. I knocked on Walt's door, which seemed to be the only one without a television yammering behind it.

Inside, his cat said something in Siamese. I knocked again, harder, then tried the door.

It was open. The big old cat stood just inside, her tail whipping in agitation.

"Cat Dancing. Hey, Cat. Where's Walt?" Maybe he'd just run out for the evening paper.

The cat arched her back like a Halloween cutout, spat, and raced away from me. Following, I glanced through the open door of the bathroom just off the entryway.

A pair of shoes lay on the tiled floor. The shoes had socks in them, and the socks had feet in them.

The feet were Walt's. The rest of his body slumped over the edge of the bathtub, which was filled with water. The water smelled faintly of chlorine. Through it, Walt's wide-open eyes stared. He was dead.

SEVEN

THERE WASN'T MUCH blood, just a dot of it high on the back of Walt's T-shirt. He wore tan cords with an elastic waistband—the jock's equivalent of the leisure suit—and gray Nikes. A tan warm-up jacket hung on the bathroom doorknob.

My gaze kept straying back to his. His expression looked hurt, as if he wondered how someone could do something like this to him. I wondered, too. Also, I wondered why.

Maybe Walt had known something he wasn't telling. Maybe someone had wanted to make sure he wouldn't. Or he might have seen something, something even he didn't realize he'd seen.

Whatever it was, he was gone, and I felt a rush of sorrow over all Walt Krusanke could have been and done, only now he wouldn't.

I took a slow, careful walk around the apartment. Nothing looked out of place. Some textbooks lay open on the kitchen table, along with a pen and a yellow highlighter. Today's newspaper, open to the sports pages, sat on a chair.

The cat had vanished into some hideout of her own. From one of the other apartments, a television announcer demanded that I take a look at all these fabulous prizes.

Instead, I sat on Walt's sofa and cried hard. When I stopped, Walt was still dead, so I called the police.

SITTING IN the back of a squad car looking through the perp grill has never been my idea of a good time, and meeting Detective Lieutenant Michael X. Malley didn't improve my mood.

I hadn't felt much like staying in Walt's apartment, so I'd dialed 911 from the pay phone near his building and waited outside for the police to arrive. Within a few minutes, squad cars stood at angles on the pavement and idled on the sidewalk. Red lights strobed the windows of the apartment buildings and the curious faces that appeared in them. Backed up to the lobby entrance, an ambulance waited, while two-way radios turned up loud spat bits of garble into the night.

I answered the few questions put to me by the patrolmen who had arrived first: my name, Walt's name, how I'd found him, where I could be reached. They wrote it all stolidly down.

Then something seemed to ring a bell with someone; a couple of significant looks and a muttered conversation later, I was invited to have a seat in the rear of one of the squads. Shortly thereafter, despite Helen's car sitting handily by, the patrolmen said they would drive me to Mercy General where Lieutenant Malley was waiting for me.

I nearly protested. Then I noticed my legs were shaking too hard to operate a clutch pedal. Tough as I like to pretend I am, finding bodies in bathtubs tends to upset me. Probably that was also why I couldn't decide between fainting and throwing up.

"Put your head between your knees," one of the cops advised me kindly, and in this undignified but fairly effective position I rode to Mercy General.

Malley met me in the lobby. He was a short, stocky Irishman with the squashed features and belligerent scowl of a chronic barroom brawler. His ears were lumpy, too, pale vegetable clumps below gray hair clipped close to his big, blunt head.

I doubted he spent much time brawling in bars, so I figured he must have been a boxer. In the service, maybe. Or maybe ears just got that way after too many years of hearing too many lies. Whatever it was, it hadn't done much for his personality.

"You know," he said in a voice like gravel being crushed in a Mixmaster, "you're getting to be a real pain in my butt." He pulled a cigar from inside his loud sport jacket. Under that he wore a navy blue rayon shirt and a red clip-on bow tie.

I looked away. Walt's reproachful expression still hung in my head like the symptoms of a bad cold.

"Now I guess forensics will have to sift your prints out of all the other crap," Malley went on. "It'd be too much to hope for, I guess, that you kept your mitts off stuff."

I told him about being at Walt's earlier; he grimaced as if this were no more than he had been expecting.

"Yeah, it figures. Christ, this is what I get for being a nice guy. Take your time, the DA says, build a good, tight case, we want it to stick. So I do that. I know better, but I do that, and what do I get?"

He answered himself. "A goddam stiff, that's what. *Another* goddam stiff, only this one is my witness, who puts my suspect right at the goddam scene. Only not any more."

"Listen," I said to Malley, "I know how things seem, but—"

"Yeah, sure," Malley said sourly. He dug a finger into his ear, gave a bored glance to the result. "People're all screwed up nowadays, you know it?"

He pointed the finger at me. "Like your friend upstairs. She's all screwed up, too. But tomorrow it's over. I'd done what I thought, this guy'd be alive, still, and now I'm doin' it."

He meant Walt. Also, he meant Helen. I wondered why he was telling me.

"Tomorrow morning," he went on, "indictment comes down, she gets turfed to corrections infirmary. She rolls on her helper, I get who killed Krusanke, maybe we make a deal. She doesn't, I don't give a rat's ass. You get me?"

I got him. He meant me to make sure Helen got it, too, when I saw her. That was why he was being so communicative.

"Lieutenant Malley, can I ask you a question?"

He made a "help-me-oh-lord" face that I took for assent.

"If you're so sure Helen killed Bill with an accomplice," I asked, "and now you think this accomplice killed Krusanke, how come you're so sure the accomplice didn't do it all alone?"

"Because," Malley said, "she was at the scene, not somebody else. She's got the motives, and she's got the method, too, from her old joy-juice habit. That's why."

The cigar had gone out. He lit it again.

"So what I wanted to tell you," he went on, "is cut it the hell out. I talk to Krusanke, you've seen him. I go to the New Age, you've been there. You're just some nosy amateur screwer-upper, from what I hear, and I don't tolerate that crap. This is the city, now, you know, not the sticks like wherever the hell it is you come from."

And that, apparently, was the other reason he'd had me dragged over here: to give me the twenty-cent lecture. It surely hadn't been to hear any of my opinions; he knew all he needed to.

Or so he clearly thought. Probably he also thought that if he threw a stick I would fetch it.

"You know, Lieutenant," I said when I could speak calmly again, "my father used to have a boat on the Mississippi river, up north around Red Wing, Minnesota."

"Umph," Malley said, puffing rank smoke from the cigar.

"This boat," I continued, "was a steamboat, and it had a little boiler, a fifteen-pound steam boiler."

"Yeah, all steamboats have boilers," Malley said, puffing more smoke. "So what?"

"So," I said, and of course I did not snatch the cigar and stomp on it, "when my father bought that boat, some damn fool had fitted the fifteen-pound boiler with a twenty-five pound whistle, and every time you sounded the goddamned whistle the boiler ran dry and the engine went dead, and you remind me of that steamboat."

Malley turned a look of pure dislike on me.

"Now I'm going to tell you," I went on, "how Helen would have killed Priest, if she had, which she didn't. First, she'd have bought a gun."

"Can't," Malley said. "Dope, remember? Convicted felon."

"Right. It's common knowledge how well you keep track of those. Getting a gun would have been no problem and you know it. Besides, I didn't say it had to be a legal gun."

"Then," I said, "she'd have shot him. Simple. Never mind plans, accomplices, all that garbage. That only screws you up."

"You've got that right, girlie."

"*Then,*" I said, "and this is the important part—then she'd have flipped out."

Malley turned to me, his expression suddenly interested.

"*And,*" I went on, "being plenty able to hire a really accomplished criminal lawyer, she'd wind up in some private psychiatric place somewhere and eventually get off scot-free."

Malley went on looking thoughtful. I should have started getting nervous right then.

"And you know that, too," I finished, "and so does anybody with half a brain. So if she were going to kill him, tell me, what would she need all this damned hide-and-seek nonsense for?''

Malley took the cigar from his mouth and frowned at it.

"You want to tell me," he inquired, "how she would pay for that? Private shrinks, hot-shot lawyer, private hospital—that stuff costs money. Up-front money."

"Oh, for pete's sake, money's the least of her problems, you must know that. She's *got* money. Lots."

He nodded slowly. "She does, huh? That what she's been telling you?"

"What are you talking about? She doesn't have to tell me . . ."

Then I stopped, because of course Helen didn't have to tell me. Also, she hadn't; not in so many words. I'd just assumed she was okay financially, because she looked it and because she always had been.

"Lady," Malley said, "your girlfriend's got no job, no bank accounts, no nothing. She's charged to the eyes at every store and credit-card mill on the East Coast, and that house of hers is carrying enough paper, it's a wonder the roof don't fall in."

I stood there feeling gut-punched.

"She's a stone liar," Malley said flatly, "and the sooner you figure that out, the better off you'll be. Now, you finished with the Twenty Questions?"

I looked at my watch; visiting hours were nearly over. I had two choices: I could go see Joey, or go wring Helen's neck. Neither choice looked nearly as attractive as a sleeping pill, a glass of wine, and twelve hours of uninterrupted unconsciousness.

"Yes," I said quietly. "I'm finished."

"Good," he said. "Let's go see the kid."

I looked at him in surprise. "Joey? What do you know about him?"

"Hey, just 'cause I ain't been talkin' to you, that don't mean I ain't been talkin' about you, you know."

"Oh. Yeah." That made sense. At the moment, it was about the only thing that did. We got into the elevator.

"Don't feel too bad," he said as I pushed the button for the sixth floor and the car started up. "I been fooled myself, a couple, three times."

He was about the last person I would have expected sympathy from, but it didn't make me feel better.

One thing was for sure: I had to talk to Helen again. But first I had to calm down enough to decide what to say to her. "I quit" was the phrase that sprang immediately to mind.

We got out of the elevator and stepped to the side of the corridor as a gurney piled high with tweeting monitors, blipping screens, beeping IV pumps, and a hissing green oxygen tank rolled by, propelled by a pair of grim orderlies.

At the center of the stretcher, nearly obscured by all the equipment, lay a man-shaped bundle of sheets with a head sticking out of one end. The head was surrounded and supported by a large metal halo contraption, secured by stainless-steel bolts.

I gathered the rest of the man was in the bundle of sheets, too, since the cardiac monitor showed a heart rate. Sort of.

"Jeez," Malley said, "do they have to wheel him around in plain view? Gives me a headache just seeing that kind of stuff."

Right about then I'd had just about enough of Detective Lieutenant Michael X. Malley, sympathy or no sympathy.

"Yeah," I said, "it gives that guy a headache, too. And since he can probably hear you, I suggest you shut the hell up."

I straight-armed the ICU doors.

JOEY WAS bathed and shaved, covered to the waist by a fresh sheet, and he smelled of Old Spice. The color in his cheeks encouraged me until I spotted the ice bags packed into his armpits.

"He's running a little fever," Twyla said. "It's probably nothing, but we've cultured him up and if anything shows we'll be starting some antibiotics."

I nodded, stunned once again by the vulnerable curl of his fingers, limp on the white sheet. His ribs splayed out painfully thin as the respirator cycled and his chest mechanically rose and fell.

Joey, I said silently to him, *forgive me for not sitting here with you every single minute.* It was a foolish thought but I was just beat enough to think it. If he'd wanted another kind of mother, he could have picked one; the family court would have let him. He had picked me because, as he said, I tried not to lie to him.

Someday I would tell him about this, too, assuming he ever woke up to listen. Twyla dumped the soapy basin, cleared her tools away, and stowed Joey's gear into his zippered kit.

"All finished here," she said. "You going to stay a minute? I've got a quick phone call."

Malley stood beside me. I still wasn't sure why he'd come along—probably just to make sure I knew how obnoxious he could be when he wanted to—and right now I didn't give a rip.

He looked as if he wondered, though. His ruddy cheeks had gone greenish and his jaw made twitchy chewing motions as if it wanted another cigar to chomp down on. Swallowing hard, he turned from the sight of Joey to the cards ranged on the bedside table, picking them up one by one and idly inspecting them.

Then he growled. "What the hell is this?"

I looked at the card he held: roses and canned verse. Too sweet for Joey, I thought, and then I saw what was pasted inside.

It was the label from a vial of pancuronium.

I snatched the card from Malley's hand and shoved past him. At the nursing desk, Twyla was hanging up the phone.

"Did this come in the regular mail?"

"What?" She took the card, looking puzzled. "No, today's a holiday, remember? There wasn't any . . . oh, my god."

Of course she knew who Bill Priest was and what had happened to him; by now, everyone in the hospital did.

"This is creepy," she said, "I set those cards out on his table, and this wasn't one of them. And no one else has been in there except me since—oh."

"Who?" Malley loomed, looking mad.

"The housekeeping aide emptied the wastebasket. Only . . ."

"Only what?" Glaring at me with murder in his eye, Malley plucked the card from her hand.

"Only," Twyla said slowly, "now that I think of it, his was the only basket she emptied." Her eyes grew wide and alarmed. "I think I'd better call the nursing supervisor."

"Call his doctor, too," Malley suggested. "We don't know this was all the cleaning lady left, do we?"

"I don't think . . ." Twyla began, then broke off and hurried back to Joey's cubicle.

"That's a good idea," I managed to Malley. "Calling his doctor, I mean."

"So," he grated, "the dumb cop's good for something, huh?"

He had a good grip on him, too, and before I could step away it was fastened around my upper arm. With short quick steps he urged me around the nursing desk and into the conference room.

"Girlie," he said, sounding furious, "let's you and me have a talk. I mean like right the hell now."

He slammed the door, yanked a chair out, and seated me with considerable force, although to be fair it wasn't as much force as I'd used putting my elbow in his gut as I went past him out of Joey's room.

Then he pulled out a chair for himself and sat down hard in it. "You made a mistake in there. You poked me, and that's assaulting an officer. For two cents I'd read you your rights and arrest you. It's what I want to do, and it's what I'm going to do unless I hear something very interesting, immediately."

He pulled out another cigar, lit it, and flipped the match into an ashtray.

"So go ahead," he said. "Let's hear it. Now."

He didn't have to be a genius—luckily for him, I thought uncharitably—to see the card as a not-very-thinly-veiled threat. And since murders and threats were of the same ilk, and since that ilk was Malley's bread-and-butter business . . .

Suffice it to say that he had sniffed the connection. I found myself almost not minding, but then my point of view had altered remarkably over the past few minutes.

Someone had got wind of my poking around, asking questions and working up theories and maybe even talking about them to the police. Someone wanted me to stop. Someone wanted to frighten me a great deal, in fact, and had succeeded marvelously.

My damned karma, I thought bleakly; it had been known to manifest itself this way before. No doubt in my next life I would come back as a case of chickenpox.

"Joey got that card because of me," I told Malley.

"No shit. I didn't figure he was in there making enemies of his own. Now I suppose you'll try to get a big blue baby-sitter for him, before you'll tell me your little tale of woe, right?"

Right. At the moment, I planned handcuffing myself to Joey's bedrail, but even I couldn't sit there twenty-four hours a day.

"Someone got close to him," I said. "They could get closer. As close as they did to Walt."

Malley looked more disgusted, but finally he gave in.

"Yeah, yeah," he said, "I got a guy, I gotta get him off the street, anyway. Hell, anything happens to the little sucker now, it's my butt in the cooker, ain't it?"

It wasn't, but I was glad he saw it that way because the threat to Joey wasn't only alarming; it was weird: the kind of thing, I thought, that might happen in a television show, or in the mind of someone who thought he or she was living in one.

A mind that was not right, belonging to a person who might do anything. That was the part that scared the daylights out of me.

Meanwhile I was still west of a rock and east of a hard place myself, and Malley liked my unorthodox location. And he was going to squeeze me there. We stupid bumbling half-assed amateur snoops can just sense these things.

"Of course," he said, "if you really don't know anything I didn't think you knew, then I guess this card was someone's idea of a prank. Stupid prank, you ask me, but it would mean the kid don't need watching, wouldn't it?"

He eyed me levelly. "Wouldn't it?"

And there he had me. When I got done talking, leaving out only the parts that would have gotten Solli and Steve in trouble, too, Malley laid his cigar butt in the ashtray and began to count slowly on his short, blunt fingers.

"Burglary. Tampering. Theft of evidence. Obstructing an investigation. Witholding."

I didn't tell him I'd recited all the charges to myself while doing the deeds; he didn't appear to want any interruption.

"And more," he said, "lots more. Jeez, girlie, I could put you away for dozens of things. I bet you've got ten years and twenty thousand on the stuff you just told me. At least."

I didn't tell him I'd photocopied Priest's checkbook and the thesis, either. Instead I pulled the originals of these from my bag, and laid them on the table.

"What I'd like to get you for," Malley said, picking them up, "is being an unauthorized royal pain in the ass, only there isn't any charge for that. They really let you get away with crap like this back where you come from?"

Again with the twenty-cent lecture. I hoped he'd make it the condensed version; I wanted out.

"I read your damn book, you know," he said. "Us dumb cops do that sometimes, for your information. This Flanders fella you wrote about in there—he's the sheriff, is he, back home?"

I nodded, resigning myself to the uncondensed version.

"Seems like a nice enough guy," Malley allowed.

Hope tickled somewhere behind my breastbone.

"He is," I said. "He's a very nice guy. In fact, if you call him I'm sure he'll be happy to vouch—"

"Nicer than me," Malley said flatly.

Hope dropped with a final *thunk* to a spot somewhere below the pit of my stomach.

"Look," I said, "if I'm trying to prove Helen didn't kill Priest, and this hypothetical accomplice also wants it to look like she didn't—"

"Why try to stop you?" Malley asked.

"Exactly."

He sighed. "Because," he said, " you are reasoning from false principles to a false conclusion."

You could have wiped me up with a dishrag.

"Hey," he said, "us cops watch educational TV, too."

His eyes were darker and more amused than I'd seen before. Also smarter. He kept doing that: surprising me.

It was like watching a jack-in-the-box pop out of a concrete block, and I didn't like it a bit.

"You," he said, "think you're looking for one thing. But maybe somebody thinks you might find something else."

"You mean," I said slowly, "that I might find out she did kill him, instead of that she didn't."

"Yeah." His Mixmaster voice had stopped grinding gravel and started in on flint chips. He got out of the chair, pulled out his wallet, and drew a card from it. Next, I knew, he would give me the card and dismiss me, with orders to call him if I got any more brilliant ideas or any more weird events happened.

Firmly I ordered myself to keep silent while hearing these patronizing words. I wasn't going to enjoy them, but if they bought Joey some safety they were worth listening to.

So I waited, and after a moment the words came, but not the words I was expecting.

"You have the right to remain silent," Malley said.

It was, I thought, a hell of a time to remind me.

"DON'T HANG up," I said. "Please don't hang up."

Whatever the New Haven Department of Police Services spent its money on, it wasn't anything frivolous like paint for floorwax. I stood in a stunningly unlovely room that contained one scarred wooden desk, six beat-up metal chairs, a metal barrel full of sand which bore the stencilled legend CRUSH YOUR BUTTS, and a pay phone.

"Don't hang up, please," I shouted into the phone. The room was an anteroom off the main desk area, and it smelled of fear, sweat, poverty, and Wildroot Creme Oil.

Out in the larger room, amidst the shouts of a harrassed desk sergeant and the staticky, incomprehensive eruptions of an ancient intercom speaker, police officers hustled miscreants from place to place and the miscreants hustled one another.

One of these miscreants, a small, shivering fellow who bore a decided resemblance to a water rat, sidled over from the desks where the others crowded, demanding their rights; he, apparently, was hustling me.

"Hey, chicky," he whispered, favoring me with a snaggly smile. His face was filthy but freakishly smooth, as if the acid bath of his day-to-day existence were slowly dissolving him, starting with every trace of his whiskers.

"Blow it out your ass," I told him, since if there is a time and place for everything this was certainly damned well the hour and location.

Looking disappointed, he went away, locating his arresting officer with remarkable efficiency and at once insisting on his right to a cell with cable TV and a color set, because he had a learning disability.

If they put me into a cell with anyone here, I decided, I was going to demand a chastity belt and a rocket launcher.

Theoretically, they allowed you one call. Theoretically, it is supposed to be to your lawyer. I didn't have a lawyer; Helen had a lawyer. Unfortunately, his card was on my bedside table and I didn't even remember his damned name.

Meanwhile, Steve Marino's telephone was busy, tied up with illegal computer communications, and I couldn't call Helen because the hospital switchboard did not put calls through to patients after ten o'clock—not that I would have trusted myself to speak civilly to Helen in any case.

I did, however, have a literary agent. Praying hard that he didn't have a publisher hankering for a first-person account of prison life, I waited for Bernie to come on the line and got his answering service instead.

"Mister Holloway is unavailable at this hour," the service deigned to inform me. "May he telephone you back?"

Behind me, a hideous scream rent the air. Little Mister Rodent, probably, finding out the jail wasn't wired for his favorite cable movie channel.

"Did you hear that?" I inquired into the sudden silence on the phone. "I'm in police custody and of *course* I'm innocent, but if I don't talk to Bernie they're going to put me in a cell down here and then I don't know *what* will happen to me. . . ."

I supposed they had cells just for women but at the moment I didn't see how that could be any better, especially since the Rodent had just pulled off his watchcap and pea coat, exposing a mass of long, knotty auburn hair and a tight pullover sweater.

The hair and the shape under the sweater, together with the baby-smooth cheeks, clued me in horridly to the truth about Rodent's gender.

"*Please,*" I said into the phone.

"All right," the answering service voice relented, "but this had better not be some sort of practical joke." After which she did get Bernie, who called his own lawyer, who called a lawyer in New Haven, who after a very long while at last came down to spring me.

Garth Harrisfaulds was fat, fair, and forty; he preferred to be called an attorney, and he pronounced the esquire when he introduced himself. Garth was clearly not happy to be acquiring me as a client; I got the impression he considered the sheer number of charges against me, not to mention their variety and type, to be in extreme poor taste. In fact, after meeting Garth Harrisfaulds, Esquire, I found myself thinking rather wistfully of the Rodent.

This, however, was almost certainly a symptom of temporary insanity, which ailment seemed to hover like a contagious cloud throughout the building, including the courtroom wing where I was scrutinized, discussed, lectured at, frowned at, argued over, and finally dismissed.

"The arrest," Harrisfaulds said primly as we walked out of the grim old structure, "was a crock. First, your statement was coerced. Also, the lieutenant clearly expected to charge you as a result of it, yet he delayed informing you of your rights until after you had made remarks prejudicial to yourself. That's a definite no-no, civil-rights-wise, and he's quite aware of it."

"In short, he was busting my stones."

"Indeed," Harrisfaulds sniffed. "A man in his position gets a free swing, from time to time, and I believe Lieutenant Malley has just spent one of his."

"Why?" I asked. "I mean, why not either yell at me and let me go, or really arrest me and make sure I stayed arrested?"

Harrisfaulds's answering look said I was a dim bulb. "You do read, don't you?" he asked. "That is, you comprehend newsprint?"

"Well, yes. But lately I haven't had time to—"

"This morning's *Chronicle* ran a front-page story on the murder of William Priest, son of Jonathan Priest," Harrisfaulds said. "As I gather you don't know, Jonathan Priest is this town's golden boy in the property-value department, New Haven's last hope for not turning into the armpit of the East Coast."

He steered me toward the parking lot. "Priest is the force behind all the downtown redevelopment we've had these past ten years, and now he's trying to do for city apartments and co-ops what he's done for offices and stores—that is, get people to move into them, instead of out of them."

I was beginning to get the picture. "And now his son's been murdered in one of the city apartments he wants folks to think are so nifty," I said.

Harrisfaulds nodded. "The *Chronicle* also ran an editorial wondering just how safe the city is to live in. The mayor didn't like that, Miss Kent. He wants people to move back into his town. He wants it very badly. In fact he wants it almost as much as Priest wants his son's killer publicly caught and put away."

"That's why Malley's on the warpath," I said. "He's getting pressure from above."

"Precisely," Harrisfaulds said as we reached his car. It was a silver BMW that looked out of place among the dusty Dodges and Montes in the NHPD lot.

"And that is why I suggest, Miss Kent, that whatever you are doing to irritate the lieutenant, you stop doing it at once. One might view his action tonight as a kindness. An uncharacteristic kindness, to be sure, with perhaps a note of expedience tossed in. After all, now he won't have to waste time in court on it."

"But next time he'll bust harder."

He looked pained as he unlocked the passenger door of the BMW. "Mike Malley is the junkyard dog of New Haven's homicide squad. He catches people by being just as mean, stubborn, and low-life as they are, a method which historically has served him very well. He doesn't solve crimes, he clears cases, which accounts for his presence on the Priest murder as well as for his unlikely rise to detective-lieutenant in the first place. Do I make myself clear?"

I assured him that he did.

"Also," Harrisfaulds said as he slid behind the wheel, "he holds grudges. Which means that next time, Miss Kent, getting out of his way again is not going to be this easy."

Gritting my teeth, I got into the car. It was my second twenty-cent lecture for the night, and I'd had a crawful. Strictly to avoid more of one, I agreed to behave myself from now on, crossing my fingers firmly as I promised this.

So maybe I wouldn't be breaking into any more apartments, I thought as the BMW bore me into the night; so what?

That still left plenty of other places—legal places, even—to go looking for trouble.

IT WAS broad daylight by the time I retrieved Helen's car, drove it to her place, stomped up her front steps, and yanked two days' worth of uncollected mail out of her mailbox. The mail consisted of bills, circulars, bills, advertisements, and more bills. There were also several skinny note-sized bank envelopes, each containing a single pink carbon. Having had considerable experience with these, I knew at once that they were notices of bounced checks.

I slammed into the apartment, wondering if having her tongue turned black might make Helen Terrell stop lying, or if lying was built into her like red hair and the ability to make me believe her.

The bathroom mirror was steamy and shaving things stood on the toilet tank; Solli had been here and gone again. I made a mental note to call him at Steve's, or stop by if the phone was busy, so that he would not begin searching for my dismembered body; it had been over twelve hours since I'd seen or spoken with him and probably he was wild by now.

I was pretty wild now, too. I went around yanking open the curtains and some of the windows, to get a little light and air into the place, since the faint scent of lavender that always hung in the rooms was beginning to smell like funeral flowers.

Then I made a pot of coffee, sat down with a mug of it, and opened all the envelopes. Helen's bounced checks totaled $2,475.23 The credit-card bills came to just about twice that amount.

Three department stores, two public utilities, a couple of mail-order places and a maternity shop were also dunning her. All mentioned collection agencies, some regretfully and some with relish. Finally, her health insurance had been cancelled—nonpayment of premium—and her telephone was about to be turned off.

Grabbing a fistful of bills and notices, I went directly to this instrument and picked up the receiver. A dial tone hummed reassuringly into my ear. Starting with the phone company, I dialled my way through ten different numbers and spoke with nine billing departments and one bank manager.

Miss Terrell was in the hospital. No, not terribly serious but quite incapacitating for the moment. Truly sorry about this mix-up and might I have a few days to get her finances in order, deposit checks, and bring her account up to date? Thanks much, do appreciate, blah blah.

And on to the next. By the end I had bursitis of the telephone ear, a sore index finger, and ten more big fat lies on my own conscience. Still, I'd bought Helen a little time to get out of the financial hole she'd apparently dug herself into.

Not that it was going to do any good, because the final envelope was from Mercy General's Department of Developmental Affairs. As her contract had been terminated, the letter said, the locks on her office door were to be changed. Did she care to remove any personal items now remaining in said office? Also, would she kindly return any keys to any other hospital areas now in her possession, *viz.,* engineering supply and work areas, lower-level HVAC maintenance and repair access areas, and the third-floor blueprint storage and reproduction rooms.

At letter's end, someone had noted rather sharply in bright red ink that this was the Second Notice.

And so much for any undeposited paychecks I'd hoped I might find lying casually around. According to the letter, Helen had been unemployed for over two months, and according to the unpaid bills, the blue-chip safety net I'd thought she had was either another of her lies or mysteriously out of order.

Which meant she didn't need the money she would eventually realize from Priest's life insurance policy—or, rather, she did, but those things took time. What she needed was money right now, lots of it.

I was staring at ten thousand bucks' worth of needing this very minute, and that was just past-due stuff.

I looked around Helen's butcher block and copper kitchen. It didn't appear to be the kitchen of a destitute person, but it surely was.

How the hell, I wondered, had Helen gotten into this? And how had she planned to get out? And what other gruesome secrets were still in hiding around here, waiting to jump at me?

EIGHT

I DON'T CARE what Arnold Bennett says; a cup of tea at an unusual hour should be punishable by flogging.

Cheerfully sipping one of these, Solli tossed rolls of film and items of clothing into a suitcase he'd dragged from one of Helen's closets.

"Come on, Charlotte," he said. "Rise and shine." He began whistling.

I have never had any difficulty with the early to bed part of the prescription. It's the early to rise part that kills me, especially when Solli whistles through it.

It was 5 A.M. I'd spent the remainder of the previous day with Joey, and had met one of the police officers guarding him. True to his promise, Malley had assigned them; if he kept it up, I thought, New Haven would have no one left to direct traffic.

This particular guard was way overweight, which I gathered was why he was no longer street-legal. Still, he looked entirely able to bean any Joey-threateners with the butt of his service revolver, all I cared about since Twyla had put herself in charge of threatener-identification, and Twyla was now so mad and so universally suspicious that she was barely letting me into Joey's cubicle.

Also, I'd seen Harry Lemon, who assured me that no district attorney or police detective of any stripe was about to take any eight-months-pregnant ladies off his medical service, indictment or no indictment, insurance or no insurance, for at least another forty-eight hours.

"Take heart, Charlotte," Harry had said. "You're dealing with a power-mad medical resident here." Then, grinning evilly, he had written orders for yet another battery of complicated and obscure medical tests, many of which would take forty-eight hours just to get scheduled, much less to complete.

Next I'd made peace with Solli, a crucial but simple process requiring only a heartfelt apology for scaring him half to death by my long and silent absence, along with a thorough news update and a promise that I would accompany him on a trip out of town.

"You need a break," he'd told me firmly, and as I had barely had strength left to nod, I was forced to agree. The fact that I was not going to get a break—not, at least, on the trip Solli planned—was something I'd figured he could find out later.

Finally, I slept for twelve hours, which just at the moment felt like about twenty minutes. The only thing that kept me from pulling the covers over my head was knowing Solli would pull them off again.

"By the way," he said, "there wasn't any thyroid connection among those thesis patients after all."

Surprise, surprise; I could have told him that. If anything good could have come of gland cases, *Home Health* would not have me writing about them.

Muttering, I swung myself out of bed with all the verve and energy of a lobotomized slug.

"Those bulging eyes," he went on, "remember those? Well, they were getting pushed by a frontal tumor. The fevers were infections. The goiter was a cyst."

He opened the camera case that Steve Marino had lent him and peered into its irritatingly well-organized interior.

"In fact," he said, zipping the case shut again, "those dead folks in Priest's thesis have still only got one thing in common that I can find."

"Let me guess," I said, stumbling into the bathroom. "Wes Brockway." Brockway's name seemed to be turning up everywhere. "Only he wasn't around when any of them popped off. Convenient for him, huh?"

"Guess so. Especially since, if he had been around, you'd be on him like a terrier now." Solli folded a flannel shirt and stuffed it on top of the film. "Even though," he added, "the guy's got no motive for killing off his own patients that I can imagine."

I closed the bathroom door gently and turned on the shower, pretending I hadn't heard. Solli hadn't had much to say about my previous evening's little run-in with the law. He'd taken it all very calmly indeed, in fact, which is normal for Solli, who likes to tinker quietly with his bombshells before he drops them.

But from his present cheery manner I could tell he thought I'd run into a complete dead end; Solli is always cheery when he sees me veering dangerously toward a black funk.

Also, he didn't like my finding corpses or getting tossed in jail. Solli thought any corpse that didn't come equipped with a tag on its toe was some sort of unnatural event, and he believed jails were dangerous, the silly man.

Ergo: real soon, he was going to start issuing ultimatums. Stop snooping, start writing.

My checkbook was issuing ultimatums, too; there are special jails, I hear, for writers who stop turning in their manuscripts. They're called regular jobs.

Thinking these things, I staggered through my early-morning ablutions and was reasonably conscious by the time I got into Helen's car.

"The thing is," he said as we crossed the Quinnipiac Bridge out of New Haven and began humming east on I-95, "I hate to discourage you when you're so determined to do something."

I thought that was fortunate, because he wasn't going to discourage me. I knew too that "in the driver's seat" is more than a turn of phrase; it was just possible that I should have insisted on being in it myself.

I also knew, however, that at this hour of the morning I was likely to ram the Datsun into the nearest abutment, just for the pleasure of becoming unconscious as swiftly and efficiently as possible. Besides, we were already going where I wanted to go.

"But," Solli went on, "I just don't see what more you can do. Priest was a selfish, self-centered, conniving little rotter. If that New Age Cafe story is true, he was worse— he was a sociopath. Heck, Charlotte, scads of people must have wanted him dead."

"Love and marriage," I said stubbornly. "Soup and sandwich. Crime and punishment. And—blackmail and murder."

Solli nodded reluctantly. "I suppose. They do go together a little too well for coincidence. Still, finding out exactly how they went together—"

"Means finding something that links those thesis patients," I finished for him. "And as far as I'm concerned, we've found the only link we need—Brockway. You said yourself I ought to follow the money, and the banking stuff shows that he was paying big chunks of it to Priest. Blackmail-sized chunks, to keep Priest from telling about Brockway's run of croaked customers."

Solli made a face. "Charlotte. I traced Brockway's trips. He really wasn't around when his patients died; he was at medical conferences in Cancun, or Washington, or Denver—at a couple of them, he was a speaker—but he wasn't at Mercy General. The only link he could've had to those deaths is a paranormal link. Besides, the money connection isn't that neat, either. The dates match pretty well, but the amounts don't—Brockway was taking out a lot more than Priest was putting in."

"We do agree, though, that someone helped those folks shuffle off this mortal coil?"

Solli's look expressed unwilling assent.

"And I don't suppose the autopsy reports added anything else helpful, other than ruling out your nice thyroid theory?"

Of course, they'd all have had autopsies; you can't conk off unexpectedly without your doctors wanting to know why, if only to deter the unpleasantness of a malpractice suit by your relatives.

"You want me to recite the causes of death for you, or just tell you how unalike they all turned out to be?"

"Recite, if you remember them, please."

"One acute diabetic ketoacidosis," Solli said, frowning ahead in concentration as three lanes of traffic began narrowing to two. "One respiratory failure. Two cardiac arrests. One pulmonary embolus, one big stroke, one status epilepticus, and a massive pulmonary edema. Satisfied?"

Behind us, eighteen-wheelers downshifted with a sound like dinosaurs clearing their throats. Ahead, a big orange highway truck crept along.

On the grass strip to the right of the traffic lanes, men in reflector jackets stabbed trash with long sticks and dropped it into shoulder sacks, cleansing the environment and reminding me just how unpleasant a regular job really could manage to be.

"Eminently," I said to Solli, "satisfied." We passed the highway truck; traffic spread to three lanes and sped up again.

"I've listened to enough of your medical blather," I went on, "to know these are immediate causes of death. They don't tell anything about contributing factors, do they?"

"Well, no. They don't," Solli admitted.

"Pneumonia, for example, can cause respiratory failure, but so can having a pillow pressed to your face. You can get cardiac arrest from a heart attack, or a knife in the chest."

"There wasn't any knife in any chest, Charlotte—"

"So they are all alike, aren't they? Unrevealing, and all different. If you were going to kill eight people and you didn't want anyone to know they'd been murdered, wouldn't you do them all in different ways, and make them look as unmurdered as possible?"

"Well, yes, I would but—"

"And if the death certificates were all signed by different doctors, and the murders themselves happened over a long period, it might very well just all go by unnoticed."

Solli sighed. "I suppose it might. There's a review board for in-hospital deaths, but there weren't enough of these to shift the statistics noticeably. And when a patient conks out on me, I don't think about murder."

He frowned. "When that happens, I think about what the hell I missed, what was going wrong that I didn't notice until it was too late. And sometimes I never find out—not often, but sometimes."

"Often enough that you might just write 'cardiac arrest' and let it go at that. Regrettable, but the fact is you don't know. There must be a reason, but you can't find it, and you're not in the mind-set to go hunting for an evil one."

He nodded, looking unhappy.

"You know what, though," he said after a moment. "There is one thing. I've been trying to think of what they all had in common. But what if it's something really common, like IV lines?"

Our eyes met briefly. "Intravenous," I said. "Fatal injection. It would do the job, wouldn't it? Just like it did on Priest."

He nodded again, looking very unhappy indeed as he turned his gaze back to the road ahead. "That means it could have been anyone, even some random nut-case. All you'd need to qualify as a victim is an intravenous line."

I shook my head. "Brockway's still the common factor. And Priest didn't die until after Marino turned the thesis in to him. I wonder if he could have rigged IV bottles in advance? So he'd be sure to be far away when they were used, for example."

By now it was nearly seven-thirty and traffic was getting thick on the Thames River Bridge, just east of New London. Helen's Datsun tootled importantly onto the huge span; below us the Thames sparkled in the sun's early slanting rays.

"I suppose," Solli said. "But it would be hard to arrange. He could spike an IV bottle in advance, but he couldn't be sure which patient was going to get it—his, or somebody else's."

"Still, let's say he did," I said, "and Priest found out about it somehow. Then he might have sent Brockway the Marino thesis as a threat—say, if Brockway were dragging his feet about paying again—to show how easy it would be to expose Brockway if the blackmail demands weren't met. And once he'd shown it, he could have used Marino again to get the thesis back, so as not to kill the golden goose."

"I don't know. It sounds too tricky." Solli merged into the right-hand lane towards Rhode Island and zoomed down the exit ramp.

"Besides," he said, "we still don't have any reason for killing them in the first place. Which puts us right back to what they had in common, which is exactly what we aren't able to find out, which is why we are dead-ended."

He fell silent, concentrating on threading his way through the warren of streets leading to Route 1. Meanwhile I refrained from telling him that I did not agree with his conclusion.

If the common factor among Priest's thesis-patients was not a medical one, I thought, then perhaps it was some other sort of factor.

That there was some link among the dead patients I remained convinced; despite steadily increasing evidence to the contrary—the sort of evidence provided by newspaper headlines like CRAZED SHOPPER AXES 3, for example—I still do believe that when person A does in person B, it is generally for some reason that person C may comprehend, even while not necessarily feeling moved to burst into spontaneous applause.

And it was that link, that reason for it all which I too still found lacking; not the what, which Solli might extract from the bloodless wires and chilly ceramic chips of a microcomputer, but the why: the sad, often messy, yet common and perfectly comprehensible motives of a heart as human as my own.

The human factor, in short, was what I wanted. And, just by coincidence—and by considerable subterfuge on my part—the human factor was what we were on our way to get.

"Anyway," Solli said after a little while, "I really do think you've done all you're going to be able to. When we get back you should talk to Mercy's chief of staff—let him persuade the police this is worth pursuing. Because to do it, you know, they're going to have to start exhuming bodies, and I doubt you can talk them into doing that on your own."

"Mmm," I said tactfully, because of course that was not quite how I saw things. And any minute now I would have to start explaining how I did see things, because we were driving into the seaside town of Stonington, which was our destination.

It was a sweet, salty little place: old clapboard houses, a village green, fish markets and marine-engine-repair shops lined up along a wharf that smelled of pine tar and seaweed. In fact it was a veritable hotbed of picturesque New England charm, all of which caused me to give Solli's camera case a guilty glance.

Lent to Solli by Steve because of course Solli had not brought any fishing gear from California, the camera was meant to provide a carefree holiday activity we could pursue together.

I, however, was not going to appear in many pictures unless Solli wanted casual shots of me interviewing the relatives of dead people. That was because, as it turned out, the data Solli and Marino had obtained held more than test results, X-ray summaries, autopsy reports, and other medical facts on the dead folks from Bill Priest's thesis.

Steve and Solli's data-thieving operation had also yielded up the names and addresses of the patients' next-of-kin, two of whom lived in Stonington and one in Noank, the next little town along the shore.

I thought I would wait a while longer to tell Solli that, though. He was happy, thinking he could wean me away from murder a bit at a time: an overnight jaunt here, a restaurant lunch there, a bit of picture-taking, shopping and strolling, just like normal people.

Soon, he probably thought, I would be normal too, or at least as normal as I ever got. It seemed too bad not to let him believe it a little while longer.

Say, at least until after that restaurant lunch.

"YOU," SOLLI said, "are the most stubborn, bull-headed, impossible... What are you going to do, walk in and tell them their relatives were murdered? And wouldn't they like to hash it over with a perfect stranger? What are you, nuts?"

Trust Solli to get right to the practical point, no matter how mad he is.

We sat on the sunny bayside deck of the Stonington Cafe. Gulls swooped and screamed as they plucked up the bread chunks I tossed them. Fifty yards out, an old man in a blue and yellow slicker was rowing a green cape dory from one buoy-marked lobster pot to another, hauling up the slat-sided traps and letting them down again.

"Actually," I said, "I thought I'd lie about that part. The murder part, I mean."

Solli slapped a roll of film into the camera and gave the advancing mechanism a vicious crank. "If Malley doesn't kill you, the hospital will, not to mention Brockway. He'll sue you up one side and down the other, Charlotte. I would. In fact, I'm already going to. Breach of promise."

I ate a buttered cornbread stick. It was delicious. "I'm not going to mention Brockway. I'm not going to mention anything. I'm going to let people mention things to me."

"Why should they?"

"Because even though some people do die of natural causes, no one ever believes it when it happens in a hospital, that's why. I'm surprised there haven't been any malpractice suits."

Solli's eyes narrowed in spite of himself. "Hmm. You think some of these people may have their own suspicions? Maybe not strong enough ones to start suing over, but..."

"Or at least some complaints," I agreed. "Which I am going to encourage them to express. Maybe while they do, they'll drop some fact about the dearly departed that I don't already know."

"Like who the departed wasn't so dear to?"

I grinned. He wasn't won over; not by a long shot. Still, he hadn't tossed his bag in the car and left me alone on the dock, which was what I probably deserved.

Meanwhile, if those dead patients had something unmedical in common—something too human to show up on any sort of official record—I wanted to know about it.

"Just don't get hurt, that's all," Solli said. "I'm mad at you now—anything happens to you, I'll dump you at a veterinary clinic."

"Who, me?" I picked up my handbag. "I have the strength of ten, for my heart is pure."

Well, the strength of nine, anyway.

"GOD'S JUDGMENT," Hattie Cranston said. "He was a *married man*. Never mind no divorce, God don't hold with no divorce."

The front walks on Stonington's Totoket Lane were edged with big clamshells. Lobster pots, broken buoys, and scraps of fishnet littered the small sandy yards and the porches; peeling flower boxes trailed a few last straggling orange nasturtiums.

"You want coffee?" Hattie boomed. She ushered me into her small, crowded living room and thumped off to the kitchen without waiting for an answer.

Paint-by-numbers religious scenes hung everywhere on the knotty pine walls of Hattie's cottage; the coffee table, a sheet of plywood supported by concrete blocks, boasted a life-sized picture of Jesus laminated to its surface. Religious statuettes crowded together atop the big color television, a plastic holy water font had been nailed into one panel of the knotty pine, and twenty years' worth of Palm Sunday palm fronds had been stuck behind the frames of the various pictures, giving the whole place an air of faded tropical festiveness.

"Here, drink some coffee," Hattie said, lumbering back with a steaming mug and a loaded plate. She was seventy or so, big and broad shouldered with a headful of frizzy, iron gray hair; she wore a flowered housedress, a red zipfront sweatshirt, and black orthopaedic shoes with one heel heavily built up.

"Eat some a that cake, too, go on. Hickory-nut cake, gathered 'em yesterday."

I sat and ate. The cake was good, and I said so.

"Hickory nuts." Hattie snorted, letting her large ungirdled form into a Lazy-Boy recliner with a sigh of relief. "Awful lot of work, like everything good. That's the Lord's price."

I'd phoned her first, still not sure what I would say, but she'd saved me the trouble of thinking up something. I'd barely introduced myself when she interrupted me, her voice crackly but vigorous.

"Ain't missus. Name's Hattie. Come on over."

Now I tried to think of some way to get around to my topic. Thinking about lying barefaced to strangers was one thing, doing it quite another.

"Hattie," I began. "It's about your sister, Agnes."

This was the sticking point. I planned to suggest that I was writing an article for which I was conducting a consumer survey, and then ask if she was satisfied with the way Agnes had been treated in the hospital.

Hattie, however, got ahead of me again. "That damn doctor," she said flatly. "Kilt Agnes, or as good as."

I blinked. "Huh?"

"Brockway," she spat. "Poor Agnes was gone on him."

I gulped, trying unsuccessfully to think of an improvement on my last comment, but Hattie wasn't listening to me anyway.

"Not him directly," she said, looking darkly wise, "but he was the Lord's instrument. *He* knew. He saw sin an' He struck down the sinner. Damned old fool," she added, and I assumed she meant Agnes, not the Lord.

Then I noticed the unusual brilliance of Hattie's dark brown eyes. They didn't shine; they glittered stonily. Her snug little home didn't seem quite so cozy, either, as all at once I noticed the subjects of the paint-by-numbers scenes.

They were all of martyrdoms. Bloody martyrdoms: arrows, swords.

"Agnes, see," Hattie boomed in her big mannish voice, "never got married. But she was always silly about men."

"And she liked her doctor," I said. "Dr. Brockway."

Hattie snorted. "You'd a thought she was sixteen. Soft in the head. He was savin' her, she said. Doin' her so much good."

She thumped the chair arm with her fist. "Why, I went in there one morning, she'd got her hair in a permanent wave, looked like a poodle-dog. They got beauty operators in that hospital, trick the old people into foolish vanities they can't afford."

"She'd had her hair done for him?"

Hattie nodded vigorously. "*And* her face. Painted like Cleopatrick. Ain't that the limit? Land, he was all she could talk about. Gentle, she said, kind an' gentle."

She snorted again. "Hah. Cuttin' folks open don't sound like no gentle trade to me, or gassin' 'em whilst someone else cuts, neither. Tempted her is what he did, an' Agnes was weak."

"But . . . forgive me, but how could she die of that?"

Hattie looked severe. "I already told ya. The Lord's retribution, that's how. That doctor might not a meant nothin' by his smilin' ways, but Agnes did by hers, an' the Lord knew it. Sent poor Agnes her death. I been prayin' for her, but I don't think it'll do no good."

Which was just about the most damn-fool crackpot idea I'd ever heard; Hattie had martyrdom on the brain. Still, she didn't seem easily upset, so I pushed a little more.

"No one was angry with Agnes, though. Other than the Lord," I added hastily at Hattie's frown. "And I don't suppose she had much that anyone would want?"

Hattie took my meaning shrewdly and fielded the question without a flinch. "No, honey, she didn't. Never owned a thing but her burial place, and she's in that now. Agnes didn't get no human shove towards the hereafter, though where you'd get a fool idear like that I can't fathom."

She hauled herself up from her chair and left the room. I heard her rummaging in a kitchen drawer, and after a moment she returned with a fistful of pamphlets, pressing them on me.

"Here," she said. "I don't know what's in your mind, with your silly questions, but this is why the Lord sent you here. To get saved. This'll answer all questions an' end all doubts."

I stood, thanking her profusely and moving toward the door. Hattie seemed to feel it quite natural that crazy women like myself would come to her door asking senseless questions, in order to have pamphlets thrust into their hands; the Lord, after all, worked in mysterious ways.

"Don't you think God might have some mercy on Agnes, though?" Hattie's version of divine retribution seemed unusually harsh, even for a woman whose God was a jealous God; Agnes's crush had after all been on her physician, not on Baal.

"I mean, maybe being sick for so long had made her weak, if she was," I said. "Surely God would understand that?"

I did not add my personal feeling on the matter, which was that having created the universe and gotten it running in the first place, Hattie's God might also just possibly bear a small portion of responsibility for the way things turned out in it.

"Ain't the way of it," Hattie replied, following me out. "That ain't the way of it at all. The Lord wants what He wants, an' He's got a fiery sword for them as tries denyin' 'im of it."

Her voice boomed out, carrying her firm convictions into the Atlantic breeze. Then as I reached the bottom step, the obvious finally occurred to her and she stopped me with a question of her own.

"How come you're around here askin' after Agnes, anyway? She never knew you—how'd you ever get hooked up in her dyin'?"

Looming in the doorway, fierce and hatchet-faced, she looked suddenly like an Old Testament prophet got up in drag.

"Hattie," I said truthfully, "it beats the hell out of me."

Hattie grinned, her expression once again darkly wise. "Now *that*," she said, "that is the way of it."

"YEAH, POOR HATTIE," said Kenneth Kruck. "She was okay until Agnes died. Agnes was a gentle soul, kind of took the edge off Hattie's Jesus routine. But now with Agnes gone, Hattie's kind of gone off the beam, too."

Kruck was a balding middle-aged man with shiny pink cheeks, blue eyes behind tortoise-shell glasses, and even white teeth that showed when he smiled, which he did often.

He was the owner of Kruck's Country Hardware on Stonington's main street; as I'd approached, a teenage boy who looked like a younger version of Kruck had been rolling new lawnmowers off the front sidewalk onto a ramped pickup truck.

Inside, a few last wire rakes stood behind a SALE sign; a carton of snow shovels lay on its side against the wall, ready to be moved up into the display. The place smelled sweetly of birdseed, machine oil, paint, fresh-cut lumber, and new tools.

"You mentioned a survey," Kruck said with a mild note of inquiry as he led me between neatly stocked shelves to the back of the store, and into his cubbyhole office.

At his invitation I sat down, then trotted out the string of lies I'd prepared, ending with "...gauge your level of satisfaction with the modern health-care delivery system."

Kruck listened carefully: head tipped, lips pursed, corners of his mouth twitching a bit as if he found something funny in my line of doubletalk.

"Well," he said at last. "My wife passed away, you know. And I guess that's pretty much bottom-line in the satisfaction department, health-care delivery-wise. Wouldn't you say?"

Then he leaned back in his old wooden chair, in front of his old rolltop desk, and watched my reaction with what I thought uneasily was a practiced eye.

"Oh, my goodness. I'm terribly sorry. Your name must have gotten on my list by mistake. I'm so sorry about your wife."

Kruck nodded. His desk's slots, I noticed now, were stuffed with papers; his shelves held pens, pencils, paper-clips, as well as Webster's unabridged, an old thesaurus, *Bartlett's Familiar Quotations,* and the current volume of *Literary Marketplace.*

I began to get a very bad feeling. Kruck got out of his chair and moved to the doorway.

"Kelly," he called down the store's main aisle. A moment later the boy's voice answered.

"Do me a favor," Kruck called, "run those mowers home, line 'em in front of the shed? Then take the rest of the day, pick me up tonight, okay?"

"Okay, Dad," the boy's voice came back.

Smiling, Kruck returned to his chair. "Now, Miss Kent," he said, settling back in at the desk, "would you like to tell me what you're really doing here?"

I swallowed hard, but the lump of embarrassment in my throat would not go down.

"Perhaps I should tell you," he went on gently, "that before I retired to realize my dream of becoming a small-town storekeeper, I was a newspaper reporter. For the New Haven *Chronicle.* And I do freelance PR for Mercy General from time to time, too."

"So you know there's no survey." I wanted to sink through the floor.

His eyes crinkled wryly. "Oh, I think there is. An informal one. And I think I didn't get on your list by accident."

He leaned back in the chair again. "Want to tell me what it's all about? Strictly off the record, if that makes you feel better. You don't look like any kind of scam artist to me—and believe me, I've met a few of them. You just look as if you're sniffing at a story, and that's something I'm familiar with."

"Yes, well, it's not a pretty story," I said. "I'm terribly sorry, Mr. Kruck. I was hoping to get some information, it's true, and I wanted to do it without really letting on—"

"Uh-huh. But I caught you at it. So now why don't you just tell it to me from the beginning," Ken Kruck suggested, leaning back in his chair and putting his fingers together in a steeple.

He looked serene, like a man who had weathered a difficult grief but come through it all right, and had put all but the good memories behind him. A man at peace, a man who had gotten his ducks in a row.

I was about to change all that, and it felt rotten. But at this point it would be worse not to tell him, so I did.

His face grew steadily more severe. When I got to the part about his wife's death being among the suspicious ones, he looked as if he might throw me out.

But by the time I'd explained about Helen, and Walt, and the human factor, he was calm again.

"A tie-in," he said, nodding thoughtfully. "That makes sense. Something that hooked them all together."

"Right," I said. "So what do you think, now?"

What I thought was that Ken Kruck didn't seem too wrought up over the idea of someone knocking off his better half. Glancing at me, he appeared to understand this.

"C'mere," he said, getting up from the chair again, leading me toward the front of the cluttered, comfortable old store. "Let me show you something about Maggie."

Margaret, her name had been. Fifty-one when she died. She'd been the one with the tumor. Out in front of the store, the boy was rolling the last mower up the truck's ramp.

"See that kid?" Kruck spoke quietly. "Where the hell did he come from? Works when he works. Cleans up when he's done. Gets all As, plays every sport known to man. Funny as hell, lots of friends. Wants to be an engineer. Going to Princeton next fall, on full scholarship."

He turned to me. "That's Maggie, there, has to be. Sure couldn't have been much me—all I knew how to do was drink and racket around. Finally quit the whole business, brought them up here. She was happy—for six months. And then she got sick. End of the line sick."

"I'm sorry," I said sincerely, hearing Hattie Cranston in my head. *That's the way of it.*

"She went in for surgery," Kruck said, watching his son. The boy tossed a wave from the truck's cab and drove off down the street.

"Afterward the doctors talked to me," Kruck said. "Couple of years, tops, they said. Maybe two, and they wouldn't be good ones. She was already in pain, and that was going to get worse. They can cure a lot of things these days, but not what Maggie had."

The truck turned a corner, out of sight.

"So," Kruck said mildly, still gazing out the window, "I started facing the inevitable—a long illness, a lot of misery. That long downhill slide."

He turned to me. "And then she went out like a light. They called one morning and they said she was gone, pretty much admitted they didn't know how or why. And now you come and say maybe you do know why. And you wonder why I'm not more upset."

He moved away from me, toward the cash register. "I'm not a religious man, Miss Kent, but the morning Maggie died I went down to church before I even went to the hospital. I lit a candle for myself, and one for Maggie. And I thanked Christ on my knees for taking her so fast. And that's the way I still feel today."

He gave himself a mental shake, like a dog coming out of the water. "And that's why I can't get too angry now. We had every good time in the world, Maggie and I; I can't grudge her not having the bad ones. And it occurs to me that you might find out if the rest of them were like her. Something someone thought they needed easing out of, I mean."

"Mercy killing." Now there was an idea; looking at Kruck, I knew it wasn't an unfamiliar one. He just hadn't had to act on it.

As we stood there, each thinking our own thoughts, two men in jeans and flannel work shirts came into the store, the little bell over the door ringing as they did so. Moving purposefully, one picked up pipe fittings, joint sealer, and a copper ball-and-float kit for repairing a toilet tank. The other stopped at wood rasps, hesitating over them.

"'Afternoon, Waldo," Kruck called to him. "That's not the rasp you want, there, if you're still working on the cabinets. Look at the ones up above, the finer ones. Uh-huh, right there."

"One last thing," I said as I was about to leave. "Would you mind telling me what you thought of your wife's doctors?"

Kruck's smile was unfooled. "Which one?"

"Wes Brockway."

He blinked, surprised, then turned to ring up the rasp and a chisel, counted out change, and wished Waldo luck on the cabinets. Waldo went out, the little bell over the door jangling merrily.

"Of all the people I saw when Maggie was sick," Kruck said when he was gone, "Brockway was the best. Flashy, but when he talked to you, he talked to you. Answered all your questions and then hung around a little bit longer so you wouldn't feel you'd imposed. Maggie loved him. That answer *your* question?"

"Yes." If there'd been anything hinky about Wes Brockway, I thought, Kruck was the man to notice it.

"He was away when she died," he went on, "but he called me when he got back. Unusual, I guess, but the kind of fellow he was I can't say I was surprised. He'd had some trouble in his own family around that time too, seems like I heard, but I was pretty distracted myself then, don't know just what it was."

Kruck began ringing up some brushes and pint cans of paint for a little boy who'd brought a list from his mother.

"Well, well, big doings at your house, hey, Billy?"

Billy grinned, exposing missing front teeth. "Yeth. Thith paint ith for my own woom. No more thithterth in with me."

"Well, isn't that just great. Guess the tooth fairy's been losing a lot of money on you lately too, hey?" Kruck said. He looked up at me.

"Give me a call, let me know if anything happens on this thing," he said. His tone was friendly, but his eyes said it was more than a request.

I promised I would, and the little bell jangled over my head as I went out.

MARIEL BRUNESI was last on my list of people to look in the face and lie to. I phoned; no answer, but the day was bright and the town of Noank just twenty minutes away, so I drove over on the chance she might be home when I got there.

Tucked away on a winding, tree-lined lane, the house was an old sea captain's mansion perched on a granite ledge overlooking a garden and the ocean. Masses of laurel and rhododendron crowded up to both sides of a curving slate path that led to the door.

A new Volvo station wagon stood on the street near the path. Its hood was still warm, so I walked down the path and knocked.

Over the distant booming of waves I could hear a stream trickling somewhere, back in the greenery which looked as if it had grown there naturally, but hadn't. Near the house, the greenery opened onto a slate terrace; oaken half-barrels full of black dirt and red geraniums stood at the edges of it, and in tubs on either side of the kitchen door. More geraniums bloomed in boxes at the windows, whose park-bench-green trim sparkled freshly against the weathered cedar shingles of the house itself.

The whole place smelled of sea breezes and flowers, new paint and old money. Through the screen, I could see the kitchen and on into the dining room. High white ceilings and country gingham; oriental rugs, brass candlesticks, and an oak harvest table with a bowl of pears in the center of it. Everything was tasteful, spotless, and expensive.

No response to the bell, however, except for a sweet-faced collie who trotted from around the side of the house and nuzzled her wet nose into my hand.

"Some watchdog," I said to the collie, who grinned. She was wearing a red leather collar and her pedigree was probably better than mine. Just standing on the back step, I got the feeling I'd need a pretty tricky genealogist to get invited to dinner here. Or maybe just controlling interest in a manufacturing conglomerate.

Then a woman's voice came from the side of the house where the dog had appeared. "Dolly! Dolly, come on now, you—oh."

She was a well-maintained thirty-five or so, with the kind of deep tan only olive-skinned brunettes ever get, and then only if they sail a lot. She wore dungarees, a gray

sweatshirt, and topsiders, and she carried a small shovel
and a hand towel. A red bandanna was tied fetchingly over
her short black curls.

I put on my most harmless look, introduced myself, and
told lies fast. Mariel Brunesi swallowed them as if they
were gumdrops.

Jill Waterhouse—Mariel Brunesi's little sister—had been
twenty-eight. She'd crushed her left ankle in a motorcycle
accident and been taken to the hospital to have it put back
together. The operation was a success, but the patient died
a couple of weeks afterward.

That had been two years ago, but it didn't seem to oc-
cur to Mariel that two years was a long time to wait before
asking about a hospital stay, or that a dead woman's sister was an odd person to ask.

When not much nasty is allowed to happen to you, I
suppose, you start thinking you can afford to take everything at face value. That might have spoiled some people,
but it didn't seem to have spoiled Mariel. Her face was as
open and pleasant as one of the chrysanthemums in her
garden.

"Everyone was so kind," she said now, leading me
around to the front of the house. In this neighborhood, the
back of the house faced the street; no sense letting trades-
people walk right up to the main door, after all, was there?

The front faced the ocean. Sloping lawns led to the garden: white stone paths, mulched beds of old roses. Mariel
had been digging dahlia bulbs, which were spread on a
sheet of newspaper. Below the garden wall, a sharp drop;
granite steps led along it down to the dock and the bath-
house. Beyond spread the view: all 3500 nautical miles of
it.

Mariel sat me down on a white wicker porch chair upholstered in sea green linen and told me about her sister
Jill: graduate student, honors in music, budding concert

violin career. Lived in San Francisco; visiting here when the accident happened.

"Of course, the shock was terrible," Mariel said. "They told us afterward that a pulmonary embolus is terribly rare in such a young, healthy woman. Complaints, though— no. None. Dolly, lie down here. Good dog."

Dolly glanced up at me and I could have sworn she winked: a dog's life, heh-heh. I led Mariel through a few more questions: Cleanliness? Noise? Too hot, too cold? What about hospital food?

Mariel made a rueful face. "Well, there was that. After the first few days, we had Jilly's meals catered, of course."

I nodded. Of course. "Quite a few people have suggested the food might be improved."

I read off some names, watching Mariel's face; no reaction to any of them. Which didn't mean Jill hadn't known them, but it was unlikely. The whole Waterhouse family, I seemed to remember, came from Oregon. Timber money.

"And the physicians?" I went on. "How did you find their services? I've got a list here somewhere, let me see . . . yes. Robert Fish was the orthopaedic surgeon, and the anesthesiologist was . . . Wesley Brockway?"

I looked up. Mariel Brunesi's face had closed itself tight and she was on her feet.

"Who sent you here?" she demanded. "My god, I was a fool to even talk to you. After all this time, I didn't—"

She was off the porch, now, aiming a finger past the house towards the street. "Get out, I don't want you here."

"Mrs. Brunesi, I—"

"All this time," she repeated. "Now I suppose you think you can get money out of me, to stop you from talking to my husband. I suppose that's what your kind of person thinks."

She glared at me. "Well, you're wrong. Your little plan isn't going to work. If I ever hear from you again, I'll make you wish to god you'd never been born."

She looked as if she could do it, too. She wasn't, after all, just a pleasant, pretty woman in a gardening outfit. Mariel Brunesi was first of all a lady with a lot of money and power at her disposal, and one who knew how to use them.

That, I reminded myself, was how folks got to live in such pleasant surroundings: by being as unpleasant as they needed to be, when they needed to be.

Dolly got up, looking queryingly from me to her mistress and back again. She wasn't a watchdog, but I could see an idea forming in her doggy brain. And she was big.

"Sorry to have troubled you," I said, and got out of there fast.

A few minutes later it was impressed on me yet again that Mariel Brunesi was not a person one harassed with impunity; not, anyway, in this part of the world.

Down Noank's main street an unmarked squad car cruised lazily past me. The cop behind the wheel nodded curtly and held my gaze a moment too long as he went by. Then he swung the squad around and followed me, two car lengths back, until I was out of town.

NINE

"Miss Kent, we have offered you every cooperation, have we not?"

Mariel's influence traveled fast. Thirty-six hours after I'd seen her, Solli and I had returned from Stonington to Helen's place, where a message had been waiting on the answering machine. The message was for me, from a hospital administrator named Howard L. Friendly.

Friendly wasn't. "And you have had access to every part of the hospital, for research purposes," he went on now, "isn't that also true?"

It seemed that Mariel's protests against my invasion of her privacy hadn't stopped with the Noank police. She hadn't waited for me to come after her again, either. Instead she'd come after me, swinging a club the size of her family's endowment to Mercy General.

Now I stood in Friendly's office, a twelve-by-twelve corner cubicle with a window looking out onto Mercy General's white concrete central courtyard. The office wallpaper was bleached burlap, the furnishings varnished oak, white formica, and bright red canvas upholstery. The bright red upholstery, just at the moment, matched Howard L. Friendly's bright red face.

"She says you barged in uninvited, damaging her property and frightening her considerably, and refused to leave when she quite rightfully requested you to do so."

His job, apparently, was maintaining communications between the Waterhouse millions and the coffers of Mercy General Hospital. Now I'd snarled them. Friendly was ticked.

"Whereupon," he continued, opening and closing his fists as if he wished he were clenching them around my throat, "you went on to badger her with questions, upsetting her and scandalizing her neighbors, only departing when Mrs. Brunesi threatened to call the police—"

Mariel, I thought, had quite an imagination.

"—all the while representing yourself as an employee of this medical center, taking some sort of a survey."

Also, Mariel had had time to think things over.

"Miss Kent, when we accepted your presence in our hospital, we were assured that you would be responsible and nondisruptive. Now the Waterhouse family is threatening to withdraw its support. They want an apology, Miss Kent, and you are going to supply one immediately."

I allowed as how I thought I could probably manage that. I suspected privately, though, that only one member of the family had been doing any threatening. Unless I missed my guess, Mariel had decided that when push came to shove it was her word against a blackmailer's. She didn't think there were pictures or letters around for anyone to use against her.

Someone was bluffing, Mariel figured, so she decided to hit back hard and fast. It was a good tactic; I had to admire her for it. What puzzled me was why she thought of blackmail in the first place. It was an unusual conclusion to jump to—unless someone had tried blackmail on her before.

"...allowing you to finish your work here, in deference to the National Hospital Association's request, and much against my better judgement," Friendly was saying.

He fixed me in his hostile gaze. "But take my advice, Miss Kent. Stick to the outline the Hospital Association sent me. No more surveys. No more field trips. Because if I hear one single whisper of complaint from anyone, Miss Kent—"

I got up looking chastened, or so I hoped.

"I understand, Mr. Friendly. I'll apologize to Mrs. Brunesi. There'll be no more problems."

"I should hope not," he said, grabbing some papers from his desktop and rattling them importantly, to dismiss me.

I left, thinking that at least I'd eaten my crow for the day and gotten it over with.

Wrong again.

"CHARLOTTE, DARLING," Bernie said, which is always a bad sign. When Bernie says darling, he means "you idiot." Bernie won't come right out and call you an idiot until you've insulted the managing editor of Simon & Schuster, and Bernie has hired guys with the silenced pistols to come and silence you.

Bernie didn't want me silenced now, though; on the contrary.

"Outlines," he said winningly. "Pages. Chapters. Books. Remember books, Charlotte, those funny gadgets with paper inside? Paper with words on it?"

"I remember, Bernie. It's just that a few things have come up here, and—"

Bernie ignored me. "The paper in books is just like money," he said, "only it's not green and it happens sooner."

Yeah, lots sooner, I thought.

"It is happening, isn't it, Charlotte? I mean, if I'm not mistaken we've signed some contracts here, made some promises, haven't we?"

Bernie's use of the editorial "we" is also a bad sign, since the editorial "we" is just like the medical "we." As in, "we're just going to have this little compound fracture fixed, aren't we?" In either case, the person saying "we" is not the one with the panicky look on his face.

Or her face. "Bernie, I'm making real good progress here."

Phrases like "real good" come tripping off my tongue when I am trying to sound terribly honest and earnest while at the same time lying my goddamned brains out. Unfortunately, Bernie knows this. In fact, it was Bernie who taught me this.

He was not lapsing into the casual vernacular at the moment, however. His tone instead was of chumminess laced with urgency.

"An intro," he said. "Tell me there's an intro, a glossary, a bibliography, even. Tell me you've got a few notes scribbled on the back of an envelope somewhere."

"Okay, I'll tell you that," I said quickly.

I did have some notes scribbled on an envelope, too, only they were about who might have tried blackmailing Mariel Brunesi. The problem was, all the notes ended in questions, and I couldn't find the envelope with the answers on it.

There was a brief silence at Bernie's end of the telephone. Bernie's silences were always brief because he is an agent, and agents deal in percentages of somethings. Ten percent of silence, Bernie maintains, is nothing, which accounted for most of the reason for this conversation.

But not all of it. "Charlotte," he said. "I know I sound like a bully, here. But by my calculations, you're going to be broke in about eight minutes. You gotta do something, kid."

He was being generous. The way I saw it, I'd already been broke for two years: last year, and next year.

"That's okay, Bernie. I know you're right. I should just sit my butt on a chair and write the damned books. The truth is, I'm all screwed up right now."

I said this because I'd learned something else from Bernie, too, which is never lie to your agent. Especially when it isn't working.

"Charlotte, what happened? You're my cleanup batter, I never thought I'd have these problems with you. Listen, you want to come down to the city? No one's around, you can stay in the apartment. Turn off, tune out, and write your guts out."

That, in a nutshell, is the other thing about Bernie. If I accepted his offer, I would find the apartment above his office stocked with the five major food groups: caffeine, nicotine, bagels, cream cheese, and alcohol. Also, with peace and quiet.

It sounded like heaven, and I nearly wept as I refused.

"So okay," he replied, "you're a martyr. But what's going on? Talk to me, Charlotte, we got a situation, here, I'm afraid."

I could hear him settling into the chair in his pink and gray office with the potted palm and the air conditioner. From his bookshelves, authors of best-sellers smiled down, concealing their winces of pain as Bernie lopped dimes off their dollars.

With many of these best-selling authors, Bernie endured long heart-to-hearts every week, which I thought was worth ten cents on the dollar since quite a few were the kind of bottom-dwelling trash-feeders you would throw back if you happened to snag one on your hook.

With me, Bernie *schmoozed* twice a year, tops. His rule was, *schmooze*-time proportional to height of dime-pile. Still, I had to sympathize with his attitude; after all, he wasn't in business for the laughs.

Neither was I, which was lucky since I wasn't getting many. What I was getting was coddling, designed to get me to crank out the book I'd promised to deliver and hadn't. This I found more than somewhat humiliating, as Bernie only coddles two kinds of clients; hot tickets, and ones he feels sorry for because they are crapping out. And I knew which kind I was starting to look like.

"Jesus," he said, when I had finished summarizing recent events. "Sounds like a blockbuster to me. Murder, money, and everyone's in love."

"Yeah," I said glumly, because it was a blockbuster I would not write. By the time I got untangled from current obligations, one of Bernie's other clients would be hyping the book on "Good Morning, America" and signing fat contracts for the eight-part miniseries.

"But don't get tied up in it," Bernie warned, confirming my suspicions.

"Yeah," I said again, "I know. Finish what's on my plate."

Bernie chuckled. "You got it. Hey, come on, you can do this stuff up in a couple of months, and then we'll get you out of the health game, find you something a little more interesting, how's that?"

Sure. Like maybe *How to Shop for Life Insurance*. Bernie would be just full of wonderful suggestions.

I sighed. "Right, Bernie. You're absolutely correct. I've got to just do it. Write that sucker."

"That's the ticket. Go get 'em, tiger." Followed by more of the same until we hung up. I was about to go out and find a nice solid brick wall to bounce my head against— Bernie's pep talks always have that effect on me—when I realized:

Bernie was right. *Everyone's in love.*

And I'd been missing it completely.

THE DRIVE back to Noank took two hours flat. I didn't stop to tell anyone where I was going, and I didn't type up an apology for Mariel Brunesi before I left, either. Instead, I intended to deliver it in person, along with some educated guesses.

The seaside lane was still charming and tree-lined, and the house still looked like a great big pile of money, all shingles and shutters. Dolly the collie let bygones be bygones, greeting me with a nose as wet and enthusiastic as she had the first time.

I thought ringing the doorbell was probably not my best move on this visit, however. Instead I walked around the house to the sunny lawn overlooking the ocean. Mariel Brunesi was down on her knees among the rose bushes, mulching with her hand trowel.

She got up when she saw me. "You must be crazy to come here again," she said, and the fear in her look said she believed it.

I held out both hands. "Mrs. Brunesi, I lied. I don't work for the hospital, and I'm not taking a survey. I'm trying to help a friend who's in a lot of trouble, and I think whoever tried to blackmail you over your affair with Wes Brockway is the one who got her into it."

Her face went flat with shock. "What are you trying to involve me in? Get out of here."

"I'm not involving you in anything, Mrs. Brunesi. You did that, and then you told me about it. Or rather, your reaction did. The thing is, whoever threatened you over it may be getting ready to do it again."

"Keep your voice down," she said furiously, so I did.

"Only this time," I went on, "you might not be able to sweep it under the rug. I'm not going to tell anyone about you and Brockway, but you might have to—because two years ago it was just a clumsy blackmail threat, but now it's murder."

"Murder." Her hand went to her lips. "Who—?"

"No one you know." I wasn't about to get her going on Jill; not until I had what I wanted, anyway, and maybe not even then.

"And," I went on, "I'm still not sure what got this all stirred up after so long. But I am sure that your experience is tied up in it somehow. If the blackmailer contacted you again, you'd have to tell your husband everything—for his safety, as well as your own."

The fear in her eyes mixed with guilt. "William? Someone might try to hurt him?" She glanced around, probably wondering how such awful things could possibly be said on her well-ordered lawn, in her well-ordered life.

"I don't know. I don't know why someone's killing people, only that someone is. Please, Mrs. Brunesi, if you can tell me anything at all about the blackmail attempt, it could help me—and maybe help you too."

She pushed the knuckle of her right thumb against her lower lip, turning to stare out at the ocean. Foamy whitecaps were bouncing on the tops of the waves. She watched them in silence for a moment, then turned back.

The look on her face when she did confirmed my first opinion of her: not spoiled. No fool, either.

"You know," she said, "I feel like falling right down here on this grass and crying my eyes out. But I don't suppose that will do me any earthly good, will it?"

She peeled off her gardening gloves and dropped them to the sheet of newspaper she'd been kneeling on.

"Come on inside," she said, "I'm going to have a drink. You too, if you want one."

"IT WAS the kind of bad time a lot of married people go through," she said, handing me a highball glass filled with ice, scotch, and Perrier. "The kind that gets better if you wait, only I didn't know that. I thought it was the end of the world, and besides, I was desperate for affection. I was staying in New Haven to be near Jilly, and—"

She took a swallow of her own drink. "Well, to put it bluntly, I threw myself at Wes Brockway and he responded. He'd have had to be made of stone not to." She gave a small, rueful laugh. "I was pretty forceful."

"What about the threats? When did they start?"

"After about a week, I started getting calls at the hotel. Calling me filthy names, and saying that if I didn't stop seeing Wes I'd have to pay a lot of money to hush it up."

She put her glass down on a napkin. "The thing was, I didn't care about hushing it up. I wanted William to find out, to hurt him as badly as he'd hurt me. When the caller started demanding money, I said go ahead, put it in the newspapers, see if I cared. Later, though, I began to feel differently.''

"After your sister died."

She nodded, biting her lip. "It woke me up, I guess you'd say. And after a while, things got better between Will and me, too—a lot better. I never told him, and now I don't ever want him to find out how shamefully I behaved. Selfishly. Stupidly.''

"I see," I said. "You hit yourself over the head a lot, don't you?"

Her face flashed anger. "You think I don't deserve it? Betraying my family, opening myself up to sordid threats, maybe even destroying my marriage? What kind of a person are you, to think those kinds of mistakes can just be forgotten?''

"Who said anything about forget? I just get tired of seeing people forgiving everyone but themselves.''

I watched as she nodded slowly, but it wasn't the kind of thing she would accept overnight. It was her Catholic childhood; I recognized the signs from my own. Once you've had that kind of guilt-training, you might get better but you never get well.

"Anyway," she said. "The calls stopped, too. I'd almost managed to forget them until you—''

"I'm sorry about that. I didn't know I'd be frightening you.''

She flicked her hand in a never-mind gesture. "I guess it's a good thing you did, though.''

Her lips tightened. "It's not true, is it, that what you don't know can't hurt you? Now at least I'll be prepared, if I do ever hear from her again.''

I stared. "Her? Your caller was a her?''

Mariel Brunesi looked surprised. "Why, yes, haven't I said so? The voice was disguised—not by much, maybe a handkerchief over the receiver—but it was a woman's voice, I'm sure of it. Yes, definitely a woman.''

DRIVING BACK to New Haven, I thought about what Mariel had told me.

The last threatening call had been on November 20; she remembered that because of what came later. Ignoring the call, she'd kept her date with Brockway the next afternoon, as planned.

If the caller had run true to form, there would have been another call that evening. Whoever it was, Mariel said, had been calling before and after each of her dates with Brockway. Eerie, she said, how the caller knew when she saw him—not that she had cared, at the time, about that or anything else.

But there hadn't been another call. Jilly Waterhouse had died suddenly, instead. That put paid to Mariel's romance—as, I now suspected, it had been intended to do.

Mariel hadn't realized that, and I hadn't enlightened her. Distraught at her sister's death, she'd just been glad the calls had stopped; she hadn't thought to wonder why they stopped just when they did.

I wondered, though. How was it so immediately clear to the caller that the Brockway-Brunesi connection had been cut off?

Unless the caller had severed the connection—by cutting off Jill's life. It was Jill who gave Mariel a reason to stay in New Haven; when Mariel's sister died, the shock stopped Mariel's affair with Brockway and sent her back home to Noank.

Just exactly as planned, I thought as I pulled into Mercy General's parking garage. Only, planned by whom?

WALT KRUSANKE'S memorial service was held on the wide square lawn in front of the medical school dormitories. Gathered with me were perhaps a hundred students, along with some nurses and a few patients, bundled against the chill to hear a hospital chaplain recite Walt's accomplishments from notes.

The chaplain's voice boomed from a PA system and ricocheted off the high brick walls of the dorm buildings. Beside me, Mike Malley stood with his face set into its usual skeptical scowl.

"Christ, but I wish that cat could talk," he said.

Cat Dancing; I'd forgotten her. "Where is she? You didn't take her to the pound, did you?"

"No, I shot the damn beast with my service revolver," he said scornfully. Then a hint of embarrassment came onto his lumpy face. "Actually, I got her at home. She's not so bad. Yowls like a damn banshee."

People were moving inside to sign Walt's memorial book; we shuffled along with them. I wasn't about to tell Malley about Mariel Brunesi; not now, anyway. If and when the time came, I'd betray her confidences so fast her head would spin, but the time hadn't come yet and I sincerely hoped it wouldn't.

"Autopsy came back," Malley remarked. "Somebody stuck him in the back with a trochar, one of those big hollow needles they take bone samples with. Once in the spine, once in the heart."

We passed through the narrow doors and on into the long wide room where, on the previous Friday night, happy hour had been held. Now it was set up for unhappy hour: discreet little plates of cookies and pastry, a coffee urn, styrofoam cups.

I glanced at Malley. "So why are you telling me?" His attitude, I thought, had mellowed suspiciously.

His gaze ranged over Walt's gathered friends and associates. I could see him wondering which one wasn't really Walt's friend. I'd have thought it was pretty cold-hearted of him, except I was there for the same reason. At the moment I had a lapful of facts and nowhere more to go with them.

"Because," he said, "it was either a very lucky poke, or somebody knew just where to put the needle."

Little chimes of hope began ringing in my heart. "Someone like a doctor, maybe?"

Malley scowled. "Cool your jets, girlie, and look around you. Anybody can find that stuff out, in this neighborhood."

"But not just anybody knows where to find a trochar. Or how to get hold of one."

"Yeah? Why don't you tell me how you'd get one?"

I looked at him. "So maybe the stupid snoop's also good for something after all, huh?" However useless the rest of my ideas might seem to him, I did know a fair amount about hospital routine, a fact that Malley seemed belatedly to be recognizing.

"Mmmph," he replied, which I guessed was the best I was going to get from him.

"Call the surgical supply room," I said. "Tell them you're a nurse or an orderly on a surgical ward; you need a bone-marrow tray, stat. Say you'll pick it up, you can't wait for a tech. Put on a uniform, get it, and take off."

It was easier than I'd thought until I'd said it.

"Like I told you," Malley agreed. "Anybody could get one." But his expression was thoughtful as he walked away.

I hung around a little longer, signed Walt's book, strolled past the coffee urn and the trays of pastry now reduced mostly to crumbs. Felicity Dunwoodie was there, pale and helpful as usual, clearing up crumpled napkins and discarded paper plates. Also among the gathered memorializers I spotted Wes Brockway, deep in serious conversation with the hospital chaplain who had delivered Walt's eulogy.

At least the chaplain looked serious. Brockway, on the other hand, looked as if he were having trouble just keeping a straight face, and when I got a bit nearer I understood why.

At three in the afternoon, at a memorial gathering for a murdered student, noted physician and medical professor Wes Brockway was drunk as a skunk.

Which struck me as passing strange. Clearly, something had upset him enough to start him hitting the white wine spritzers—or something stronger—a few hours early. I wondered what it was, but before I could march up to him and ask, the chaplain led him tactfully away.

He had, however, given me an excellent idea for the rest of my afternoon, because I was tapped out. After a quick stop at the hospital to check on Joey and Helen, I headed for her place, thinking hard and hopefully of a heating pad, a puffy quilt, and a good hot toddy or two while I tried to make sense of recent revelations.

When I arrived there, however, I found none of the privacy needed for such a project. Instead, her house was full of people.

"THAT LOVE stuff," Myron Rosewater said, "gonna mess your head up every time."

I glanced at him, surprised, but his remark was directed at Harry Lemon. Love had apparently reared its head in a number of local camps lately, and many of them seemed at the moment to be pitched in Helen's living quarters.

"What," I demanded of Solli, "is going on here?"

Solli smiled innocently. "It's Steve Marino's birthday," he said. "You wouldn't want him to celebrate it alone, would you?"

I was quite sure that it was not Steve Marino's birthday. More likely this was another of Solli's efforts at improving my social skills while distracting me from interests of which he did not approve, such as solving infuriatingly insoluble murders.

Now Myron stood at Helen's sideboard, taking small polite spoons of everything from the serving dishes Solli had arranged there. In his pink button-down oxford cloth shirt, navy cords, and Hush Puppies, Myron was transformed from the jive-talking street kid I'd met just days earlier. He'd cut his hair, too, and wore a single gold chain and a high-school class ring instead of the beads and studded leathers he'd so recently affected.

He caught me watching and grinned. "Camouflage," he said wickedly, and I thought he'd done an awfully good job of it. Myron the Civilized was even more frightening than Myron the Mugger, because he had transformed himself so effectively, so fast.

I found myself hoping it wasn't all camouflage, put on in order to use Harry Lemon for some sly purpose. Harry was so sure that a layer of civilization improved almost anyone, he made a perfect Henry Higgins sucker for a clever Eliza-type con job.

Harry himself stood before Helen's record shelf, searching for something to put on the stereo. The selection, like everything else about Helen's place, entranced him.

"Ah," he said, plucking down a jacket. "Vivaldi, just the thing. And by heaven, it's the Stuttgart, too. Charming." Placing it on the turntable, he sighed with satisfaction, looking around once more at the rose chintz sofa and chairs, the valenced curtains and brass-potted green plants, the antique hooked rugs perfectly placed on Helen's polished hardwood floors.

"What a wonderful environment," he said as the first notes of "Spring" trilled into the room, and I could see him imagining himself with slippers, pipe, and book, comfortably at home in it. The happy domestic scene in his head needed only a certain absent redhead to make it complete.

The redhead in question had not had much to say during my most recent visit, only that she was sorry for making such a mess of everything and for not telling me about it sooner.

Her money troubles, she confessed, were due to a couple of disastrous stock market forays; she'd lost her job by exploding in a temper when Mercy's director of development had insisted on adding his alcoholic, color-blind sister-in-law to Helen's staff.

It appeared as if the development director was a local mover and shaker, too, because after she'd told him what she thought of him, the old boy network had gone to work with a vengeance, frankly blackballing Helen from several other projects and convincing her it was hopeless to try for others.

She'd been too embarrassed to tell me about her run of bad luck, she said, when I'd clearly thought she was on top of the world as usual, and had my own troubles besides.

And that too was a typical Helen story: reaching for the moon while skidding on the brink of disaster, relying on herself to carry it all off somehow as she always had.

The only difference was, this time she hadn't. This time she'd skidded off the brink of disaster right into the soup. Meanwhile, I was coming rapidly and unhappily to what seemed an avoidable conclusion: I wasn't going to get her out of it.

In short, I was stumped. I knew in my bones that something was fishy with Wes Brockway, but I didn't know what or how I could find out without tipping him to my interest in him. The best I could think of now was to follow Solli's advice: take it all to Mercy's medical director and dump it in his lap.

Then of course I would have to take Solli and get out of town, to avoid being prosecuted over it myself; sometime much later, with any luck, Helen's defense attorney would be able to use some of it, to instill some reasonable doubt into a jury.

And after that, twelve strangers would decide the fate of my friend, her baby, her home, her career, and her life. Meanwhile she would wait in the women's correctional institute while the baby went into some sort of foster care, since neither Helen nor I now had the kind of cash it would take to bail her out of that little kettle of fish....

It was not a cheery train of thought. I poured myself a drink and collapsed into a chair, unable to stop thinking it, which was where Steve Marino found me, plumping himself down on the ottoman with a beer in one hand and a Camel unfiltered in the other.

"Oh, god," he moaned. "I'm doomed."

I refrained from wishing him a happy birthday, as I was sure this would only confuse him, an idea he confirmed by wishing me one, at which I shot Solli an evil look, and he grinned.

Across the room, Twyla McKay was delicately devouring a ham sandwich, drinking a cup of tea, and laughing at a story Rawlins was quietly telling her.

Joey, at this moment, was under the care of Twyla's sister, also a registered nurse; at eleven this evening Twyla's mother would take over. Twyla's family, I gathered, contained enough nurses to staff the battlefields of the Crimean War, a fact for which I continued to thank Hattie Cranston's god along with any others who happened to be listening.

"Doomed," Steve groaned theatrically again, and took a gulp of his beer and a drag off his cigarette. Hastily, I handed him an ashtray.

"I'll never get this thesis done in time, now. Maybe I should shoot myself in the foot and write that up. It's my only chance to get out of this town this year."

Personally, I thought Steve had shot himself in the foot when he hired Bill Priest to write a thesis for him. But I did not say so; he already felt bad enough.

"It's too late," he said, "to bother starting a new one. And now that we're done sifting through all that Manners-Moreheim stuff, I don't have anything else to distract me. Two more terms in New Haven—oh, god."

His gaze wandered disconsolately about the room, at last lighting on Twyla. Food had revived her from her day's labors; now, curled in a corner of the sofa, she resembled a bright-eyed kitten.

"Actually," Steve said, cheering somewhat, "there is one thing that could distract me." Then his face fell again. "But hell, who am I kidding? What would a girl like that want with a guy like me?"

"Stranger things have happened," I said with more optimism than I felt, and got up to rejoin Solli who had returned from the kitchen. Prettily arranged on the tray he carried were eight Hostess chocolate creme-filled cupcakes and an equal number of Twinkies.

"My hero," I said, taking a cupcake. Better living through chemistry: when I am truly miserable, there is nothing like a dose of processed sugar and chemical preservatives to improve me.

And I was truly miserable, because the more I learned the less I understood. The patient deaths from Marino's thesis were a fine reason for Priest to have been blackmailing Brockway, and the financial facts suggested strongly that he had been doing so.

That, it seemed to me, gave Brockway a motive for killing Priest. It did not, however, provide a reason for Brockway to have killed his patients in the first place, even if he had been in the vicinity when they died, which he hadn't.

Furthermore, the only link among the patients themselves, other than that they had all been Brockway's patients, was that they—or in Mariel's case, one of their relatives—seemed to have been nuts about him.

I was willing to bet that among the rest I would find more members of the Brockway admiration society; love and death, lately, seemed to be going together better than the proverbial horse and carriage.

But that didn't make a motive, either, at least not all by itself, and now along with a solid jolt of the human factor I'd been setting such naively hopeful store by, Mariel Brunesi had thrown another wrench into my monkey-works: not just a voice, but a woman's voice on the telephone, warning her to stay away from Brockway.

It was all just too maddeningly confusing for words, these it seemed being the only things left that could help me as long as they were arranged in the form of a nice neat confession.

I recited all this to Solli, who listened in sympathy; then, morosely, I folded the cupcake frosting in half and took a bite out of it. Across the room, Rawlins sensed the young master's approach and withdrew tactfully from conversation with Twyla, who was now eyeing Steve with clear bemusement.

"Poor Charlotte," Solli said, noting my mood. "Sit down and I'll fix you some dinner to go with your dessert." He returned with a loaded plate, and while I picked at it I gave him the rest of the account of my horrible, terrible, very bad day.

"And," I finished, "there's something else, too, while we're on the subject of misery. Do you think I should start looking into long-term care for Joey? I mean, he's just not improving."

At this, Solli shook his head firmly. "Way too early for that," he said. "It's only a couple of days after surgery, after all. I mean, give the kid a chance."

"Do you really think so?" I took a bite of potato salad, which hunkered down in a sullen lump at the bottom of my stomach and began making irritable remarks.

"Of course I think so, or I wouldn't say so."

I began to feel more hopeful; unlike most people, when Solli says that of course he really does think something, he always does of course really do think it.

"Look," he said, plucking a cherry tomato from my plate, "I'm not handing out guarantees. But I have a strong hunch that Joey is going to be up and about and driving you crazy for many years."

A faint pang of hunger replaced the mean growl in my middle.

"You sound pretty sure of yourself," I said doubtfully.

Solli shrugged. "I've seen a lot of sick people. Besides, I talked to Claire Bogan while you were out. She says this morning's CAT scan looked like the swelling's down some more. They're going to do another scan and then try waking him up."

A bolt of pure happiness struck me, wiping out misgivings on other topics for the moment; suddenly I was very hungry indeed. I took a bite of roast beef, meanwhile silently promising Joey that I would feed him roast beef for the rest of his whole life; I would write bodice-rippers and even dragon fantasies to finance every gourmet taste he could imagine, if he would only get well.

Meanwhile from one end of Helen's rose chintz sofa Harry Lemon was telling Myron that the neighbourhood Myron lived in was marginal, and that Harry did not intend to venture there again. Myron, apparently, had persuaded Harry to make a number of house calls, some of Myron's friends being too mistrustful of authority even to visit clinics.

"Nothin' marginal about my neighbourhood," Myron retorted, balancing a paper plate on his spiffy corduroy knee as if he had been doing it all his life. "Somethin' marginal about your mind, is the problem. Shoot, man, I put the word out. You the safest white dude in this city. You could walk down Park Street stark naked with a ruby in your hand, man, wouldn't nobody touch you.''

He laughed. ''I'm the one gotta worry, I come around your place. Cops think I'm a mugger.''

''You are a mugger,'' Harry said, but his tone was indulgent.

''Not any more,'' Myron responded. ''I made a career change. From now on, I steal the legal way, just like you white guys.''

Looking pleased with himself, Myron bit into a cupcake. But when Harry's back turned Myron's expression changed, becoming one of such simple affection that I abruptly lost my worries about the two of them.

None of which solved my other problem, which now that I felt better I was getting frustrated about all over again. And looking at Myron, I felt the problem sorting itself into plain terms.

Anyone, I thought, could accuse Myron of anything and be at least halfway believed until Myron proved that wasn't true. That was too bad, but the fact was, that was the way things worked. The same, although to a lesser degree, went for Twyla, or Rawlins and Steve, and to an even lesser degree for Harry Lemon; also for Solli and myself.

A black street kid, a student and his mob minder, a nurse; one overworked, underpaid physician-in-training; one longhaired hippie commie phone phreak who, to look at him, no one would ever believe was a surgeon at all, much less a truly gifted one. And me: a hustling, hump-it-to-the-deadline freelance writer, for god's sake, some sort of ludicrous have-pen-will-travel quick-script artist with a stubborn yen for justice and an unerring nose for the messiest sorts of problems, paradoxes, quandaries, complications, contradictions, and general human disasters.

A hackwriter, in short, with no degree, no local references, no credentials, and most of all, no money.

And then there was Helen: broke, pregnant, and in trouble, she was a third-act comedy complication of purest ray serene, only it wasn't a comedy and it wasn't funny.

Finally, there was Wes Brockway: so warm and wonderful and white-bread; also so rich, well thought of, and well connected. No one would ever dream of casting him at the middle of a messy murder plot, or even dare to suggest it to him. He could walk down Park Street stark naked with a stolen ruby in his hand, and the police would ask him respectfully if he wanted an escort.

God, it made me mad.

"Look," I said to Solli, "there's only one way I'm going to find out how Brockway's hooked up in all this."

Solli's face took on a familiar, stubborn look; he backed away from me, his hands raised in a warding-off gesture.

"Oh, no," he said, "that's out. If he is involved, you'll be calling his attention to you, and if he's not he'll have his lawyers all over you like ants on molasses. You don't walk up to guys like Brockway and accuse them of murder, Charlotte. You just don't."

"Maybe I wouldn't have to accuse him," I said slowly.

"Charlotte—"

"I mean," I went on, "up until now, I've avoided asking him anything, because I didn't want him to know that I suspected him. And without real evidence, you're right, I couldn't very well accuse him. Him being so eminent and well defended, and all. I mean, anesthesia guys like Brockway have got whole buildings full of lawyers on retainer, am I right?"

"Charlotte..."

"Which," I said, "is exactly what's starting to burn my tail past enduring."

I got out of my chair, grabbed the phone book off Helen's kitchen counter, and looked up an address.

"Because," I said, flipping madly through the pages, "we know he's mud to the neck, don't we? We just don't know how."

I found the address I wanted, snagged my jacket and bag, and headed for the door.

"Only we can't say so, which is what he's depending on, isn't he? The idea that he's just too goddamned respectable to suspect of anything, so normal and natural and successful. And if we even whisper a word of anything else, it could hurt his professional reputation and he can sue our wits out, on top of everything else that could happen to us."

I rummaged in my bag for Helen's keys and found them. "But I have had it to the eyes with respectable, Solli, I really and truly have. He's just too damned good to be true, on top of which he isn't. The only reason we haven't got something on him is that he's too damn slick to get a handle on—until now."

I hurried down the front steps with Solli at my heels. By the time he reached the car, I had it started.

"And," I said, "there is absolutely no way I can think of to find out the things I have to know, except to face him and ask him. So I'm going to, and lawsuits be damned. I haven't got anything he can sue me for, anyway, and if I get tossed in jail again maybe I can get some writing done there. Are you coming or staying?"

Solli hesitated, trying to think of something to stop me or at least slow me down. No one else has ever been able to either, so I didn't think any less of him as he swung into the front seat and slammed the car door.

He peered through his fingers as I gunned the Datsun across Grand Avenue and onto Elm Street, past the old New Haven *Chronicle* building and Prospect Cemetery and up Prospect Hill past the Yale ice rink.

"Besides which," I said, "I have had it personally, too. I am tired, I am worried, I am angry, and I am broke. And the real reason I've avoided Brockway, if the truth be told, is that I have been letting him intimidate me. He's got letters after his name, and I don't. He's somebody around here, and I'm not. And I've been letting it put me off, and damn it, it stops here."

I pulled the Datsun into a parking space halfway up Prospect Street and yanked the hand brake.

"I am," I said, "ready to quit. I admit it. I think Helen is the one who will wind up in jail, and there is probably nothing in this world that you or I or anyone can do about it."

I yanked the keys out of the ignition. "But I am not quitting until I ask Wes Brockway what *he* thinks is going on here, because I think he knows and until he tells me differently and I believe him I'm going to go right on thinking so."

I slammed the keys into my bag. "And that, damn it, is that."

Breathing hard after this outburst, I sat with my hands on the steering wheel, looking across the street at the windows of Wes Brockway's private medical office. The windows were lit, which meant that Wes Brockway was probably behind them.

"Scared?" Solli asked. Trust Solli to get to the root of an outburst.

"You bet I am," I said. "This guy's either going to sue me for slander or slit my throat. I really can't think how I got my ego so deep into this, but now that it is I also can't seem to give up without a fight, so please excuse this little attack of extreme bullheadedness. Oh, and by the way— thanks for coming."

"That's all right," Solli said generously.

"No, it's not." I looked at my hands, still gripped on the wheel. "None of it's all right, and you're being ungodly nice about it."

Solli said nothing. He knew what I meant. It's just that he's too graceful to complain, most of the time.

"I demand your presence," I went on, "and then I use you or ignore you. I worry you half to death, and barely apologize. I trick you or bully you into doing things you don't want to do, and I'm rude and unpleasant about doing ones you do want to do. Worst of all, in the over two years that I've known you, I've never, ever let you be certain about anything."

"Oh, now," Solli said, "you're not as bad as all that."

"Well, I'm bad enough. Bad enough to think that when I look in this guy's eyes, I might see something I recognize from the bathroom mirror: terminal selfishness. In kind, anyway, if not in degree."

I turned to face him. "Why you put up with it all is more than I can imagine, to tell you the truth, but I'm awfully glad you do. Really, I really am."

"My, my," Solli said, his eyes amused. "Is this an appeal for reassurance? A request for protestations of undying love, in spite of your many flaws? How encouraging you are this evening, Charlotte—I was beginning to think I would never hear anything like this from you."

"Wait a minute," I began, but Solli had already seized a handful of my hair. Then he kissed me, a task which took him quite a long, thorough time.

"Now," he said when he was finished, "if we've beaten back your insecurities for the moment, shall we get this over with? Seeing," he added, "as it was your dumb idea in the first place."

TEN

"Now, LET ME just make sure I've got all this straight," Wes Brockway said, holding up some clean, well-manicured fingers.

His private practice was a pain-control clinic, and we got in to see him by sitting in his waiting room until the last of his patients had been dealt with and had departed. His receptionist hadn't liked it, but we hadn't picked our noses or torn pages from any of the magazines fanned out on the low walnut tables, so she'd let us stay.

"One," Brockway said, after smilingly welcoming us into his consulting room and hearing what I had to say to him. "I killed—how many?—eight patients. Because they liked me more than patients generally do like their doctors."

He wrinkled his brow in pretended thought. "Hmmm. Unusual motive. It would have been simpler just to ask them to pay me a bit extra, don't you think?"

The room smelled faintly of rubbing alcohol, and held a big oaken desk, leather chairs, and bookshelves full of reference works and bound medical journals. Framed diplomas and certificates hung about on the paneled walls; whatever else he was, he was thoroughly sheep-skinned. It struck me also that he was being awfully genial about the whole thing.

"Then," he went on, "a student named William Priest discovered my nefarious doings and blackmailed me over them."

He waggled his eyebrows mysteriously; a nice touch. The trouble was, I didn't believe him for an instant, any more than I believed in the rest of him. Close up, Brockway looked like a friendly, intelligent fellow, a bit tired after his long day, but still willing to be polite and helpful if at all possible.

Which was exactly what bothered me. He should have tossed us into the street ten minutes ago.

"So I killed him, too," Brockway went on. "And then I killed . . . what was his name? Walt Krusanke. Who may have seen or suspected something of my killing Priest."

He shook his head in dismay. "So much for the Hippocratic oath." Then he smiled some more.

"Aren't you worried about being here yourselves? My receptionist's gone home now, you know. I might have a trigger behind this desk, to make your chairs drop through the floor into a hidden pit, or a button that fills the room with poison gas to which I've somehow managed to render myself immune."

Solli glanced around. Brockway's office did not look as if it contained poison gas or hidden pits. Brockway didn't look as if he contained any, either, but I still thought he did.

"I don't have those things, though," he continued. "Because I'm not at all what you think I am. The fact is, and I hope I'm not too immodest—the fact is that many of my patients do like me a great deal. I hope they go on doing so."

He got up from behind the desk and moved to the window. "It's too bad more doctors don't inspire the kinds of feeling I seem to. It's a real collaboration, you know—the healing process."

He fiddled with the draperies, drew them aside and looked out into the night: a man alone, pitted against human suffering. Any minute now, the violins would start playing.

"I don't apologize for it," he went on. "I'm glad they have the feelings they have for me. It helps them get well—

doing what I ask of them, wanting to please me. I'll go on inspiring my patients for as long as I can."

Then he turned, his craggy face serious. "I'm familiar with Manners-Moreheim, but in the cases you've mentioned I can only think the system must have been applied improperly. Priest was a student, after all, not a fully trained scientist. He must have made an error—an error, I must add, of which I was unaware. I never saw his thesis. I haven't seen it yet; in fact, I have only your word that such a thing exists. And I did not kill anyone. I am, as they say, an innocent man."

Yeah, and I was the Dalai Lama.

"Sorry to have troubled you," I said as Brockway ushered us pleasantly from his office. Considering what I'd been accusing him of, it was damned inadequate, but he responded graciously.

Too damned graciously.

"I'm not in the slightest offended. In fact, I'm glad you could be honest about your feelings. I wish I could hand you a culprit on a silver platter, but I'm afraid I don't think there is a culprit in the sense you mean. Good luck in helping your friend, though. Where would we be in this terrible world without friends?"

He smiled one last time and shut the door on us.

Out in the car, we sat in silence. Brockway's office lights began snapping out.

"So," I said to Solli. "What do you think now?"

"I think," Solli said, "that smiling sonofabitch was lying through his pearly whites. For one thing, he talked too much."

I thought so too. And for another, Brockway knew perfectly well who Walt Krusanke was; he'd been at the memorial service. And it had upset him enough—or something had—to make him take a few belts before he went to it.

On top of which, despite all his studied politeness, the look in his eye had been frantic, the look of a small animal wondering how it had gotten into a cage, and how it would escape.

In short, Wes Brockway's gracious sincerity had been enough to make me want to put my finger down my throat.

"'Honest about your feelings,'" Solli snorted. "That guy was scared. He was trying not to show it, but he couldn't wait to get rid of us. Let's see where he goes now."

My sentiments exactly. In a few minutes, the last of the office lights went out and Brockway strode out into the street. I had the Datsun running, ready to follow him, but he didn't get into a car.

Instead, he walked down Prospect Street in a hurry, and went into a tall Victorian house that had been converted into offices just a few doors down the hill from his own.

We followed. It was past nine P.M. now, and only one set of office lights in the big house was on, but the building's outer door was still unlocked.

Inside was a cramped vestibule. A dozen mail slots and the building's office directory hung on the wall. The listings were for family counselors, psychologists, an eating-disorder clinic, a hypnotherapist, and several individuals whose names were followed by strings of academic degrees all ending in "M.D."

It was a shrink building, and the office on the ground floor was also the only one whose lights remained lit.

I consulted the directory once more. It confirmed what I'd thought I'd read the first time. Either Brockway had given us the slip, or he was consulting a child psychiatrist.

"I THINK you'd better leave," Jane Blackwood said.

Her outer rooms were furnished with a toybox, kindergarten pine chairs, picture books, and paintings in primary colors hung at the eye level of a seven-year-old.

"I think I'd better not," I told her. The whole suite was arranged so that patients leaving did not meet patients arriving; I'd waited on the "in" side until Solli, sitting on the hall staircase, signaled me that Wes Brockway had gone out, and that he hadn't seen us.

Blackwood was a slender, fiftyish woman with salt-and-pepper hair, sharp dark eyes, and a severe expression. She wore a black turtleneck sweater, a long gathered suede skirt, and a necklace of big turquoise chunks.

She'd looked upset when she came to the door, and that look intensified when I told her who I was and what I wanted.

"I am not going to discuss anything with you," she repeated, and began closing the door to the suite's inner room.

"Brockway came to you because he's scared," I said quickly, improvising all the way. There were plenty of other reasons Brockway might have gone to see her, but her face looked too upset to fit any of them.

"I don't know how you got involved," I told her, "or with what, but I'm starting to think he's committed some serious crimes. If he is your patient and you believe he's dangerous, concealing that is a crime, too, if I'm not mistaken."

The door opened a crack. Behind it, Jane Blackwood's face grew even more hostile. "I'm aware of my professional responsibilities. One of them is maintaining confidentiality. My patients' identities are none of your business. In fact, you have no business here, and if you do not leave at once, I will call the police. Do you understand?"

There was a file folder lying open on the desk in the room behind her, but I wasn't going to get at it by any means short of knocking her down. As if reading my mind, she stiffened, then shut the door firmly in my face.

"Damn the woman," I fumed to Solli as we headed back up the street toward the car.

Ignoring my remark, Solli eyed me curiously. "What's that noise?"

I stopped. A faint, strangled peeping came from somewhere nearby. In fact, it was coming from me.

"Your bag," Solli said. "It's in your handbag."

"Oh, my god." I rummaged the bag. At the bottom of it lay my beeper, silent and nearly forgotten since the day Joey had come out of surgery.

It wasn't silent now. Grabbing the squealing thing I hauled it from among crumpled tissues, stray stomach tablets, sticks of chewing gum, scribbled notes, and all the other trash I haul around with me on the theory that, if I clean the bag out, the one thing I need will be the one thing I don't have at the moment I need it.

At last, fumbling, I found the button on the beeper and pressed it.

The squealing stopped, replaced by a short burst of static and then by the message.

The voice was Twyla McKay's, and even through the beeper's tinny-sounding fuzziness it was urgent and frightened and close to tears.

OUTSIDE JOEY'S cubicle stood a stretcher half-covered by a rumpled sheet. Beside it was a cardiac defibrillator with loops of EKG paper dangling from it. Empty glass ampules, used syringes, and a black rubber resuscitator bag lay on his bedside table.

Near the nursing desk, Mike Malley was angrily questioning the plump young patrolman I'd met earlier. Twyla caught sight of me and interrupted her conversation with a nursing supervisor to hurry over.

"It's okay now," she said. "Big scare, no damage done."

But she still looked upset. "I'm sorry if I frightened you, but I thought you'd want to know. And for a minute there..."

She didn't finish the sentence, but she didn't have to. For a minute there, things had looked dicey indeed.

Now, though, Joey looked just as usual, except for evidence of recent hasty action all around him. The emergency-medication tacklebox stood open on the floor by his bedside, and a couple of the other nurses were watching him cautiously as they gathered papers and equipment from where they were strewn in the cubicle.

"What happened?"

Twyla lifted her hands in a who-knows gesture. "No one's sure. I stopped by to see my sister and let her go down for coffee, and she did. Then patient transport got here, to take him down for the second CAT scan—the scanner's been jammed up all day with emergencies, so this is the first they could get to it."

She stopped and took a deep breath. "Well, we got him on the stretcher and almost to the unit doors when his heart rate dropped. At the same time, the respiratory therapist who was bagging him—breathing for him, with the resuscitator bag?"

"I know. Go on." Solli stood at the nursing desk behind me, and Malley came over to listen, too.

"Well," Twyla said, "the therapist said his color looked bad, and it did, so we hustled him back into the room. By then he was really looking rocky and his blood pressure was dropping, so we called a code. But by the time everyone got here and we had medications running into his IVs and all, he started looking all right again."

The nursing desk was littered with lab slips from blood drawn during the emergency; no one had yet had time to put them into Joey's chart. As he listened, Solli glanced over them.

"His heart rate and pressure came back," Twyla continued, "his color pinked up, and now he's fine. I can't understand why he bottomed out like that, or why he came back so fast. And then another patient crashed out on one of the cardiac floors, so almost everyone had to dash off to that emergency, and they're still there."

"You sure the resuscitator bag was working, and there was oxygen in the tank you were running the bag off?" Solli picked up one of the lab slips and frowned at it.

Twyla turned, nodding. "Same bag I used earlier, and the gauge on the tank reads nearly full. And yes, the tank was turned on; we checked."

Malley moved past me to Joey's cubicle. To his question, the other nurses replied that no one but Twyla's sister and Twyla had been near Joey all evening—the unit was so busy, no one had even been able to stop in and chat—until the patient-transport aide had arrived to get him onto the stretcher for the CAT scan.

"I'm going to find that aide," Malley said, "and then I'll be back. I've had just about enough of this mysterious crap." Scowling at me as if it were all my fault, he stalked out.

"You know," Solli said, still holding the lab slip, "I think he's starting to believe you may be right about all this."

"He's a little late," I snapped. "What's that?"

Solli smiled. It was a mild, dangerous smile, the quiet one he wears when his worst suspicions have been confirmed and he's truly furious about it.

"This," he said, "is a blood gas slip."

He turned to Twyla, and pointed at a small green cylinder standing outside Joey's cubicle. "Is that the oxygen tank you were using to move Joey?"

Twyla nodded, looking puzzled.

"And," he went on, "is there somewhere you could put it, without attracting a lot of attention?"

Enlightenment dawned on Twyla's face; her eyes grew large with interest.

"Sure," she said. "In my locker, in the conference room. Should I watch out for fingerprints?"

Solli shook his head. Twyla strolled casually into the cubicle and began to help out with Joey, keeping a sharp eye on the small green oxygen cylinder as she did so.

"Solli," I demanded, "what's all that all about?"

"That," he replied, "is about this—the results of Joey's blood gas test, on this lab slip, drawn while he was in trouble. It's a measurement of the oxygen and carbon dioxide in his blood, see? Normal for oxygen's a hundred, for CO_2 it's about 45."

According to the slip, Joey's oxygen level during the time of the emergency had been 43. His CO_2 had measured 97.

"These are backwards," I said. "You can't get numbers like this unless you're not breathing at all. Or unless..."

I looked at the green cylinder Twyla was now toting past me. No one else took any notice as she vanished into the conference room with it.

"Right," Solli said. "Unless you're breathing CO_2. In fact you can't get that much CO_2 into a breathing person's blood any other way."

I stared at him.

"So," he said grimly, "the question is: what color is a green oxygen tank?"

"Green," I answered. "Unless—it's not an oxygen tank? Unless it's some other kind of tank, painted green?"

"You got it," Solli said, tucking the lab slip firmly away in his hip pocket.

"There's a pin-index safety system for the oxygen gauges," I objected; I'd learned about it doing research for *Tricks for the Sick!* "You can't just stick an O_2 gauge on a CO_2 tank."

"Sure," Solli replied, "but the system is perfectly easy to defeat—chip the gauge-pins off with a chisel. Then an O_2 gauge will work on any tank."

Tricks for the murderous, I thought; Wes Brockway would know how to rig a tank like that.

"But even if you did," I asked Solli, "how could you be sure Joey was the patient who got the rigged tank?"

"Stand it in the corner of his room," Solli answered. "It's not like IVs, where there's a pretty strict quality-control system for the mixing and preparing. People just grab whatever tank is handy, and the transport aides don't always bring them. Stick it in his room, sooner or later you know it's going to get used."

"And if they'd gotten him into the elevator before he went bad..."

"They'd have kept right on using the tank," Solli said, "instead of going back to the oxygen from the wall outlet. And unless I'm very much mistaken, if that had happened Joey wouldn't have survived it."

In Joey's room, the respirator continued pumping through its steady cycles; Joey's chest rose and fell. The tracing on his cardiac monitor was slow and regular, too, and his IVs dripped steadily, while the room itself had been returned to its state of nonemergency neatness.

Nothing now, in fact, betrayed how close I'd come to losing him, or how close someone had come to killing him.

The anger began in the pit of my stomach and spread like a gasoline fire through the rest of me, with an intense, absolutely physical glowing heat that kept on swelling and growing. This, I thought distantly, was rage: the pure stuff, strong and sudden as heroin.

Solli eyed me narrowly. "Charlotte," he began in warning tones.

"Stay here," I told him. "Watch Joey, and talk to Claire Bogan and Twyla's sister when they come back. Tell Malley what we've figured, too." I headed for the door.

"Charlotte," Solli called after me, "wait a minute. Where are you going? What are you going to do?"

I answered without turning. "I'm going to nail that bastard to the wall."

I meant it, too: My heart was pure. I had the strength of ten.

Also, I was mad as bloody hell.

THE TANK room was in the hospital basement, near the central supply rooms, the morgue, and the loading docks according to the janitor I asked on the way.

I took the staircase down, feeling confident. My first burst of fury had settled back to a fine, slow fire, and I was sure of what I would find now.

Carbon dioxide was used for calibrating lab instruments, among other things. Colorless and odorless, it was also the perfect gas for murder, assuming you had a way to get some, and to administer it. An anesthesiologist, I thought, would have no trouble with either task.

Finding the tank room itself took a while, however; the utility end of the basement was unpainted concrete block and bare concrete floor, with no signs or markers to tell me I was going the right way.

People who had any business here knew the way already, or so the theory apparently went; I kept plodding, however, and after a couple of wrong turns, dead ends, and backtracks I did find the tank-storage room.

Beyond the gray metal door, a teenage boy with watery eyes and a bad complexion sat at a counter reading a comic book. The boy looked up vexedly as I entered. From a large radio beside him came a sprightly little lyric about the devil's death cult, to the tune of someone destroying metal trash cans with a hammer.

"Help you?" the boy asked, not closing the comic. His eyes held the kind of dismissive, all-purpose hostility I never know what to do with, so I ignored it.

"Maybe," I shouted over the radio's insistent racket. "You in charge here?"

His shoulder-hitch indicated that he was.

Along the sides of the unpainted concrete-block room, tall tanks of various gases stood chained to the walls or propped on wheeled metal dollies. The tanks were yellow, silver, green, gray, and combinations of these colors. Each color indicated the kind of gas in the tank.

Smaller tanks, also of various colors, lay on their sides on the grubby linoleum floor or stood in wooden racks. Metal shelves at the center of the room held piles of chrome-plated gauges for the different kinds of tanks.

"I don't suppose you were here earlier today, though," I said. On the counter near where he sat, a large black-bound book lay open.

"I was here." His gaze had returned to his reading matter. "Doin' a double shift. Need the bucks."

"Do you happen to remember who might have come down to pick up a CO_2 tank? Today, maybe? A small tank?"

The boy looked at me as if I'd just arrived from Mars.

"Never mind. I'll have a look at the charge ledger, would that be all right?"

His look told me clearly what I could do with the charge ledger, and to please get out of his face; couldn't I see he was trying to read, here?

Tanks that went out of this room, I knew, had to be charged for. The ledger on the desk showed date, size and type of tank, the name and charge number of the department using it, and the name of the person who had signed for receipt of it.

I flipped pages. In the past week, eleven small CO_2 tanks had been signed out. Two had gone to the cardiology lab, five to the pulmonary lab, and three had been charged to the anesthesia department.

That made ten. The eleventh tank had been taken by someone whose handwriting, except for numerals, was illegible, but the numerals matched the charge number that had been listed three times on the lines above, for the anesthesia department.

"Thanks," I yelled as I turned to the door, but the kid had already returned to Flash Gordon's illustrated adventures.

I could see why; the gloomy, grimy concrete-block tank room certainly wasn't very exciting. Except to me.

There was no reason at all why the anesthesia department should not have CO_2. But all the other tanks that had gone to that department in previous days were signed for by someone with clear, firm handwriting.

The last one was different. Whoever took it had end-stage spasm of the writing hand, or didn't want his signature read.

Physicians, I seemed to remember, had notoriously poor handwriting. But why, if Brockway had taken and rigged the tank, had he not signed it out against some department other than his own, just to cover his tracks a bit more? Surely he could find out plenty of other departments' charge numbers, and use one of them.

Except that was just the sort of thing that could screw him up, if questions arose later and the tank-room kid remembered him. Better, I realized, simply to take the tank and sign it to his own department, thus maintaining at least the appearance of innocence.

Meanwhile, anyone who saw Joey's screwed-up blood gas results—anyone not looking for murder—would think it was just that: a screwed-up result. Labs made mistakes; not often, but often enough to make it the first conclusion to jump to.

And even if someone thought otherwise—me, for example, because after all I had been warned—there was no way to prove the tank in question was the same one signed out of the tank room by Wes Brockway.

If he had, because damn him, I still couldn't pin him inescapably down.

But I was getting closer, so I headed for the elevators and Lieutenant Mike Malley again. By now Malley would be back in ICU, and if recent events had changed his attitude as much as I suspected, there were lots of things we could profitably discuss—such as the probable contents of a certain oxygen tank, and how there happened not to be oxygen inside it, and who might have arranged matters that way.

At least, I meant to head for the elevators, but once again the unpainted, unlabeled basement walls confused me; deep in thought, I walked for several hundred yards and made a few turns—how many, I wasn't sure—before I realized that I had turned the wrong way in the first place, coming out of the tank room.

After that I'd turned left, right, and left again.

Or maybe it had been right, left, and right.

Now I found myself at the end of a blind alley, between a door that said ENGINEERING—locked—and one that said DANGER—CONSTRUCTION—no doorknob.

The surrounding decor, meanwhile, was deteriorating into something that resembled early Paleolithic; I half-expected to start seeing blue cave paintings daubed on the grim concrete.

I turned another corner. The corridors here were low, dim and dungeonlike, lit at long intervals by naked bulbs dangling from drop cords. A few more doors bore signs, but the sign I wanted said THIS WAY OUT and there wasn't one of those.

Reversing directions and remembering not to panic, because of course that was silly, this was a public *building*, this was a much-frequented, thoroughly civilized *place*, I walked back the way I had come. I did not, however, re-

member passing the door marked RADIATION AREA—
DANGER—DO NOT ENTER or one behind which an electrical generator hummed. Nor did I recall several more that
were secured by large, rusty-looking padlocks, or the one
stencilled BIOHAZARD—INFECTIOUS AGENTS—NO ENTRY
WITHOUT PROPER AUTHORIZATION.

By now I would have happily joined the germs, infectious or not, because it was clear at this point that I had
gotten myself lost. Still I tramped steadily on, remaining
certain that sooner or later I must find an elevator or
stairway somewhere.

Meanwhile, however, even though a few of the corridors did sport glowing red exit signs, these seemed meant
only to lure me on to further exit signs, not to actual exits.

This was, I realized, an underground warren of labs and
work areas set deliberately out of the way, so that no casual visitor would be in danger of blundering accidentally
into them.

Now I had not only blundered in, I was blundering
deeper, and at last understanding this, I stopped.

The corridor I stood in had looked at first as if it might
lead somewhere useful, but now it stretched away silently
in both directions as if it went on forever. Several nearby
offshoots of it suggested possible routes for further explo-
ration, but I had no way of choosing among them; also
they looked rather dark.

A crumpled paper cup on the floor raised my hopes for
a moment—perhaps I might follow bits of trash as if they
were breadcrumbs—but closer inspection showed cob-
webs on the cup.

I had traveled past the out-of-the-way into, it seemed,
the abandoned. If even the janitors didn't come here, then
this area of the basement wasn't only little used; it wasn't
used at all.

Cursing my notoriously poor sense of direction, I now
began considering whether I ought not simply to begin to

yell for help; no doubt the hospital's security people came here, or within earshot, even if no one else did. And while yelling would be embarrassing, it would also be effective.

But something about this idea felt inexplicably wrong. For one thing, now that I was standing still, the deep, unbroken stillness of the place held me back. It was a solid, vacuumlike silence such as I had never felt before, created not only by the absence of sound but by the insulation of concrete-block walls, inches thick all around me.

If I shouted in that silence, I would not be able to hear—

But that really was silly. There was, I told myself sternly, no reason at all to be frightened. Deserted as it seemed, the hospital was after all full of people, any of them not far away, and I would certainly run into one of them very soon.

This thought proved less than completely comforting as, in the next moment, I realized: It *was* awfully quiet. It was so quiet that I could hear my own breathing. In fact, unless I was mistaken, I could also hear someone else breathing.

To test this unpleasant theory, I held my breath. Someone else didn't.

Someone else rushed suddenly forward, instead.

The figure sprang out at me from one of the side passages, so fast and so forcefully that I barely glimpsed its costume—baggy green scrub pants and shirt, flapping green gown, surgical cap and mask—before it was upon me.

I did get a good close look at the knife it was gripping, though. For a moment, in fact, that knife occupied my whole attention as it plunged with wicked accuracy toward my neck.

In the next moment, however, my nerves and muscles unfroze enough to take my brain's urgent message of advice. Zipping in a rapid synaptic flash down routes labeled Highest Priority; For Use In Life-Threatening Emergencies Only, this message read:

(A) hit, and (B) run.

For what followed, I can take no credit. It is simply amazing what the human body can do when faced with a big sharp knife. My balled fist flew out, striking the figure's mask with inspired force. This surprised me considerably, but not anywhere near as much as it surprised the figure. The eyes above the mask opened wide for an instant, then shut as my attacker staggered back.

Then I turned and ran, my sneakers drumming the floor and my heartbeat drumming in my ears, a percussion duet in the key of scared witless. My right arm felt as if I had stopped a train with it, but I figured what the hell: if you're going to get hurt you might as well do it in a hospital. Later I planned to howl with pain for an hour or so.

Meanwhile I heard nothing from the rear, which was just fine with me. After about fifty paces, though, I risked a glance over my shoulder, as it occurred to me that I didn't know where I was going and my attacker probably did.

After all, whoever it was had followed me very efficiently without my noticing, a fact which suggested some knowledge of this entire basement including the side passages.

The figure struggled up, a bright bloom of blood spreading redly on its facemask. It didn't look crippled, and it didn't look happy.

Also, it still had the big knife. I swung around a corner and accelerated down a hall as blank and unhelpful as the one I had left, passing several doors all equipped with locks, some of them padlocks and some of them big stout Block cylinders, none of which I felt I had sufficient leisure to stop and test.

Behind me, feet thumped the floor as someone threw off the shock of a punched nose and began picking up speed. What I needed was a way to get inside one of the rooms I

kept passing, a way past one of those big shiny locks that
kept glittering and winking at me, taunting me. What I
needed was a tank, a bazooka, a small thermonuclear device....

Keys. I needed keys. And I *had* keys. I had Helen's keys,
jangling in the bottom of my bag with my every panicked
stride.

The trouble was, I didn't know what they fitted, or how
I would get hold of them while flinging myself wildly
around another corner and slamming madly down another long, dim, deserted corridor.

Some of the overhead bulbs here were burnt out, but
through the gloom I could see a set of green double doors
about fifty yards away, big and windowless with tall black
print stencilled across them: BASEMENT LEVEL II.

Also, they were the only doors in the corridor. I was in
a blind alley.

From the rear came the sound of my pursuer, breathing
hard but not falling back much. Not falling back at all, in
fact; closing the gap, instead.

As I ran, I dug through my bag: Kleenex, pens, papers,
loose change. I swore on my life that I would clean this
damn thing out, if I only got the chance, and then my hand
closed on a metal ring with a bunch of keys attached to it.

Helen's keys. Twenty yards, now, to those solid-looking
doors; I could read the smaller black print warning on
them:

ENGINEERING   MAINTENANCE   ACCESS   AREA—
AUTHORIZED ENTRY ONLY—THESE DOORS LOCKED
BETWEEN 5 P.M. AND 7 A.M.

Feets, don't fail me now.

Beyond those doors, in the sub-basement, lay hospital
wiring and plumbing: things Helen would have had to
know about. And those doors, unless I missed my guess,

were ones she had keys to: keys the hospital office of developmental affairs had written to her about, to demand that she give them back.

Which meant they were on this ring.

Either that, or I was mincemeat.

House keys, car keys, office keys, a half-dozen more. Some looked big enough; in fact, several did, which was too bad because I didn't have time to stand around trying them one after another. Behind me, footsteps pounded nearer.

Five yards; four. I raised the biggest, fattest key, slammed full-tilt into the big green double doors, jabbed at the lock and missed. The end of the key took a jagged scratch out of the door's paint. From behind me came the swish of that long green scrub-gown.

I stabbed at the lock again. This time the key went in and stuck. Wrong key. My hands felt like silly putty. Next key; wrong again.

Come on, come *on*, shrieked the helpful message-sender in my brain. Last key. I rammed it in, twisted it. The lock turned grittily and stuck. Meanwhile a harsh ripping sound came from below my right ear.

I glanced down; my sleeve was slit from collar to elbow, cloth flapping. The masked, scrub-suited figure was right on top of me, raising the knife again. This time it would ventilate more than my outfit. This time, it would ventilate me.

In one instant, I was gaping at the unbelievable malice and fury in the narrow gray eyes above the surgical mask.

In the next, I gave that key one last vicious twist.

The lock snapped open. The door creaked outwards. I yanked it wider, kicked out at the figure, flung myself under its arm and through the door, and dragged the door shut behind me.

The figure yanked it open again. I lunged, hauling it shut, holding it that way with all my weight while slamming down a rusty, disused floor bolt with my foot.

Trying to, anyway. At last the unwilling bolt slid down an inch or so into its grit-clogged slot. Suddenly silence, broken by the rumble and hum of the huge building's inner workings:

Steam-hiss and water-hammers, faint clickety-clicking from electrical panels, distant roar of an enormous generator somewhere.

Unhappily, I regarded the doors I had been so anxious to get behind. There was now no way of knowing if the figure had gone away from the other side of them—at least, not without opening them, and the chances of my doing that, I calculated swiftly, were approximately zero.

Meanwhile behind me a half-dozen concrete steps led down into what seemed little more than a crawl space, lit by a series of grimy fifteen-watt bulbs widely spaced along a jerry-rigged drop cord.

I have never been very fond of tunnels. But then, I have never been fond of psychotic knife-wielding killers, either, and that was what awaited me on the other side of the doors.

Unless of course the aforementioned psychotic knife-wielding killer was already on the way in here. Whoever it was seemed awfully familiar with the basement layout, I realized with fresh dismay.

Which ruled out just sitting here and waiting on the steps until morning, when the engineering department supervisors would open the doors for the maintenance workers on the dayshift. By that time, I could easily be past all possibility of maintenance, except of course for the kind performed so cheerily and expertly by Louie the morgue technician.

The more I thought about it, in fact, the more I realized: My only real chance with the tunnel was getting out of it before my attacker managed to get into it.

Thus, shuddering, I descended to the crawl space.

ELEVEN

AFTER FIFTY YARDS or so, the crawl space widened to a passage a little over five feet high and perhaps seven feet wide. The dim bare bulbs stretched ahead for as far as I could see, illuminating steam pipes and bundled wiring that snaked along the low ceiling.

The air in the downward-sloping passage was hot and stagnant, smelling of old dust, and as I stood breathing it I began to think a map would come in handy. Now that I was no longer frightened half out of my wits, but only about a third of the way out, I remembered the newspaper accounts of the Dungeons and Dragons games and the boy who had gotten lost down here while playing at them.

Even the maintenance men who worked here regularly didn't know where all the tunnels went, the newspaper articles had said. Some tunnels ran clear to the university's main steam generators, way across town. One was rumored to end under Prospect Cemetery, where in olden days grave robbers had stolen corpses and spirited them back to the hospital for illegal dissections.

Which was just about the last thing I wanted to think about. To distract myself, I began trying to decipher the markings on the steam pipes above me. I could only hope that someone had done some comprehensible labeling of these conduits, because it seemed I was going to have to find my way out of here by following them.

Squinting upward for this purpose, I stumbled on a stray chunk of mortar, fought to keep my footing, and sat down hard in a sort of niche that had been dug into the passage wall.

The niche was dark. To push myself up I put my hand out and something skittered crisply away from my fingers.

I stifled a small shriek. Then the tunnel was silent again. Only not completely silent.

In addition to the rumble of basement workings—it was, I reflected, rather like the sounds Jonah must have heard, trapped in the belly of the whale—there was also a faint, papery rustling, almost inaudible but still very present and continuous, from the niches cut into the walls on both sides of this length of the underground passage.

Roaches big as rats, said a nasty, unwelcome voice in my head. And rats, I thought unhappily, rats as big as collies.

Then I steadied myself with an effort: bugs. Even a mouse, maybe. Big deal; who's afraid of a little . . .

Something moaned, furious and challenging, a scant foot from my head, whereupon all my blood flash-froze in the pit of my stomach.

I turned my head slowly. If whatever was crouched at the back of that niche took a swipe at me—or a bite of me—I was going to come out of this scarred like a Masai warrior, assuming I came out of this at all, which I thought was getting to be a fairly optimistic expectation considering the way things were going lately.

Gradually my eyes adjusted to the niche's gloom. It was a hole about two feet wide and four feet high, built originally perhaps for some kind of large pipe to run through. Just at present, however, it held a large, snarling cat, which I supposed represented the top of the food chain in these tunnels.

At least, I hoped to hell it did. All right, I thought: I will now assert my human superiority.

The animal's hot yellow eyes held mine, reading my purpose while communicating without flaw or impediment just exactly what it thought of human superiority.

"Nice kitty," I croaked.

Its battle-shredded ears flattened back on its bony white head. It snarled, and then it leapt.

Human superiority, I thought while the horrid moment went on, is one damned highly overrated commodity. Give me a nice fat club or a pile of throwing-rocks any day; yes sir, if it's good enough for the great apes, it's fine with yours truly.

Meanwhile the cat kept sailing at me, resembling a living buzz saw equipped with two enormous yellow headlights, and time just kept stretching out the way it will in the moments before a fatal car crash.

Then, inches from my face, the cat changed direction abruptly in midair and vanished with a final yowl back into the pipe hole.

Time started up again. The whole thing had taken perhaps three seconds. Slowly I peeled myself off the floor and let out my breath, astonished to find that I still had any.

What I didn't have was illusions; I hadn't scared that beast one damned bit. In the few moments I'd spent fixed in the crosshairs of its gaze, I'd felt it measuring me into cutlets, its carnivorous interest still crawling on my skin like the dotted lines on a meat chart at the butcher shop.

I brushed at my arm, then at my neck. And then I realized those crawly feelings weren't dotted lines.

They weren't imaginary, either.

They were ants, and there were quite a few of them. And just about the time I got most of them swatted off, I noticed that one had strayed carelessly quite some ways up into my pants leg.

Correction: not an ant. Bigger. More legs, too; lots more.

At least it wasn't wearing a tiny little mask or carrying a knife, I thought as I shook out my pant leg, and that was about the only good thing I could say for it or for the next hour during which I crept onward—slowly, itchily, and nervously. The whole experience, in fact, was much like snooping in general: frustration and discomfort punctuated by moments of terror.

Soon discomfort and terror were livened up even more by a complete absence of bathrooms, which I wouldn't have cared about except that there was no bathroom tissue, either, and I had tossed away all my old Kleenex while digging for Helen's keys, and the only thing more I want to say about it is that I started out wearing eight items of clothing, including two shoes and two socks, and ended up wearing seven items, never mind which ones, although I did mind, very much.

The entire trip by that point had gotten almost as bad as the alternative, and not long after it got even worse as I fell yet again, this time landing on a heap of sheets that turned out to have Bill Priest's body all wrapped up in them.

Fortunately, this experience did not last long, although it scared almost all of the remainder of the living hell out of me.

The final bits got scared out a moment later, when a hand came suddenly from behind me and seized my shoulder.

"HI, CHARLOTTE," Steve Marino said.

Of course I did not know at first that it was Steve; for all I knew, it could have been the shambling ghost of a body snatcher. By then, though, I would have welcomed a body snatcher if it knew its way out of the tunnel and was willing to snatch me there, the steam-pipe method of navigation having turned out to be a complete bust.

Behind Steve stood Solli.

"Hi, you guys," I gasped. "What are you doing here?"

It was, I must say, one of the more humiliating moments of my life. I had been very frightened. Left turns and right turns had multiplied, fueled by my compelling but erroneous sense of direction. A moment earlier I had nearly walked flat-faced into a wall, after a determined three-hundred-foot march that I had been certain would lead me into the medical school dorm basement.

The dead-end wall had been quilted with spiders. Big fat white ones. It was as I hurried away from them that I had tripped over Bill Priest's sheet-wrapped corpse.

"Stupid idea," Steve said, indicating me and the tunnel.

"Shut up," I explained.

"Hey," Solli said in tones of gratified interest, crouching by the heap of sheets. "Look at this."

Personally, my interest in corpses decreases directly with the amount of time they have spent lying around unembalmed. Solli for once seemed to feel no such qualms, however, and after a moment Steve bent beside him.

Carefully, they began removing Priest's wrappings. The body looked sad and defenseless on the raw concrete floor, and I began feeling sorry for it, something I had not been able to do earlier. I'd told myself Bill Priest had not deserved murdering, but I'd been too angry with him really to believe it.

Now I believed it. Curls of his dark hair brushed the floor. His hands lay open, fingers helplessly half-curled. His face, white and bloodless, stretched in an openmouthed rictus of horrid surprise. He would have hated being seen this way, and the reason he didn't deserve it was simple: no one could. Beside him stood a wheeled canvas hamper, the kind the hospital's aides used for taking soiled sheets to the laundry.

Something clinked on the concrete floor.

"Bottles of saline," Steve mused, picking up one of three glass half-liter jugs that had been hidden among the sheets. "A hundred-cc syringe, rubber tubing...."

Understanding spread on his face. "Gastric lavage. It's a stomach pump setup."

"Why isn't he, uh—"

Solli looked up at me. "Decomposing? Good question. Maybe he was somewhere else first, somewhere cold, and someone hauled him recently to pump his stomach in private. I wonder why."

His face grim, he picked up the big syringe and the tubing. "Let's find out."

My own stomach turned over. "Listen, guys—"

It was a terrible idea. It would screw up the evidence, it would infuriate Lieutenant Malley, and it would hogtie some struggling defense lawyer, some day when all this got back onto its official tracks and into a court of law, if it ever did.

Also, the sound effects weren't attractive.

I explained all these things, but Solli continued doing what he was doing. Precisely what that was I wasn't quite sure.

I could imagine, though, and that was bad enough.

"Charlotte," Solli said, "I just don't care." His face as he worked was frowningly intent, and it had that look again: the one Solli gets when he just doesn't give a rat's ass.

A look down at my own shoulder told me why: My attacker had come a little closer to success than I'd thought. Fear had kept me from feeling any pain, but I began feeling it now.

An inch higher and to the right, and I wouldn't be feeling anything. As it was, a long, nasty red arrow pointed directly at my jugular vein, clearly the intended target. The bleeding had stopped, but my torn sleeve was a red, soaked mass, beginning to stiffen with dried blood.

I looked again at Solli, meaning to tell him that I was all right. Then I looked away once more, because he already knew I was all right, and besides, what he was doing wasn't only unwise; it was also revolting.

"*And*," he went on, "whatever's here is what our murderous friend wanted hidden. Therefore—"

A truly terrible sound made me swallow hard.

"Therefore, I am going to reveal it."

A few moments of silence followed.

"I'll be damned," Steve Marino said.

"Me, too," said Solli. "Thoughtful of him to die on a nearly empty stomach, but what the hell is that?"

I peeked. Both of them were bent over something on the sheet. I couldn't tell what, and the last thing I wanted to do was get any nearer, to find out. Soon, however, curiosity overcame squeamishness; I crouched down with Solli and Steve. Bottom line was, I wanted to know even more than I wanted to be ill.

And after a few moments more, I did know. "Cherries," I said. "Maraschino cherries. The kind that come in little jars?"

"You know," Steve said, "I think she's right. I ate a whole bottle of those things once, when I was a kid. And that night I—"

"Never mind," I said hastily. "Cover his face up and let's get out of here." Then another thought struck me. "How *did* you guys find me, anyway?"

Steve's grin was shamefaced as from his pocket he drew a small object that resembled something smuggled out of Bell Labs. I recognized it: the gadget he'd been assembling in his room.

"If you look in the bottom of that satchel of yours, you'll find the other part of this," he said. "It's about the size of a thumbtack."

I stared at him, comprehending and furious.

"I have to admit it took me a while, though, to figure out where you were. On the screen it looked like I was right on top of you, which of course I was; my room is directly above us."

"The screen," I repeated flatly.

Steve nodded. "Plots distance and direction from the signal, lays it on a grid, superimposes the grid on a rough map."

"Which is to say, you were spying on me. Electronically."

I evil-eyed Solli, who was carefully not looking at me and also not saying whether he had known of the Charlotte-tracking project, although of course he had. Probably, in fact, it had been his idea. Then I glared at Steve again.

"Come on," he said, "if it weren't for this, you'd have been wandering around here forever. You're lucky I even remembered how to get out. Which reminds me—"

He glanced at his watch, then at Solli. "Time to go."

"What do you mean," I demanded, "what's so—"

"Listen," Solli said, "Steve's right. We really should go."

I faced him. "I'm not sure I want to talk to you. You let him spy on me. You probably encouraged him."

"Hospital's on another one of its cost-cutting campaigns," Steve went on, stepping along ahead of us rather briskly, I thought.

Solli took my hand. I yanked it away again. "Listen, what's going on? What aren't you guys telling me?"

"Well," Solli began, "the thing is, it's almost midnight."

"And," Steve added, "the only people who are ever supposed to be down here at all are hospital engineers, and their last shift gets off at midnight."

"So," Solli said, and then as if to finish his sentence all the lights went out.

"WHAT WE need," I said, " is a confession."

Luckily, Solli had brought along a flashlight. Following its beam along with Steve's arcane knowledge of the hospital's nether regions, we had made our way eventually to the dormitory basement and up to main floors.

"On paper," I said, "or on tape. Tape would be good."

My fears about my attacker coming into the tunnel had been empty, apparently; at least, we spotted no scrub-suited lurkers along the way. Nevertheless, I was delighted to reach Marino's dorm room, even though it was as full of electronic gadgetry as it had ever been, and as empty of creature comforts.

A chair whose seat was not stacked with floppy-disk boxes, for example, could not be found, nor could his bed be precisely located amidst heaps of printout, lists of unpublished phone numbers, and loops of shielded cables, wires, and unidentified black boxes into whose purpose I did not care to inquire.

What could be found was a bottle of scotch, a hefty dose of which Steve poured out for me, whereupon I swiftly surrounded it.

The room also contained Rawlins, looking spiffy in uniform as usual; looking alert, too, and perfectly comfortable with that cannon he carried around under his jacket. I'd never quite understood the value of a bodyguard before, but I did now.

"You know," Solli mused, unceremoniously sweeping an armload of clutter onto the floor and sitting down, "I'll bet you could get a fair amount of chloral hydrate into a cherry."

"Shoot it in," Marino agreed, "with a needle and syringe. A couple would do it. But why hide it? Anyone can buy cherries, and plenty of people can get chloral hydrate."

"Because," I went on, although no one seemed to be listening, "we don't know why he killed them. And we don't know how he killed them. So without a confession..."

"You don't," Rawlins pointed out, "even know *that* he killed them."

I looked up, surprised. It was the first unsolicited remark I remembered ever hearing out of Rawlins, and I was about to pursue it when Steve interrupted.

"Oh, come on," he said. "Of course we know. We've got bank statements; Priest was blackmailing him. And all the dead patients were *his* patients. And Priest didn't die until after the thesis about them hit Brockway's desk. And the tank-rigging deal—I mean, Christ, Rawlins, what more do we need?"

Rawlins's eyebrows rose a genteel quarter-inch. "Proof, sir."

"He's right," I said. "I'm not even sure it was Brockway who attacked me. It could have been, but I was too busy ducking the knife even to think about yanking on the mask."

Steve made a face. "Sure, and it's just coincidence that right after you confront him, someone tries to do throat surgery on you."

"One thing we do know," Solli said. "It took nerve to get Priest's body out of the emergency room. Simple, when you think of it: put on a housekeeper's outfit, stroll into the resuscitation room once everyone's gone out, tip the corpse into a hamper. Then stroll out again, pushing the hamper. Not hard—just ballsy."

"That's the nuttiest idea I ever heard," I said.

"We're not talking about giving out the mental health award of the year, here," Steve pointed out.

"I guess not," I said doubtfully. "And he's not a real big guy. A wig, some makeup, and the outfit—I suppose he could have done it, assuming he really is that nuts, and as long as no one looked too closely at him."

"Which no one would," Solli said. "Heck, no one looks hard at the housekeeping staff. Especially when things get hectic—then they're like interchangeable parts."

"The thing I keep wondering, though," I said, "is why? Here we thought Priest's body was going to have some big wonderful clue in it, and all it's got is cherries. Like Steve says, why hide that? What's it supposed to mean?"

Solli nodded. "I can understand wanting to cover up a lot of murders, too," he said, "but my big question is still why he did them in the first place."

Steve made a noise. "The guy's clearly bonkers—that's all the reason he needed. But as you point out, Rawlins, proving it's going to be something else again."

"So," I said slowly, "a confession. What if we got it on tape? Steve, you must have some contraption around here—don't they call it a wire?—that I could wear if I went back to see him again. I mean," I added scathingly, "you're such an expert at electronic surveillance."

Steve beamed, apparently taking this as a compliment.

But Solli frowned. "That sounds dangerous. Besides, if we know we can't prove anything, he probably knows it, too. Why would he incriminate himself?"

"Right, but what if he didn't know? What if he thought that someone—his psychiatrist friend, maybe—had already told the story, or was getting ready to? If we tell him enough of it, he might think we know the rest. And if that happened—"

"He might spill the rest himself." Solli's frown deepened. "I'm still not sure, Charlotte. He's no fool. He'd have to figure you were trying to trap him, unless he's dumber than we think."

"He's not dumb," I said. "What he is, though, is tired."

Saying it, I remembered the look on Brockway's face when I'd seen him earlier: the confident smile contradicting the look in his gray eyes.

The eyes in the basement had been gray, too: furious gray eyes peering murderously over a surgical mask. I wasn't sure those eyes had been Brockway's, but they were like his—very much like. If they were the same ones, then Steve Marino was right: Brockway was bonkers.

Because one thing I did know: they might or might not have been Brockway's eyes in that basement, but it hadn't been Wes Brockway looking out of them. Oh, no; not at all. Behind the hate-filled glare had been someone else entirely.

Someone who, even in memory, scared the living bejezus out of me.

"AND YOU think *he's* bonkers," Solli said an hour later as we piled into the Datsun.

We'd gotten the taping equipment together, then sent Steve and Rawlins up to the hospital to watch Joey, since by this time I didn't know who might try what and I no longer trusted Malley's minions to stop anyone from anything.

Another hour, I told myself; two hours at the most and it's over.

"I'm the one who's nuts, going along with this," Solli grumbled as I started the car.

"Look," I told him, "I just don't think we've got a choice. We still can't go to Malley with all of what we know, because we still aren't supposed to know it. All we can do is try to stick Brockway with it, pretend we know what those damned cherries mean and scare him into getting stupid. You could lose your medical license over that stunt with Priest's insides, you realize, aside from what they could do to you for the phone stuff."

Solli looked rueful. "Right. Heck, though, somebody dumped that kid in the tunnel like a pile of garbage. I got so mad and so curious all at once—you know how it is."

"Right," I said quietly, "I do."

I glanced sideways at him. The look on his face was one of sudden, quiet comprehension.

This, I saw him thinking, was why Charlotte kept poking her nose where it didn't belong, asking impertinent questions and taking damn-fool actions and generally hanging her tail out to swing in the breeze while some nutcase ran around threatening people with cutting implements.

So mad, and so curious. But mostly mad. The whole thing was so damned gut-level offensive: the coldness, the arrogance of it. The sheer, insane, egocentric power trip of it: me, Me, ME.

Only not any more; not if I worked it right with Brockway, made him believe I knew more than I really did.

Just keep pressing him, I told myself as I guided the Datsun past Prospect Cemetery and up the hill; find his soft spot and poke it.

It was still, as Solli said, a crazy idea and probably it wouldn't work. But it was all I could come up with: harassing him until he finally said or did something. Sometimes when you want apples, all you can do is shake the tree and hope what falls out doesn't crack your skull open.

Brockway's home address was listed in the telephone book. It was a prosperous, well-ordered neighborhood: big old houses, ancient elms that had somehow escaped ravaging, no toys on the front lawns or junkers in the driveways.

"Lord loves an idiot," I said to Solli, "I hope."

He checked the tape machine a final time. The wireless mike was in my jacket pocket.

"Yeah, but I love one, too. And I don't like this a bit."

"Don't worry. He'll know you're out here. I doubt he'll try anything with a witness just a few feet away."

That, I could see, did not convince Solli much. It didn't convince me much, either, as a matter of fact. Nevertheless, I got out of the car and headed up Brockway's front walk.

At two in the morning, everything was dark and silent except for a few dry leaves whickering in high branches over the street. The feeling of people sleeping in houses all around was palpable, like a thick blanket of dreams. Brockway's house was a big old two-story Greek revival, tall evergreens standing like sentries at intervals on either side of the long front walk. Bay laurel and box hedges crowded at the windows; behind heavy draperies, a lamp burned in one of the first-floor front rooms.

I had a good mind to ring his doorbell and run. Instead I rang it and didn't. Inside, two notes chimed distantly, and I was about to ring again when the door opened.

Well, at least I hadn't gotten him out of bed; not unless he slept in cashmere sweaters and gray wool slacks.

He scowled at the sight of me. "If you think I'm going to let you in here at this hour—"

Behind him I could see a red-tiled foyer with cream-colored stucco archways leading to the dining room and kitchen. A small lamp burned over a hallway table; on the table stood a candy dish and some silver-framed photographs.

"You're in trouble," I said, stepping past him onto the red tiles. My heart was slamming against the insides of my ribs and I prayed he couldn't know.

"There are things I didn't tell you earlier," I went on. "Then someone tried to kill me. I think it might have been you, and I want to talk to you about it."

I pulled my collar aside to reveal the gash in my shoulder. His wince was faint but unmistakable, and it gave me a moment of doubt which I brushed away: of course he wouldn't like having his nose rubbed in it.

He looked past me and saw Solli waiting in the Datsun.

"Perhaps your friend would like to come in, too? Since you seem to have invited yourself."

"My friend prefers waitng outside. He can wave the police cars over, when they start arriving."

I paused in the foyer. The house was very quiet. There were candies in the candy dish: foil-wrapped Hershey's kisses.

"That's ridiculous," Brockway said, but he didn't sound as if he thought so; not quite. I could feel him waiting for me to tell him why else I'd come back.

"Your psychiatrist, Jane Blackwood, doesn't think it's so ridiculous." I walked on into the lit room off the foyer.

It was a den, much like his consulting room but bigger, with a fireplace, overstuffed chairs, oriental rugs. Bookshelves lined the walls; framed photographs of sailing boats hung over the mantel.

"Say what you've come to, and get out," he snapped. "Your accusations are nonsense. I don't have to listen to—"

"Your medical records say you've had at least eight unusual deaths among your patients. Your bank records say you were paying hush money to Bill Priest. Your psychiatrist says you've got a great big problem, and your face says you know just what I'm talking about."

Disdain crinkled the corners of his mouth. "No one has ever been convicted of anything on the basis of a facial expression, that I know of."

"And," I finished in quiet tones, "there were doped cherries in Bill Priest's stomach."

It was still a guess about the dope, but he looked up sharply.

"So what? So you badger me with ludicrous accusations? Stringing together a lot of silly suspicions and coincidences?"

He took a step towards me. "Patients die. Doctors spend money, too. Sometimes they even visit psychiatrists."

His voice turned bitter. "None of it means they are guilty of murder. Jane Blackwood wouldn't have said I was, either, for the simple reason that it's not true."

While he spoke, I let my gaze wander around the big room and wondered why Wes Brockway kept suffering my intrusions; once again, just as earlier, he'd put up an initial fuss and then let me walk right into his place.

This time, though, I thought I understood why: he had to know what *I* knew, to keep a step ahead of me. More photographs stood on the shelves behind his desk; I moved nearer to examine them.

"As for candied cherries or some such ridiculous thing," he was saying, "I haven't the faintest idea what that could mean, or how you could know if it did mean something."

One of the photos was a family group, fifteen or twenty years old from the look of Brockway in it. He stood with his arms around a pretty woman; both aimed forced grins at the camera as if to convince it that things were all right.

The two little girls in front of the grown-ups were not grinning, however, and neither of them thought things were all right. One was ill, skinny and sad-eyed, with the dry thinning hair and pasty complexion of the advanced chemotherapy patient.

The other, dark and sturdy with a baseball cap jammed onto her Buster Brown hair, a catcher's mitt lying at her feet, was angry. She tried to hide her feelings behind a smile so taut it looked nailed-on, but her clenched fists and smoldering eyes told the truth: no joy in Mudville.

The rest of the photographs were more recent: no sick little girl, no smiling woman. I remembered Ken Kruck's remark about family troubles. Brockway and the other child, though, were still represented, and later, the child alone. Through the photographs, she grew older: eighth-grade graduation, a prom snapshot, a studio portrait that probably had been taken for her high-school yearbook.

She was pretty; still sturdy, but in a healthy way. Physically healthy, at any rate; that resentful curl in her lip was still there, and the suggestion in her eyes was that she was not getting all that she thought she ought to have.

And her eyes, like Brockway's, were gray.

He was still talking: hurriedly, defensively. I wasn't listening, though, because all at once I recognized the pretty girl in the portrait.

Suddenly a lot of other things made sense, too: the candy dish in the hall, the box of toffees on a shelf behind Brockway's desk, the shiny foil wrapper in the wastebasket by my feet.

And Brockway's own remark.

"Felicity," I said. "Felicity Dunwoodie is your daughter. Why is her name different from yours?"

He stopped dead. "My daughter went through a period of being, shall we say, less than fond of me. She took her mother's maiden name legally, years ago. Although I don't quite see what that has to do with anything."

"Oh, but it does. It gives someone else a reason to do things I thought you'd done. You see, I didn't mention candied cherries just now, only cherries. The candy was your idea, or rather it was Felicity's. To get chloral hydrate or something like it into Bill Priest."

"I have no idea what you mean," he said stiffly.

"I mean," I said flatly, "they weren't maraschino cherries. They were the chocolate-covered kind, only the chocolate had dissolved by the time I saw them. That's why you've been so upset lately, isn't it? Because you suspected what she'd done."

He collapsed into the chair behind his desk. "You'd better get out of here. I'm not going to stand for any more of your—"

"She knew about the Marino thesis," I went on. "Bill Priest wasn't only blackmailing you; he was hitting Felicity, too, to pressure you into paying. I didn't know she was your daughter, but he did; it's the kind of thing he would have liked knowing, and hers is the kind of vulnerability he liked, too—the kind he could manipulate. Or so he thought."

Brockway shook his head wordlessly.

"So he told her about the thesis, and that was his mistake: pushing Felicity just a little too far. She went to his place, got him to invite her in. Maybe she said she had the money he'd been demanding, and somehow she tricked him into eating a couple of chocolates. The cherry flavoring in them is quite strong—he might not have noticed anything else about them."

"Idiotic," Brockway spat. "Why would he accept anything edible from someone he was blackmailing?"

"Because he was arrogant," I said, "and for all his academic brilliance, quite stupid in his own way. It was a game with him, really, he had no idea of other people's feelings. Besides, he thought he was such a hot ticket. It just wouldn't have occurred to him that someone might actually try to hurt him back."

"And," I added, "Felicity can look quite harmless when she chooses. Can't she?"

Brockway shifted in his chair. My mention of his daughter's acting ability had made him uncomfortable. Probably she had used it on him, too—maybe until he caught wise.

I almost felt sorry for him.

"Once she got into his apartment, though," I said, "the chloral or whatever she used hit him harder than she expected. Walt Krusanke heard him fall, and came up to find out what had happened."

"Nonsense." But he didn't sound convincing.

"She got the drug into him," I went on. It was all falling together like puzzle parts now; it all made sense when you had the missing piece.

"And then everything really came apart. Walt started hammering on Priest's door. Pushing thirty cc's of anything into a vein takes time, and she knew Walt would be back. She couldn't stay to finish what she'd planned."

All it needed was Felicity. Brockway hadn't known I'd met her, or he'd never have let me in where her picture was displayed.

"Everyone who knows Felicity knows she loves candy," I said. "And she knew there'd be an autopsy; even without suspicion of murder, there's always a post-mortem exam in sudden deaths."

Or maybe he was even more tired than I'd suspected; too tired to go on. He might even have forgotten the photographs were here: forgotten accidentally on purpose.

"Right from the start," I said, "she meant to get the cherries back. Of course that wasn't necessary. But Felicity is so much the center of her own universe—in her mind, those cherries might as well have had her name written on them. She's so compulsive, so obsessed with details and especially with herself. That's why it all went so wrong and got so out of control."

Brockway put his elbows on the desk and lowered his face into his hands.

"Probably she slipped out of Priest's place just as Walt was returning with the keys. She thought he might have seen her, and that later he might begin putting two and two together. He hadn't, as it happened. But she didn't know that for sure, and she couldn't stand taking a chance."

She'd raced to the hospital, got herself up as a housekeeper, and stolen Priest's body with a daring any daylight robber would envy. She'd taken his body through the tunnels to the library building, and from there to the grad-school labs. That got rid of the evidence she'd been so obsessed with, that she'd thought would damn her.

Then she'd gone back to Walt's to fix her other mistake: letting Walt get a glimpse of her. Or so she feared. And that was where Walt had made his mistake: the same one people had been making with Felicity all her life. He'd turned his back on her.

"But these cherries—they were there, you say," Brockway objected feebly. "Why go to all that trouble and then not remove this supposedly damning evidence?"

One thing you could say for him: he went down fighting.

"Because she made one last fatal error," I answered. "She was in a hurry, and getting rattled—things just weren't working out at all the way she'd planned."

I parted one of the draperies. Out in the street, I could see the Datsun, Solli's head a dark shape in it.

"She meant to use the lab crematorium," I went on, "to dispose of the body for good. But it was broken, so she stashed the corpse in a freezer in one of the grad-school labs. She'd know which labs weren't being used, and she had all the keys. That gave her time to figure out what to do next—and what to do about me."

In the car, Solli's shape remained motionless.

"But the other labs started needing more freezer space," I finished, "and when Felicity heard about that she knew the body would be discovered soon unless she moved it again. Meanwhile, his stomach contents froze with the rest of him—and you can't pump ice cubes with a syringe and a rubber tube."

Brockway went on listening in silence.

"The thing she had going for her," I went on, "was knowing her way around. Joey's crash was her doing, and she followed me to the tank room to have another crack at discouraging me for good. She'd been following, I'll bet, since Solli and I went to your office. Probably she was listening at the door there; that's what made her so frantic all over again."

I crossed the room to Brockway's desk. "But with all of that, there's one thing I can't figure out."

I leaned over the desk. "Your daughter was protecting you, hiding the murders Priest's thesis would have begun exposing."

Small dark splotches appeared on the desk blotter; he was weeping.

"Why?" I asked him. "Maggie Kruck and Agnes Cranston—mercy killings? And Mariel Brunesi's sister, Jill—did you kill her just to get rid of Mariel? And who warned Mariel away from you? Was it you, after all, disguising your voice better than Mariel thought you could? In short, Dr. Brockway, I don't understand why you killed all those people—or how, when you were out of town when each of them died.''

"But he didn't kill them, you see," Felicity said. "I did."

I turned. She didn't look harmless or useless, now, and neither did the .22-caliber pistol she gripped in her right hand.

She hadn't only been listening outside her father's office. She'd been outside Steve Marino's dorm room, too. She'd known I was coming here, and what I would learn.

"I got it from your desk," she said to Brockway's astonished look at the pistol. "Don't you know not to leave guns lying around? Especially," she finished bitterly, "with children in the house?"

Brockway held out his hands. "Honey," he said.

"Shut up."

He looked as if she'd slapped him. Also he looked frightened. Suddenly I wondered why he'd had the gun. Maybe he'd been suspecting that he had a tiger by the tail, or that one had him.

"That's where the rest of the money went, wasn't it? The withdrawals from his bank records were lots bigger than the deposits to Priest." I put the question to Felicity, afraid that if I asked Brockway and he answered, she might really shoot him.

She looked angry enough to do it, and quite mad. Bonkers, as Steve Marino had so concisely expressed it.

And that, of course was the heart of it: mad love. "Was he paying to take care of you, Felicity?" I asked it gently. "To a private hospital, or a clinic somewhere? And maybe to keep Jane Blackwood silent, too?"

She didn't answer me, though. Instead she kept talking to him. It was as if some cracked and crumbling dam had broken at last, spewing forth a muddy, torrential wave of grudges.

"That's right, isn't it, Daddy? All the money you spent, slapping it on like one of those filthy bandages you put on all your filthy patients."

The psychiatric hospital would have been very private, very discreet. And of course there had been one. You just didn't get as sick as Felicity was without going indoors—for a while, anyway.

Only in her case a while hadn't been quite long enough. Maybe Brockway had even agitated for her release; probably he'd thought he would be able to handle her.

I could imagine it: first put her away, hide her crimes and make sure there would be no ruining scandal. Then, later, a quiet job, arranged by him. Secure home, not much stress, fairly close observation and most likely medication, too.

Of course he'd thought he could handle his own daughter; he was a doctor, after all.

Unfortunately, it had been like putting mercurochrome on a cancer: ineffective, and it had stung. The psychiatric drugs, meanwhile, made her fat, sallow, and pimply. And Wes Brockway just wasn't one who could show much love to such an unlovely creature, even if she was his child.

Or maybe because she was.

"I did it for him, you know," she said. "So he'd have the time he was always saying he wished he had, time for me. All the attention all the sick ones took away."

Her hand shook as she leveled the pistol, its small dark eye fixed on Brockway. "Well, now you'll have to pay some attention again, won't you?"

"Priest saw you," I said. "He saw you doing something to them. That was how he knew from the start. But what was it? It seems impossible. How did you even get near enough to them?"

Her lip curled in a sneer. "*He* brought me. My father. He took me on rounds with him, in the hospital, back when I thought I might be a doctor, too." She shook her head.

"I was your shining light, wasn't I, Daddy? As long as I turned out just like you, so perfect. And that's how I saw the way they all looked at you. That's how I found out where all the things I needed were really going—to all of them."

She turned to me. "I did it different ways. Insulin. An air bubble. Whatever came to hand. It was easy, and no one ever suspected me. After all, I was the doctor's daughter."

Solli, I prayed, I hope you're paying attention.

"And then," her voice hardened, "*he* found out. And had me put away. Only Dr. Blackwood knew why, and he paid her not to tell."

She grinned. "I fooled them both, though. I got better. Didn't I, Daddy?" Her lips twisted on the word.

"I got so sane, Blackwood couldn't keep me in there any more without telling somebody why I was really there. And she's too damn greedy to ever do that. At least, she was until tonight."

A chill went up my back.

The admission seemed to trip a switch in her. It was eerie, listening while all the furniture inside her head crashed into itself.

"How sick do I have to get, Daddy, before I'm a real, live sick person, the kind you like so much? Before you'll love me?"

Her face contorted with fury. "Tell me, you sonofabitch. How sick do I have to be before you start taking care of *me*?"

She put her other hand around the pistol grip, to steady it. Her index finger began contracting on the trigger.

I kept thinking there was something I could do, some magic word I could say to flip the switch back again, but there wasn't.

Her eyes were the ones I had seen in the basement, above the mask: the eyes of a furious, unrepentant child. A mad child.

Solli, I thought. Solli, where the hell are you?

Brockway just kept looking at her. There was an odd, smooth look of relief on his face, as if he had always known this would happen and now he would get it over with.

"I'm so sorry," he began.

Behind Felicity the front door flew open and there was a sudden commotion in the foyer, cut off by the pistol's explosive report.

Felicity turned. I threw myself down and scrambled toward her, hoping the shock of the moment might immobilize her briefly. But by the time I reached her, her arms had been firmly seized by Lieutenant Michael X. Malley, and the pistol lay on the rug.

"Christ," Malley said in disgust. "What the hell do you people think you're doing here?"

"What," Solli asked him, "are *you* doing here?"

"Well, I think it took you both plenty long enough," I said as I fell into a chair.

Brockway crawled out from behind his desk. Blood stained the sleeve of his sweater, but he didn't look mortally hit. He gazed at his daughter, who wept softly and monotonously in Malley's grip. Then he looked away.

Solli crouched beside Brockway and examined him briefly, but Brockway waved him off.

"Nothing major," he said in dull tones.

So Solli took off to call him an ambulance, and Malley took Felicity out to lock her in the caged back seat of his car, and I took a deep breath and leaned back into Brockway's overstuffed chair and took my eyes away from him for just a moment.

"Transplants," he said.

I opened my eyes. ''What?''

He sat cross-legged with the gun in his hand. ''Organs,'' he said mildly, as if that explained it all. ''Mine are perfectly good. Use 'em.''

He stuck the gun in his mouth and pulled the trigger.

TWELVE

MYRON ROSEWATER LOOKED disbelievingly into the face of
the tiny creature in his arms.

"He's in there, ain't he?" he said in wondering tones,
peering at little Carl Walter Terrell as if trying to fathom
what cunning trick made the infant work. "He's in there,
man, lookin' right out through them baby eyes all by his
ownself."

"Of course he is," Harry Lemon said irritably. "What
were you expecting, a wind-up key?"

"Hey, man," Myron said, "I never seen such a brand-
new one before, that's all. This little dude is somethin'
else."

Six weeks had passed since the night in Brockway's
house. During that time, Helen Terrell had been released
from the hospital and Felicity Dunwoodie had been committed to one, pending her first mental-competency hearing.

The consensus was that if Felicity had been taking her
antipsychotic medications as prescribed, none of the murders ever would have happened. The consensus was, once
she got back on an antipsychotic regime, and was supervised on it, no more ever would.

Personally, I had my doubts, but then I have never been
a fan of the consensus; none of that, however, was any
longer any of my business, a fact for which I was supremely grateful.

Meanwhile, as the waning year's first snowflakes began
drifting delicately down, Helen had returned to Mercy
General where her son was born; soon after that he was

brought home, and at his baptism Helen had named him after Walt Krusanke and me.

Another sort of birth had occurred during those weeks, too: a rebirth.

Shortly after Carl Walter's appearance, Joey Rosen had begun coming out of his long sleep, opening his eyes and moving at first his fingers, then his arms, at last his whole upper body.

His legs had not moved, however, and it now seemed unlikely that they ever would.

"Do you think he should sit up for so long?" I asked Solli, watching Joey reach out to accept the baby from Myron.

In Helen's living room, whose decorating scheme had swiftly been transformed into what I could only call 'early pablum,' Joey sat in his new lightweight wheelchair, a chrome and leather model with wire wheels that Myron had pronounced "bitchin' transport."

Wearing a Jefferson Starship T-shirt, denim vest, and jeans, Joey looked older, wiser, paler, and much more tired than I liked.

"Hey, Walter," he said softly to the infant he was cradling, "Hey, you want to learn how to play the guitar? I'll teach you, huh, guy? When your fingers get longer."

A stroller and a carton of Pampers stood in the entry-way, and a playpen had replaced one of the rose-chintz chairs. Tiny items of clothing fresh from the laundry were stacked on one end of the elegant sofa, a baby backpack had been carelessly tossed on the other, and a Sesame Street mobile dangled from the record shelf under the Vivaldi collection.

Joey put his finger into the baby's fist, which closed firmly on it.

"I think he should sit up for as long as he wants to," Solli said. "You're going to have to let him find his own limits,

now, Charlotte, let him fall and hurt himself. Don't treat
him as if he were sick any more, because he's not."

I nodded, biting my lip. "I wish he were sick. So he could
get better, so he wouldn't have to be like that forever."

"I know. And maybe he will get better, who knows? It's
early days, yet. But either way, it's going to be fine. It's not
going to be like you planned, but he's a strong kid. You'll
see, he'll be all right."

Solli put his arms around me just as Steve Marino came
in from outdoors, slapping his arms around himself and
complaining about the January cold snap.

"Christ, a person could die in this climate," he blus-
tered. "I was supposed to be doing an internship in Miami
by now."

Behind him, Rawlins and Twyla McKay crowded into the
little entry too, stamping their feet and making noises of
pleasure as the room's warmth hit them.

"You said you didn't mind staying." Twyla spoke mock-
accusingly, coming up behind Steve and slipping her arm
through his.

I looked at her face, pink-cheeked and bright-eyed, and
then at Steve's. He glanced down sheepishly.

"Well, sticking around does have its compensations." He
drew a small circle on the floor with the end of his shoe,
then glanced shyly up at Twyla. "I mean, if I left now, I'd
never be able to play you my whole collection of Russian
tuba music."

"Beast," she said, but she gave his arm a squeeze before
she let go of it and went out into the kitchen.

"Oh, my god," Steve breathed, watching her go. "I still
don't believe it. I've died and gone to heaven."

"Remember what you said about washing her feet," I
warned.

"With a Q-tip, if she wants," he replied in helpless tones
that I thought boded well for Twyla.

Rawlins said nothing, but I detected an unusual twinkle in his steely blue gaze.

"You know," I said to him, "I haven't had a chance to thank you for your help."

It had to be Rawlins, I felt sure. He and Steve had run into Mike Malley in the hospital, after I'd left for Brockway's that night. And while I couldn't imagine Malley listening to much that Steve had to say, Rawlins was another matter entirely.

"How did you get Malley to believe I was in trouble, though?" I went on. "Come to think of it, how did you know?"

Rawlins glanced sideways as Steve followed Twyla into the kitchen, out of earshot.

"That was young Mr. Marino's doing, I'm afraid. You see, the microphone he gave you transmits to more than one listening device. And Lieutenant Malley happened to be present when Mr. Marino and I arrived at your young gentleman's hospital room."

"Steve bugged me," I said. "He spied on me again."

Rawlins pursed his lips austerely. "Quite so. But only for your own safety, I assure you."

"So Malley heard me talking to Brockway—"

"Indeed. It disturbed him considerably, I might add. When he left the hospital, it was with the expressed intention of, ah, 'tossing your stupid meddling butt in the can and junking the key.' I gather, though, that once he encountered Mr. Solli, his intentions altered."

"That's putting it mildly." I shivered, remembering. Then I thought of something else.

"Rawlins. Steve doesn't have any more homemade listening devices hidden around me anywhere, does he?"

Rawlins permitted himself a small smile. "No, ma'am," he said. "Mr. Steve's interests have begun developing in another direction, you see."

I saw. In the kitchen, Steve and Twyla slid sugar cookies fresh from the oven onto a plate, amidst much laughter. With them was Helen, smiling too, pouring something from saucepan to pitcher. Hot spiced wine, it looked to me.

She wasn't over Bill. She wasn't over any of it. But she was beginning to see it all a bit more clearly, and even to make plans for working again. Until she did, the bank had floated her a loan on the strength of the life-insurance benefits she would soon begin receiving.

On top of which, I have noticed that there is nothing like a brand new, much-wanted baby to occupy a woman's entire attention and console the living hell out of her if she is at all inclined to let things work that way, which luckily Helen was.

Hot spiced wine, I thought, feeling pleased. "Twyla's a nice girl, isn't she?" I said to Rawlins.

"Eminently nice, ma'am," Rawlins replied. "Indeed."

Helen came to the kitchen door, wearing a flowing caftan in emerald green. Her hair shone like polished copper in waves that fell loosely around her face; her cheeks, bright with health and stove heat, resembled burnished apples.

"Come and get it, everyone," she said, after which we ate cookies and toasted Carl Walter in bits of baby talk, which he seemed to enjoy. Helen did a great deal of smiling, which for all her talents and foibles has always been one of the things she does best; Harry Lemon sat next to her on the sofa between the baby clothes and the backpack, making no overtures but clearly planning many, while Steve looked meaningfully at Twyla, at the baby, and then at Twyla again, making Twyla blush.

Solli asked Rawlins if he liked fishing; Rawlins's face relaxed in a look of pleasure. Soon they were deep in talk of rods and reels and the relative merits of graphite over bamboo.

Myron wanted to know how fast Joey figured he could really go in that thing, anyway, and Joey said pretty fast,

he thought, especially when he got his arms built up a littl
more.

I would have liked hearing more of this, the better t
thwart any plans for atrocious velocities, but the telephon
rang.

"Charlotte," Bernie said in the warm, fruity tones h
always uses to persuade me into awful projects. "Char
lotte, you're a genius."

"Huh?" I said, which was my second mistake, right af
ter answering the telephone in the first place.

"Glands, Charlotte, you really made glands come alive.'

I averted my mind's eye from his unappetizing thought
Out in the living room, I heard another arrival.

Two arrivals: Lieutenant Michael X. Malley and his new
feline sidekick, Cat Dancing.

"So where's this alleged baby?" Malley demanded.

"Meerowyowwow," Cat Dancing agreed.

"No," I pronounced firmly into the telephone.

Steve Marino had not only insisted on paying me mor
than the rate upon which he had originally agreed, plus
substantial bonus, he also threatened to burn the money up
in an ashtray if I tried to give it back. So I took it.

With it, and the advance checks for two very-nearly-
finished Home Health books, I was set up for quite a while.

"No," I repeated.

"Tut-tut," Bernie said. He actually pronounced syllables like "tut-tut," especially when he was pushing a project he had originally lined up for someone else, while at the
same time promising a publisher that half a dozen truly
abysmal books would swiftly get written by that someone
else, at which point the someone else had crashed out on
Bernie's project, ruining his deal along with his credibility,
a commodity that had never been exactly sterling in the first
place.

Which was why he was calling me.

"Charlotte, I hate to bring up a subject like this, but…"

"Go ahead, Bernie," I said, feeling sudden foreboding. When Bernie says he hates to bring up a subject, it means he is thanking his stars he has it to bring up, because it will win the argument.

"I just wondered if you'd filed your September quarterlies, is all. Because I know you missed summer, and that means you're two tax payments behind—"

Three, I realized sinkingly.

Somehow—if I knew how, I could solve all my money problems forever—the IRS has learned to take 15 percent of a writer's yearly income, that is, next to nothing—and turn it into a tax bill of over five hundred dollars, four times a year.

Twice in a row I hadn't had a cent to send them; the last time, I'd spent it on the trip East. Which meant the amount I now owed, as Bernie was so slyly and strategically reminding me, came to nearly three-fifths of my current bank balance, not counting the checks I had written but which had not cleared yet.

Aluminum wheelchairs are expensive. So are the kinds of triple-A municipal bonds one buys for the son of one's friend on the happy occasion of his birth.

So, additionally, were items of clothing I had rashly gone out and purchased, as the rags I had been wearing were threatening to fall in a mossy heap at my feet.

"Okay, Bernie," I sighed. "What is it this time?"

Bernie told me.

Which was why it was not until much later, after I had contemplated and rejected the relative merits of suicide versus writing a twelve-part series entitled *Pennies From Heaven: Your Astrological Guide to Stock Market Millions,* that I went into Joey's darkened room and sat down on his bed.

"He got you again, didn't he?" Joey said drowsily.

"Yeah. He did. We need the money."

As my eyes adjusted to the darkness, I could see his face: dark eyes, dark hair, soft shadow of wispy adolescent beard. His room smelled of three-in-one oil from the wheelchair wheels, leather from its new padded seat. Over it all was the smell of warm clean boy.

Suddenly I loved him so much that I almost couldn't breathe, and I didn't know how I would take care of him.

"Jesus, Joey," I said.

He knew what I meant. "Yeah. It freaks me out, too. I'm just kind of feeling my way into it, bit by bit. I have dreams where I'm running."

I said nothing. He hauled himself upright, laying his head on my shoulder, one arm looped around me for support.

Down the hall, Carl Walter began to cry. Helen padded in to him, her voice coming in soft, indistinct murmurs.

"Solli wants to marry you," Joey said.

"Yeah? Did he say that?"

His head moved. "He's afraid you won't, though. He says you're independent as a hog on ice, and he's afraid you might say no on account of that."

"Well, what do you think?"

No answer. Slowly, his body relaxed.

I rested my cheek on his hair. Beyond his window, the night sky was milky with reflected light.

"Joey," I said, "do you think I ought to do it?"

But he was already asleep.

HOOKY GETS
THE WOODEN SPOON
LAURENCE MEYNELL

First Time in Paperback

HOOKY HEFFERMAN WAS MUCH BETTER AT GETTING GIRLS IN TROUBLE THAN OUT OF IT.

His passion for the fair sex and English pubs aside, he had been known to solve a crime or two as a private investigator, profiting from the idiocies of this comic adventure called life.

Now he's been hired to find a rebellious, poor little rich girl who has taken up with some unsavory characters. Dad isn't comfortable swimming the murky waters of London's underground. Hooky, however, feels quite at home.

He's never minded helping out a pretty face—and Virginia Chanderley is that—but young and angry, she's also easy prey for a professional crook planning to steal a priceless painting. In fact, lovely Virginia has got herself into more trouble than even Hooky Hefferman—London P.I. and soldier of fortune—knows quite how to handle.

"Laurence Meynell had a gift for creating recognizable characters and ingenious plots."
—*The Independent*

MURDER
HAS A PRETTY FACE
JENNIE MELVILLE

The raped man had drowned. No one claimed him. Nobody wanted him. Least of all, Police Inspector Charmian Daniels. Why did he have her name and telephone number on a card in his pocket?

Several large-scale robberies of furs and jewels and a mysterious, garishly made-up woman lurking about town add to the bizarre caseload. Charmian is convinced the crimes are connected—but how? A chance visit to a local beauty salon puts her on the trail of a diabolic gang of criminals—and leaves no doubt that even the prettiest face can mask a ruthless heart as cold as steel.

FRIGOR MORTIS

RALPH McINERNY

Author of the Father Dowling Mysteries

From an actuarial point of view, death comes eventually. But Stella can't wait. She doesn't love George Arthur. She never has. She'd married him for his money, and now she would kill him for it.

Actually, it is Roy Hunt, the town's bank president and Stella's longtime lover, who commits the cold-blooded act of shoving poor George through a carefully cut hole in the ice-covered lake. But the three million dollars in George's safe-deposit box mysteriously disappears and is hidden under some steaks in his devoted secretary's freezer.

As friends, lovers and killers alike play a wily and nervous game of "money, money, who's got the money," Stella is bludgeoned to death with a croquet mallet. It's further proof that a boiling pot of jealousy, greed and rage fuels this icy tale of murder.

MYSTERY

WORLDWIDE LIBRARY

TM

BACKLASH
PAULA GOSLING

Winner of the John Creasey Award for crime fiction

THE TASK THAT FACED GENERAL HOMICIDE SEEMED MONUMENTAL

They had four dead cops from four different precincts, all shot through the head. The headlines were screaming cop killer. Rookies were making sudden career changes, while veterans of the force were anxiously eyeing retirement dates. Panic was growing.

For Lieutenant Jack Stryker, the pressure was coming everywhere: up from below, down from above, and in from the outside. And with each new death, the pressure increased. Was the killer shooting cops at random...or was there a more sinister reason for the murders?

But when Stryker is hit and his partner is almost fatally wounded...Stryker knows it's time to forget procedure and put an end to open season on Grantham's finest...before he becomes the next trophy of a demented killer.

"Gosling's novels have all met with critical acclaim."

— *Library Journal*

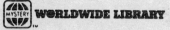

WORLDWIDE LIBRARY

A SENSITIVE CASE
ERIC WRIGHT

AN INSPECTOR CHARLIE SALTER MYSTERY

THE BIGGER THEY ARE THE HARDER THEY FALL

The murder of masseuse Linda Thomas was a sticky situation—her clients included big people in high places. It was a case for Special Affairs Inspector Charlie Salter and his chief investigator, Sergeant Mel Pickett. They delicately kick open a hornet's nest of hostile, secretive suspects, including a provincial deputy minister, a famous television host, the tenants of the woman's building, a nervous academic, a secret lover and an unidentified man—the last person to see Linda alive.

A lot of people had a lot to hide—and even more at stake than their careers. To make things more difficult, Salter is worried his wife is having an affair.

It's a sensitive case, both at home and on the job. Charlie's doing a lot of tiptoeing around—with a killer lurking in the shadow of every step.